Teach Me to Forget

Erica M. Chapman

MERIT PRESS
NEW YORK LONDON TORONTO SYDNEY NEW DELHI

Merit Press
An Imprint of Simon & Schuster, Inc.
1230 Avenue of the Americas
New York, NY 10020

For information about special discounts for bulk purchases, please contact Simon & Schuster Special Sales at 1-866-506-1949 or business@simonandschuster.com.

The Simon & Schuster Speakers Bureau can bring authors to your live event. For more information or to book an event contact the Simon & Schuster Speakers Bureau at 1-866-248-3049 or visit our website at www.simonspeakers.com.

Manufactured in the United States of America

10 9 8 7 6 5 4 3 2

Library of Congress Cataloging-in-Publication Data has been applied for.

ISBN: 978-1-4405-9457-1
ISBN: 978-1-4405-9458-8 (ebook)

1

6 Hours

My breath feels like a solid mass as it travels from my lungs into a whisper. "Bye, Jackson Gray."

I always call him by his first and last name. It makes him sound like a movie star. And he hates when I call him that. A film of tears coats my eyes, making his face blur like I'm staring into a funhouse mirror. Even blurry, his smile is always so perfect and sincere. I wonder if mine will ever look as endearing as his, especially while I'm faking my way through the rest of the day.

He crooks his mouth to the side and gazes at me like I've grown horns. "Are you crying? I know leaving me is hard, but . . ." he says, letting the sentence fade out like he always does. He displays a goofy grin, showing white teeth that contrast with his olive-toned skin.

I clench my fists, urging the tears to dry. "It's the wind."

He searches around the parking lot as if trying to catch sight of the breeze before narrowing his gaze back to me. "Okay." He shrugs.

The tree branches stop swaying in the wind, and my hair suddenly lies flat from its previous wild abandon. I push it out of my face. Jackson gives me a confused glance, looks down at his cell, and takes off. "I'm coming over," he yells halfway to his car.

I chase after him. "What?" I try to mask the tone in my voice so it sounds more normal.

He whips around, his nose still in his phone. "Jaclyn called me and said we needed to talk. I need to know what to do."

I give him my *you're an idiot* expression. "Talk to her?"

He looks up and laughs, rubbing his stomach like he's hungry, which he usually is. "Okay, okay," he says as a concerned expression takes over his face. "Hey, are you really all right? You seem a bit . . . ." His voice is laced with worry. Maybe he's figured out I'm saying goodbye for the last time.

I laugh because that's what *Happy Ellery* is supposed to do. "I'm fine, you doof."

"Look." He punctuates the word with his hand for emphasis. "I need your advice and I don't want to talk about it in the parking lot. I know you said you were busy tonight, but, it'll only be for a sec—"

"No," I say too quickly, cutting him off.

"Yes," he says with a smirk on his face, his dark hair blowing in the wind.

"No." We always do this—go back and forth until the other one caves.

He narrows his eyes and folds his arms across his chest. "Yes."

I sigh. He's changing my plans. *This* is our goodbye, not at my house where memories creep around every corner. "No."

He smiles at me again. "Yes," he says, soft and sincere.

He's not going to fold. I can tell. I groan, and he knows he's got me.

"See you in a few," he says, cranking open the door to his rusted, piece-of-shit car.

Just a year ago the world cornered me, but now it's swallowing me whole, digesting me slowly, like the gum I swallowed at lunch. I look down at my shoes as they make ridges in the soil, one deeper than the other. I spot my Ford SUV in the parking lot, and stand in front of it for a moment to remember all the times I've had in it; the time Jackson taught me to drive, the time . . . . Is this what today's going to be like—me standing in front of my life, breathing in memories and saying goodbye to inanimate objects?

Sliding into the front seat, I wrap my hands around the wheel, squeezing the leather, taking in the last drive I'll make away from school. It's Wednesday. I would have picked to kill myself on a Friday, but Mom works the weekends, and I don't want her to have to worry about cleaning up my dead body on a Friday. A Wednesday is better.

I flip on the radio and listen to my favorite song. It's full of loud guitar chords and yelling. It's perfect. I turn it up and roll the window down, letting the cool wind of Grand Creek, Indiana, whip brown strands against my face, slicing into my skin like little hairy knives.

The plan is done. I've set some money aside (not enough, but it will help) for the funeral, so my mom won't have to pay for all of it. I'd been saving for a year to pay for a trip to Paris, but since I won't ever make it to Paris, I figured this is a good investment. I don't deserve Paris, anyway. I've booked the cleaning crew for tomorrow morning, telling them it's a surprise for my mom, who always does the cleaning. They even congratulated me on being a good daughter. I had to place that memory in a compartment to keep it from haunting me for the last twenty-four hours. The gun is in my closet. It only has one bullet in its chamber.

A sliver of dread burrows through me, a lost feeling, not unlike the one I had the day I decided this would be my last. It's been happening ever since. The ebb and flow of the unknown variables in my plan. I'm waiting to feel numb. Jackson will hurt. We've been best friends since he climbed my tree and broke his leg in second grade. He'll get over it. He'll find another friend. Someone who deserves him more than me.

I make it home and run to my room, passing Mom in the kitchen cooking something that smells like a cross between cabbage and apple pie. I cringe as the odor wafts my way and speed up the stairs before she can pull me aside to eat whatever she's killed in the kitchen. I never had the heart to tell her I've been a vegetarian for the last six months. Now she won't have to know. She yells something up to me I don't understand. I slip into my room and frantically gather the items I'd stored away in preparation. I toss clothes and books around the room, hoping it looks more lived in than it did before I packed it all up.

A hollow knock on my door makes me jump. "Honey? Jackson's here. I'm sending him in. Are you decent?"

"No, I'm naked."

I hear her tell Jackson I'm *indisposed*.

"I'm not naked, Mom. It's fine. He can come in."

"I knew *that*," she says in a playful tone.

The door opens tentatively and Jackson's tall frame enters the room. He runs a hand through his hair. It's always been shaggy in that cool way, like he forgot he had it for about ten years. His shoes are dirt-stained, and the laces are always untied. His shirt is wrinkled above his muscled chest, fabric that bears some strange football saying I don't get. He never changes. I think that's what I like best about him—his predictability.

"All right, Jackson Gray. What'd you do this time?" I tease. I'm getting so good at faking.

He plops onto my bed and looks around the room, his eyes adjusting to the emptiness. "Are you moving?" His eyebrows crease in confusion and his posture changes to that of someone suspicious. "Where's the Duran Duran poster I got you?"

I was born in the late nineties, and even though I love some good grunge, I am a child of the eighties. I love everything about that era. Jackson got me the Duran Duran poster for my birthday last year. It's signed by all the members. Mom thinks it's hilarious and "so me" that I love bands she loved when she was a kid.

I need to come up with a lie to keep Jackson clueless. I search my brain for a thought. He used to be able to tell when I lie, but I've gotten pretty good at it. "I'm going to paint my room," I say, avoiding his eyes, hoping he buys it.

"Not pink, right?"

I smile. "Not pink."

"Cool." Jackson accepts things so simply. He never asks for an explanation. He's kind of the Goldilocks of people, middle in almost everything. He's average at football, but doesn't strive to be better. He's average at school, but doesn't care to get past a 2.8 GPA. He's not the captain of anything.

We have this in common. But that's where our similarities end.

"You came for a reason, yes?" I ask, grabbing a book and placing it neatly on the empty shelf.

He looks around again and nerves perk in my chest. "Something's seriously off, like . . ." he says, narrowing his eyes.

Perhaps I underestimated him. "Tell me about Jaclyn. She kissed Jeremy, right? That's what this is about?"

He purses his lips. "How'd you hear?" he says, flipping a pen he found on the ground between his fingers. "Eh, that relationship is over anyway. Come on, you had to have money on it ending." He makes a sound in his throat that's half chuckle, half too-cool-to-laugh. "What's up with you, anyway?"

My whole body freezes. I'm an iceberg about to crash the *Titanic*.

He doesn't wait for me to lie to him again. "You've been acting strange for days. What the hell is up with you? You're not . . ." he says, leading me to confess like he usually does.

You're not . . . *losing it like before.* I finish the sentence for him in my head. *Happy Ellery* isn't doing her job. Seething anger builds in me and threatens to burst. I can't have anyone ruin my plans—months of preparation and deceit. I calm, and put on an unaffected face. "Jackson Gray, you and I both know I'm strange. That's why you love me," I joke, hoping it convinces him that nothing's wrong.

"I do love ya." His tone is deadly serious as his gaze follows me suspiciously around the room.

"Anyway. Since you're clearly not here to listen to my sage advice on love, I must get with my first love—homework." I hug my calculus book to my chest and nod toward the door.

He sits up from the bed and stands, placing his hands in his pockets. "Fine. I'm leaving. So should I break up with Jaclyn, then?"

I laugh and nudge him lightly in the leg. "Yes, she kissed another guy."

He nods slowly, as if really trying to consider the decision. "Yeah, okay. I'll see you tomorrow?" he asks.

I nod, unable to tell him another lie.

2

5 Minutes

The moon is in the middle of the sky, dancing in the fog, attempting to hide its bruises. It speaks to me. *Ellery,* it says. *You never chose to be born, but you can choose to die.* It reflects my scars, my quiet resolve. It doesn't change. When I'm gone the moon will still shine in the sky and disappear behind the clouds, crying for the morning sun. It's a comforting thought tonight.

The wind is cold against my thin shirt. I adjust the sleeves, covering my scars, and check my phone.

Five minutes.

I decided I would start preparing at 8:13 P.M. That gives me just enough time to prep myself and get the job done so I can pull the trigger at 8:27 P.M. I didn't want to die on the hour—that's such a cliché. My death will not be a cliché, although I suspect it already is.

Nothing I can do about that. It won't matter in five minutes.

The wind whistles through the dark as I lean against the beat-up railing on the back porch. The night is mesmerizing, with bright stars clustered together to form constellations I wish I knew. A light shoots across the sky and I don't wish. I don't need to. It's probably a satellite or a plane anyway.

I glance down at my phone again.

8:13.

I stare at the numbers and watch them blur before turning my gaze to the blackened sky. My heartbeats echo in my ears and throat while the wind rustles the crispy leaves that are close to falling off the trees. Closing my eyes, I smile, take one last breath, then turn to go inside.

Mom's nursing shift ends at midnight. I have plenty of time. A quick shade of doubt snakes through me as I enter my bedroom. I shove it down into the pit of my stomach and lock it away with the rest of the memories I've tried to forget.

There's no room for doubt.

I often wonder if in the split second after I pull the trigger I'll have changed my mind, decided I should live. This haunts me, but I know only one thing. I don't deserve to live. It's as simple as that. The world will be better without me in it. Cars will drive by my house, kids will kick their soccer balls, best friends will still share secrets.

Sisters will still go to the zoo.

I open my closet door and kneel down, my knees cracking like brittle sticks, and retrieve the gun. I read somewhere that women like to use pills to kill themselves. I've always thought that was a cop-out. If you want to die, this is how it's done. One shot and it's over. No chance of coming back.

The shotgun's long and its hard angles shine in the dim of the lamp's light. I hate that it's so long. I wish it was a handgun, but they're almost impossible to get here. If I lived in a bigger town, maybe I would have been able to get one illegally, but since I live in this tiny shithole I'll just have to work with what I have. It will do the job. I check to make sure the bullet's still in it, then take a long breath and go to the bathroom. I unfold the navy blue towel I picked out (for its dark color) and lay it out. I sit in front of the toilet and slide down to the rug—the ugly pink shaggy rug that makes my legs itch.

I won't miss that rug.

Air is coming faster and my heart is beating like it knows its thumps are numbered.

Nice try, heart.

I secure the shotgun, pushing it against the vanity. It's awkward and clunky and I have to maneuver myself into a different position to get it to fit right. I shove the tip into my mouth, rearranging it to make sure the trajectory will hit my brain.

I don't want to be injured, that's my greatest fear.

The cold metal tastes like a dirty penny. My mouth is small and the ridges of the gun scratch my teeth. I stretch my arm and put my finger on the trigger.

Then I swear I can feel her, smell her shampoo in the air. "Tate?"

Silence.

I close my eyes as stills of people and disjointed memories whirl in my mind.

Jackson's hugs after Tate died.

Mom telling me she was sorry.

Dad telling me it was all my fault.

You don't have to do this.

Tate's laugh as she chases the goats at the zoo. Her sweet laugh.

Tears fall violently down my face.

The gun clatters against the vanity, vibrating the barrel in my mouth. I look down and realize my hands are shaking it.

I close my eyes.

The bridge.

Tate screaming.

Falling.

I have no other choice.

I pull the trigger. Happy Ellery is no more.

3

Click.

No shot.

Am I dead?

I feel around my body. I'm still alive.

"What the fuck?" I remove the gun from my mouth. It's wet with my tears and saliva and slips a little. I check the chamber again. The bullet's still there. I put it in my mouth again and pull the trigger.

Nothing happens.

I pull it eight more times before jerking it away.

Why didn't I test it first?

I can't even die right. And now I'm going to have to call Merry fuckin' Maids and cancel everything. My plans are ruined.

The room shrinks as I search for a razor blade, finding that it's harder to locate than a gun on a foggy Saturday night at Kmart. I pull the vanity's drawers out, find nothing of use, then slam them closed. I slide down onto the floor, grasp the broken gun, point it to the ceiling, and pull the trigger. A loud crack sounds in the air as I fall backward. Plaster falls into my hair, turning the brown to white instantly. A small hole appears in the popcorned ceiling.

How in the hell?

When I fling the gun onto the tile, it echoes through the room like a broken bell. Ten times and the fucker didn't go off.

Please. Just let me die.

Tears don't come now. I am not weak. Another plan. I just need another plan. I snatch the gun off the ugly pink rug, get off the floor, and head to my room. It's so bare, so naked with nothing to show who I am.

I check my phone.

8:32 P.M.

Kmart's still open and the guy I had buy the gun gave me the receipt. I couldn't buy the gun myself, since I'm seventeen and you have to be eighteen to buy a shotgun. He didn't seem to care what I was doing with the gun. I should've been more disturbed by that, but honestly I just wanted it.

I think I can fake being eighteen.

My scruddy SUV sounds like it's about to break down as I travel across town to Kmart. There are exactly four cars in the parking lot; three of them are old and rusted. One is a white Escalade that looks brand new. Light from a lamppost flickers, creating moving shadows onto the gray asphalt. I hop out and grab the bag I'd shoved the broken gun pieces in. I Googled how to take the gun apart so it won't look like I'm trying to shoot up the place. I use my elbows to open the glass door, careful not to let any part of me touch it. A clear slime of what looks like mucus is dried on the handle.

Gag.

The service desk is opposite where I parked. I walk up slowly and lean the bag against the front of the counter. A thin girl looks down at me with stringy hair and eyes sunk into her skin so far it looks like she had them gouged out with a spork. She's as tall as Jackson. A twinge of something roils through my stomach when I think of his name. I recognize the guilt, but I ignore it. I have no choice.

Her nametag says Clementine. "What can I do you for?"

"I need to make a return."

She slides a pad of paper toward me. "Fill this out," she says in monotone, like she's bored and thinking of the time she will get off, or maybe when she's able to quit and dance at the bar full time.

That's such a bitchy thing to think. I'm going straight to hell.

I fill out the form and reach for the gun parts under me, only realizing after I'd pulled them out what it looks like I'm doing. The gun muzzle barely makes it to the counter when Clementine's face goes as pale as the wall behind her.

"I'm not going to rob you. I need to return it. It's broken."

She stares at me like I have snails crawling out of my ears.

I reach into my pocket and retrieve the receipt. "I have a receipt."

She continues staring, angling her neck to the side, scrutinizing me.

I'm holding the gun muzzle in one hand and a receipt in the other, and I feel stupid. "Look. It's obviously broke. I just want to exchange it or get my money back. It's been a long night."

She sighs. "Listen here, girl. I'm like, five minutes from closing, and you come in here brandishing a gun?"

Did she just use the word brandishing?

"Yeah, I know all that, but can I get my money back or a new gun?"

She grabs the receipt from my hand. "This is a Walmart receipt." She tosses it back to me.

Oh, yeah, Walmart, not Kmart. She looks so offended, like I just told her Ted Nugent left the NRA.

"Sorry, got my marts mixed up."

"I don't even think we sell guns," she says.

"My bad."

I shove the muzzle back in the bag and make my way out of Kmart, set on Walmart and getting my money back, or at least a new gun.

An arm grips me and pulls me backward. "Come with me. Now," a male voice says from behind me. It sounds authoritative.

"This is about the gun, isn't it?"

4

The room I'm in is small, and the walls are littered with flyers about safety and worker's compensation. I didn't think my evening could get worse, until I find out the security guard is Colter Sawyer from my AP English class. He's taken my gun and is on the phone in the other room. Nerves snake around my body and I fight to breathe normally. I shove my scarred arms under my legs so he can't see them, or he'll know. Maybe he already does. The room's silent save for the gurgle of the water cooler in the corner.

I'm afraid to touch anything.

Steps echo in the hallway, and the door opens quickly after.

Colter regards me carefully, looking me up and down. A flash of familiarity crosses his face. He's figured out where he knows me from but he's not going to say anything. "What were you doing with a gun, Ms. Stevens?" he says, sitting in the squeaky chair across from me.

Ms. Stevens? Really? He's a senior and I'm a junior, come on. "I have a receipt. I wanted to return it. It's broken." His eyes narrow as he takes in my statement. He doesn't believe me. He thinks I wanted to rob the place. Seriously, what the hell would I take? "Having the wrong receipt doesn't make me a criminal."

He licks his lips once and leans back in the chair, making it screech so loud I want to cover my ears. His appearance makes it look like he's trying too hard to blend into the crowd. His wavy dark hair is sticking out from under a Yankees cap and his jeans are torn at the thigh. A walkie-talkie that crackles every five seconds is attached to his side. A memory from class pops into my mind. He once told Mr. Kramer he was clueless for thinking that Shakespeare wasn't a pervert. I remember laughing at that. He has to have a sense of humor somewhere under that sweat-stained baseball cap.

He writes something down in an official-looking binder. I try to peek, but he moves the paper to the side and gives me a look of contempt. I pull my sleeves down past my scars just to make sure they're covered and lean back against my chair.

He closes the binder and sets the pen down on the top of it. "Who can I call to pick you up? Are your parents at home?"

"I have a car. My mom's at work." I start drumming my fingers in an uneven beat on the desk. "Do I get the gun back?"

He lets out an exasperated sigh. "No," he says with a surprising lilt in his voice. He leans over and his face nears mine. He smells like a mixture of cologne and sweat. His eyes roam over me again. "I know you."

"That's most unfortunate."

"I could have you arrested."

"I bought the gun," I lie.

His lips purse again and he leans back in the chair causing it to squeal like a wheel needing oil. The sound shrieks in my head. He scrutinizes me. "There's no way anyone sold that gun to you. We both know that."

I shift in my chair and cross my feet, and for the millionth time I have to say, "I have a receipt."

"I'm going to ask you again. How did you get that gun?"

"I. Bought. It."

He can't prove otherwise, but his third degree is making me feel like wood in a bonfire. I swallow and turn to the water cooler.

He rubs the back of his neck and lets out a breath. "Let's say I believe you. Why would you want to return it?"

"It doesn't work," I say as non-snotty as I can make my voice.

He throws his arms in the air. "You know what? Fine. But someone still has to come get you. What about your dad? Mom?"

I don't want to call Jackson, but I have no one else. "I can just leave."

"No. You're . . . ." He thinks about his next words carefully. "Unstable, at best."

Not the worst insult I've been given.

Static from his walkie-talkie makes me jerk in my seat. I quickly recover and hope he doesn't notice how jumpy I am. "I can call Jackson." My voice groans when I say it.

"Jackson Gray?" His face looks contemplative as he quirks his lips to the side and glances into the air. He blinks once, then his gaze travels back to me. "It's really supposed to be a parent or guardian."

"Please. My mom works nights and I'd rather not have her . . . involved."

His sympathetic expression tells me everything I need. He's going to let me go. "It's fine. But I'll call Jackson."

I give him Jackson's number and within ten minutes Jackson's standing in front of me fuming, red-faced and ready to let me have it. Colter tells him what happened, and the whole time Jackson sneaks glances at me and shakes his head. We're the same age, but you'd never know it. Jackson is millenniums older than me. It's obvious to everyone but him.

He grabs my arm, just like Colter did, and hauls me out of the back room and into the crisp night air.

"Is that Colter Sawyer?"

"Yes." I'm going to call him Tom Sawyer if I ever talk to him again, I bet he hates that.

"What in the fuck were you . . . ." He trails off.

"It was broken."

He spins to face me, his face full of rage, his fists clenched tight. His knuckles have turned white. "What were you doing with a shotgun?"

There's no lie I can tell that would make any sense. I could pretend to faint. Maybe I could just run away. He's fast and would catch me. Instead I say, "I found it." I can hear the lie in my voice, it seeps out. It's so obviously not the truth that I want to smack my own face for being so stupid. I was here to return it.

I need to have a plan for my lies too.

"Come on, Ell. What the hell is going on? You've never liked guns, and now you're trying to return one in the middle of the night to a Kmart on the east side. Are you nuts?"

"It's not the middle of the night. It's only ten." He glares at me; it stings me, I feel his stare deep within. I don't want to let him down. "Someone's stalking me. I have it to keep me safe."

His rage transforms into concern then back to the rage again. "You really expect me to believe that?"

"It's true."

"Why the shotgun? It's not like you can pop it out easily. Why would you need a gun? If there's really a stalker, I'd know."

"Someone got it for me."

That wasn't a lie. I'd found a guy outside the Walmart and asked him to buy it for me. I had originally thought it was Kmart because they kind of look alike and Walmart is only a block down the street. It was so easy to get the guy to buy it for me. I had a lot of money saved up for my trip, so I just offered him an extra twenty bucks and that was enough for him. I never learned the guy's name, but he gave me the receipt, and it didn't have his name on it since he'd used the cash, so I thought I could return it. I just got my marts mixed up, like I'd told Clementine.

"Are you capable of telling the truth?" He looks at me sternly and I have to come up with something quick.

"I'm taking shooting lessons. Thinking of trying hunting, you know, make a trip up to Michigan with this hunter I know who's from there." I nudge his shoulder with mine. Jackson loves to hunt and doesn't understand why anyone wouldn't want to. He'll buy this lie.

He nudges me back. "That's crazy. I didn't know you wanted to hunt."

I shrug. "Wanted to surprise you. You ruined it, *jackhole*."

He smiles and shakes his head at the same time.

I often wonder why he keeps protecting me. Our friendship has become one-sided and he hasn't noticed. His standards are much too low.

"So, where's the gun now?" he asks.

"Colter took it from me."

The corners of his mouth turn up slightly. "You really thought you could return a gun with a receipt? And a Walmart one at Kmart?" He chuckles.

My insides lurch into wonderful convulsions at his voice. His laugh could heal the world if it were bottled and given out like a Coke.

"Not my finest moment."

He curls his arm around my shoulders. "You never cease to entertain me."

"Were you on a date?" I ask.

"Yeah, Ginger Speilman. Total hag. She smokes too much. I felt like *my* lungs were burning."

"You still slept with her anyway, didn't you?"

"Of course. I have needs."

Happy Ellery laughs.

5

1 Day After

I dread going to English 'cause I know I'll have to see Colter and I've never talked to him, except last night; haven't had a reason to.

The collective voices in the room sound like buzzing bees as I stroll through the door. I make my way to my usual seat in the back of class, and hike my bag up over my shoulder, skimming through a positively titillating conversation two girls are having about Jasper Collins, the guy whose dad was on the TV show *Big Brother* last season. They think if they get with him they will somehow be famous.

Pathetic.

Colter's not in the classroom yet, but I'm already sweating over everything, literally. It's running down the back of my neck and pooling in my sweatshirt. I stare at the clock as perspiration collects between my breasts. With each tick, my stomach burrows deeper into my body. I was too nervous to eat breakfast. Mom had no clue what went down last night. After I got home, I called and canceled the cleaning crew, and patched up the hole in the ceiling as best I could.

My mind didn't change when the sun came up. I'd read that somewhere. *If you just believe the sun will rise again, you won't want to kill yourself.* I call bullshit. I don't care about that. I know it's selfish. I know I'll probably go to hell, but I just don't want to do it anymore. Feel it. The pain, the feeling of dread when I open my eyes in the morning. The guilt and shame. That cringing, scraping pit in my stomach that won't go away because of what I've done.

I sit up higher in my seat as Colter strolls in and fist-bumps some guy who's in my history class before sliding into his seat three desks from the front. He turns around, searching for someone, looking worried he won't find them. His gaze lands on me and stops.

I sink down into my seat. That feeling of dread magnifies ten times when his gaze penetrates me. Shit. What does he want? Does he know? Now I have to worry about a fucking hall monitor watching me.

Mr. Kramer sits tall at his desk and twists his red pen in his fingers, waiting, watching for the next victim. "Flanders?"

Jason Flanders cowers in his chair. "Yeah, Mr. Kramer?"

"Yes," Kramer corrects him.

"Yes, Mr. Kramer," Flanders says, gritting his teeth.

"Is Beowulf the only hero in this piece?"

Flanders starts to stutter, "Uh . . . yes, I mean, no. He's . . . uh." He wipes his palms on his jeans.

Kramer rolls his eyes. "Mr. Flanders, you have managed to look more incompetent than you did yesterday. I think congratulations are in order." His gaze leaves Flanders and lands on me.

Shit. Not today. I was supposed to be dead by now. I'm not supposed to be here. I kind of loathe *Beowulf.* I glare at him for picking me today.

"Ms. Stevens, what do you think the author is trying to say about Grendel in this passage?"

I sigh and bite on my lip. I feel something bubbling up and I know I'm going to get in trouble. "I don't know, Mr. Kramer, that he's sick of Beowulf? That maybe he's a freak? I don't really care, to be honest." I cringe a little at my words.

Kramer regards me carefully, spinning his red pen in his fingers. "Care to try that again without the attitude?"

I roll my eyes. I'm fed up. Kramer's a jerk and I'm in a rotten mood. "Care to stop being an asshole?"

Groans and *oooo*s fill the room. Kramer's expression can only be described as amused anger. He slowly stands up and walks over to my desk. My heart is thrashing in my chest and the sweat I've collected drips down my back.

He leans down so his bright blue eyes are even with mine while his coffee breath wafts toward me. "You're right. I am an asshole." He grins. "But you're the one that's going to be in detention this week. Hope it was worth it, Ms. Stevens."

I sigh again and sink back into my chair as Kramer walks back to his desk, his red pen swirling in the air.

I'm just so damn tired of fighting my own life.

The bell rings at the end of the hour. I'm anxious to get out of my seat. The room has been closing in on me the entire class like I'm in a trash compactor. Life has become a trash compactor, pushing and crushing me into its folds. It won't release me. And now I have a week of detention. I should care about that, but I don't. The look on Kramer's face was worth it all.

I hurry to the door when I feel someone behind me, close.

"Ellery?"

It's Colter's voice. Damn.

I whip around and give him my best *Happy Ellery* fake smile. "Tom Sawyer? Is that you?"

He gets that look on his face again, the stern authoritative one I bring out in everyone, it seems. "Very funny. We need to talk."

"No, we don't." I turn and walk toward my locker across the hall. The air buzzes as students file in and out of class, lockers bang, people yell. I want to cover my ears. Every sound is magnified.

His body heat radiates behind me. I wish he'd just leave me alone.

"Ellery," he says close to my ear.

I turn around again and clench my fists, my patience waning with every breath I take. "Look, I'm sorry about last night. I have since seen the error of my ways under your expert tutelage of security guarding." I grin.

He rolls his eyes, then his expression becomes concerned. It makes me pace in place. "Nice job in there. What? Do you have a death wish?"

A nervous chuckle escapes me. "Something like that."

He shoves his hand through his hair, breaking up the stiffness of the strands, and leans against the locker beside me. "Why'd you have a gun last night?"

Someone bumps into me and I almost topple into him. "Seriously? We're going to do this again? Why do you care?" My voice sounds froggy, like something's stuck in it. Nerves bounce around my body as if in a pinball machine. I can't get them to stop. The little coiled shooter just keeps knocking them into me.

"I just find it kind of weird, you showing up with a gun at a store that doesn't sell guns." He arches an eyebrow.

"It was an honest mistake. Both stores have the same crap in them—easy to confuse." I fold my arms across my chest and glance away from him briefly.

He scrutinizes me and shakes his head. "You're lying."

"Why do you care? I don't know you. Just leave me alone," I snap, lifting my chin up to look him straight in the eyes.

He sighs again. "You're right. Why *do* I care? Clearly, you don't." He runs a hand through his hair again and gives me that pitiful look I hate. The *so sorry about your crap life, I'd like to help if you'll just let me in* look.

It's so condescending.

I narrow my eyes at him. "Just go off to whatever practice you have and be the dutiful athlete we both know you are."

He jerks upright from the locker. "You should think before you judge." His lips purse and it looks like he's going to say something else, but instead he storms off, mumbling something about why he even tries.

I bang my head against my locker.

Jackson comes up as soon as Colter leaves. He's wearing a University of Michigan football jersey with a grape juice stain across the yellow M—correction, the *maize* M, he'd kill me if I even thought the color yellow. Jackson's always talking about how awesome Michigan is. Grand Creek isn't far, maybe a couple hours, but he tells me often that life here is different.

His eyebrows lift. "Making friends?"

I retract my forehead from the metal, yank my calculus book out of my locker and shove it in my backpack. It's the one class I always have homework in. "Don't I always?"

"What was he saying?" he says, leaning on the locker next to mine.

"He was professing his undying love for me." I slam my locker door; it echoes in my head like I closed an iron gate.

"He was asking about last night, huh?" he says. "You don't think he's your stalker, do you?" he teases.

I give him a deadpan look. "Do you think he needs to stalk anyone? Especially a five-foot-five, average-looking, brunette loser with mismatched socks on a good day?"

"You don't give yourself enough credit. Brush your hair more often and maybe put on some makeup, you'd be surprised how hot you'd look."

I throw my arms in the air. "Oh! Makeover?" I grab his arms and squeal, garnering a few glances from other hallway patrons.

He laughs. "You seriously need a friend that's a girl."

"A girlfriend?"

"Stop, I'm serious," he says through another laugh. "Also . . . ." He gets that serious look in his eyes like he wants to pat me on the head—*poor little Ellery.* "My mom's expecting you on Sunday. Don't think you're going to get out of it like last week." He gives me his stern glare.

I groan. "I know. I'll be there." Jackson's mom is pretty much the perfect female specimen. You can't hate her. But she turns into a barracuda if she wants something. My mom works Sunday nights, so back when we were younger, Jackson's mom found out I was eating alone and invited me for perpetual Sunday dinner.

The bell rings, a warning for sixth period. Sociology, my favorite class. Something I'm good at.

"I gotta go," he says. "Think about it. The friend part, not the makeover. And Sunday?"

I nod. "Got it."

I don't need any girls as friends. I don't need anyone else to miss me when I go. I've been slowly trying to separate from Jackson for months. But he's like taffy, it's never going to happen. He sticks to you, to your ribs, gets caught in your teeth.

I need to think of another way to die. I need another plan.

6

Sociology is my favorite class. Something about learning people's behavior makes me feel smart. I slide into my seat next to Dean Prescott, an old friend of Jackson's and mine. He never talks and looks about how I feel most days. The rumor last year was that he tried to kill himself. I'm kind of obsessed with knowing why and how he did it, so I still try to talk to him.

I'm a masochist.

"Hey, Dean," I say.

He looks up at me and the bags under his eyes dominate his face. He nods a hello.

Mr. Fellows, a short dude with a bald head, takes his seat on the desk and hikes up one leg onto the dark wood. "Today we're talking about structure and agency. Free choice. What does that mean to you?"

A few people raise their hands and talk about generic choices, like, between Pepsi and Coke. I'm sure that's not what he was talking about.

Free choice.

Free and choice shouldn't even be together. Choice already represents freedom. If you choose something, you're taking a stance, you're exercising your freedom. So it really should just be *choice*.

I search the room as the next hand raises and I spot Dean. He's scratching at his arm. Curious, I stare at what he's picking at and I hold my breath.

Scars line his wrists up and down like he drew them on.

His gaze darts to mine as he quickly slips down his sleeve, cowering lower in his chair. He glances at me again and opens his book, pretending he's paying attention, but I know.

Dean Prescott has scars on his arm. Scars that look recent. Scars that look like mine.

I used to cut myself to feel pain, to feel *something*. My skin was too perfect—silky-soft and pure, except I wasn't pure anymore. I wanted to tarnish it, mess it up so my outside would match my inside. The first time I cut myself was to die—it didn't work, obviously. It didn't take long for my skin to match my heart. I had thought I won against the demons inside. I'd finally inflicted the pain I deserved. But my scars were a shining beacon to let everyone know I was fucked up. That's when Dr. Lamboni came into my life. I've worked hard to fake him out, and finally have. After that, I decided the only scars I'd inflict on myself would be invisible.

Class ends quickly and I try to talk to Dean. He shuffles out the door and I follow behind him.

"Dean. Hey, Dean."

He turns around, his light brown hair falling in front of his gripping green eyes. "I have class," he says quietly. He turns to walk away from me.

"Wait."

He doesn't stop and I'm left alone in the hallway while my fellow students churn around me.

"You're not alone," I say to myself.

The smell of popcorn from the nearby theatre is choke-worthy in its butteriness. Mom must have noticed my penchant for evading her. She's dragged me to the mall. I know. I know. I'm a girl.

I'm supposed to love the mall. Honestly? It makes me tired. All the walking and looking and trying on shit. It's just not for me. I try to concentrate on what my mom is saying over the hum of people in the store. I grab a neon belt and wrap it around my waist—too small. There are at least fifty other belts. I didn't know there were that many shades of neon. I guess the eighties really are back.

"What about this one?" Mom says, holding up a hideous, sleeveless aqua dress.

"Did I turn into a mermaid overnight?"

She frowns and puts it back on the rack. "That's the tenth one. I'm starting to get the feeling you don't want a dress."

I place the belt back on the rack. "What gave it away?"

She smiles despite my attitude. I love that about her, but there's a sadness in her eyes, like she knows she could be shopping with two daughters instead of one. She grabs a hair clip off the counter and scrutinizes me while flicking the clip over and over. "Aunt Sue wants you to join the choir."

"Mom, I told you—"

"I know. But your voice is so beautiful and she needs one more soprano."

None of this matters.

"I can't."

"Why? You have nothing else going on. If you're not sleeping, you're doing homework. I don't know what to think of you anymore. I'm worried you're not getting out enough. Maybe you should talk to Dr. Lamboni again."

Shit.

She gives me that look. Like if I don't join choir she'll send me away. Try to find someone else to get through to me, since Dr. Lamboni just put a Band-Aid on my life.

"Okay, Mom. I'll transfer to a cappella tomorrow."

She sets the clip down and sweeps me up into a huge hug. My fingers get caught in the fabric of her long, hippie skirt. I pat her on the back a couple times and she whispers in my ear. "Thank you."

"Aunt Sue owes me one."

"Yeah, yeah. Put it on her tab." She laughs.

I roll my eyes.

"How about a smoothie?" she asks, fingering a neon-green shirt that looks like it could glow in the dark.

"Banana Orange Creamsicle?"

"Don't you ever want to try something new?"

"No."

"Fine."

7

28 Days

I have a plan.

It's not going to be neat. It will be messy and awful, but there's no way it can fail. I picked a date. October 31. Halloween—the day my life changed forever. Everyone will be wearing costumes and no one should notice me. I'll jump from the Dover Bridge. It's fitting since that's where it happened—fitting and maybe a little clichéd. I'm okay with that. The job will be done.

A putrid smell pulls me away from my calculus homework. I tromp down the stairs, practically tripping on the last step. Mom's in the kitchen cooking something that smells like fish and cabbage. She's clanking the spoon against the pan when I walk in.

"Smells awesome," I lie.

She continues scraping the pan and empties the contents onto a plate with a motherly grin that says I have no choice but to eat it. "You'll like this."

I groan.

She places the pan in the kitchen sink; it ricochets off other dishes. "Almost ready." She sits across from me and places the plate of gross in front of me. Her hair is graying a little on the sides, but her face is wrinkle free. I wonder how she does it—how she looks so young. I know I'm the reason for the few gray hairs she does have. She had me when she was twenty—a product of a spring-vacation fling that turned into more. She'd met dad in Florida and said it was love at first sight, but I don't believe her because if it was he wouldn't have left. People who "fall in love at first sight" don't ever leave each other. That's what that means, I think.

I don't know a lot about love, though. I've only had a couple of boyfriends, but never long. They were more the *let's hold hands and go to the movies, make out on a Saturday night, and break up a few weeks later* type. It's better I didn't have more. I would hate to have to leave that kind of love behind. The kind where a boy loves you and you can only think of them and what they're doing and of the next time you're going to see them. That slow burn that ignites each time you see each other. Yes, I've read romance novels. I should feel deprived that I never got that, but I'm content with not having it. I have to be to die. It's the constant guilt-love that I have to carry around like luggage. That's the love I can leave behind.

I lift my fork and scoop out a bite of the soggy fish and stare at the substance, contemplating how awful it must taste. The plate's chipped on the side, gouged out at some point in time or knocked on the counter. I can't remember if I did it, or if she did, or maybe Dad or . . . . There's imperfections all over the house. The stair that creaks too loud, the cabinet door that hangs when you open it, the fridge door that doesn't shut all the way unless you close it gently. It's not even an old house.

"Eat," Mom says, forking the sludge on her plate. "How was school?"

"Fascinating."

She shoves the food into her mouth and chews, scrutinizing me. "Something's different about you."

I perk up. Can she see the desperation on me? I quickly change my posture and lift my chin so I look more put together.

"Did you do something different with your hair?"

I let my back slouch. "Yeah, it's parted on the right instead of the left," I lie.

She nods.

I poke at the fish and taste the cabbage. It's atrocious, but I eat it all because that's what a good daughter does—a daughter who isn't thinking about killing herself.

When we're done, she gathers our plates and puts them in the dishwasher. "I need to get ready for work. You know the rules," she says, closing the dishwasher door.

"No boys, no sex, no fun."

She laughs. "Fun's allowed." She walks by and squeezes my shoulder. "It won't always be like this. When you go to college . . . ." She laughs again. "Good Lord, help me. I don't even want to think about the shenanigans you'll get into then." She glances down at me with a thoughtful expression.

"You said shenanigans, Mom. I'm so proud."

She laughs and walks out of the kitchen. "I thought you'd like that," she yells, clomping up the steps.

A twinge of guilt wiggles into my heart, but I tamp it down. I've gotten good at that. When my heart's mission is to stop beating, I can't let anything get in the way, not even Mom and her big words I never thought she'd use.

I run upstairs and plop down on my bed, sinking into the comforter, and slide my earbuds into my ears. I turn on the TV so there's more noise in the background. I hate the silence; it reminds me of the voices I've heard. Mom's comforting tone. The clink of dishes as she makes her awful meals. My little sister Tate's laugh as she ran down the hall, chasing our old cat, George. Her tiny voice calling me *Sissy*. I used to hate when she called me that, but now her voice haunts me like a permanent echo.

I open my calculus book, stare at the same page for five minutes, then close it. I'm not going to need this anymore. No use torturing myself.

Out of nowhere, Dean pops into my head. I grab my laptop off the floor and flip it open to do some cyber-stalking on him when my phone rings. I glance at my phone and Jackson's picture's not there. Instead, a number I don't recognize is. I debate answering it, but slide the answer button to the side.

"Hello?"

"Ellery?"

It sounds like . . . shit.

"It's Colter."

What the hell is he calling me for? And how did he get my—

"I got your number from Jackson."

Fucking Jackson.

"What do you want?" I say, trying desperately to sound nice, but sure I sound like an asshole.

"You're so pleasant. I can't imagine why you don't have any friends."

"Jackson's my friend."

"Jackson's a puppy who follows you around for some reason."

Oh, he's trying the tough love thing. I've seen this on TV. I can play too, Tom Sawyer. I laugh. There's something about him that makes me want to listen. "Okay. Really, what do you want?"

"You haven't told anyone I let you go, have you?"

"Let me go?"

"I could get in big trouble if someone finds out I didn't give you to the cops when you had that gun."

Ah, okay. This makes more sense. Maybe he doesn't want to save me. Could I have misjudged Mr. Do-Gooder?

"I'm not going to tell anyone. Your secret's safe with me."

The phone crackles with his breathing. It sounds intimate, like something I shouldn't be able to hear.

"Okay."

It's silent. I'm waiting for him to hang up.

He doesn't.

"What are you doing?" he asks.

I pick at the spine of my calculus book. "Aw, are we friends now, Tom Sawyer?"

"Jackson must have masochistic tendencies to hang out with you all the time."

Covering the phone's speaker, I laugh. "He must." I adjust the phone to my ear. "I don't know what you're hoping to accomplish by calling me, but you've made your point. Your heroic image is intact. I won't tell anyone you broke the law for me." I tear paper off the book's spine and roll it in my fingers.

"Trust me, I'm no hero."

What the hell do I say now?

It's silent again.

"Couldn't fool me. This conversation's been a blast, but I do have to go," I say. "Other insults to sling and lives to ruin, you know."

There's a pause.

"Oh, okay. I guess I'll see you tomorrow then."

"Yep. Bye."

We both hang up at the same time and the air that's been trapped in my lungs finally escapes.

I turn back to my computer and type Colter's name into Facebook. His profile is a group photo with him and some friends from school. He has over a thousand friends and his most recent status update says, *Ghosts have a way of showing up when you least expect them.*

What does that mean? Apparently I'm not the only one confused by his update. Several of his friends asked what it meant. He never answered.

I type Dean's name into the search bar. His profile pops up and I realize I'm not connected with him, and he only has ten friends. My throat dries a little at that. I grab some water from my nightstand and browse his pictures. There's a few random ones with a girl with bright red hair who I don't recognize. He looks so uncomfortable in his body, his skin, like he wants to shed it like a snake.

He looks like me when I look in the mirror.

8

27 Days

I slam my locker closed, distracted. It echoes, so I cover my ears, dropping my book on the ugly, blue-tiled hallway floor. When the noise in my head diminishes, I retrieve it and start to walk to my next class. Someone taps me on the shoulder.

Not again.

I turn around expecting Colter to berate me on my sunny personality, but instead I'm facing three of the bitchiest senior girls in school.

Janie Reynolds, who once drank a whole liter of Mountain Dew on a dare in seventh grade. She threw it up pretty quickly after. Confirmed gossip girl Dee Simmons, who basically lives in the biggest house in town, and Kirstyn (with a Y) Matthews, the mayor's daughter, and also, interestingly enough, Colter's ex-girlfriend.

"Can I help you?" I say, clutching my torn book in my arms.

Kirstyn glares at me. "Yeah, you can tell me why your number is on my boyfriend's phone."

Great.

"I thought you broke up?"

She flares her nostrils and flips her blonde hair behind her shoulder. "Why was it there?" she demands, her voice going a few octaves lower.

Dee gives me a snotty glare to match hers.

"He's in love with me," I say straight-faced.

"You're such a loser. I have no idea why he would call you anyway."

"I don't either."

She looks confused for a moment. "Right. Well, uh . . . ."

"Leave him alone," Dee says, pointing her French-manicured fake nail in my face.

Janie glances at something to the side, avoiding the conversation. I point to my English class. "I have class."

Kirstyn huffs a couple times then walks away, her minions following close behind.

I take my seat in English, fuming. Why did Colter have to call me? Was it really just to make sure I wouldn't tell anyone? I mean, I'd get in trouble too. Now I have the bitch patrol on my ass.

Colter walks in and his gaze finds me again. He shakes his head, like the disappointment is bothering him. It's annoying. He shouldn't care. I need to get this asshole off my back, and his girly minions too.

I take a breath in and stand. My legs shake as I walk up to his desk. "I need to talk to you after class," I manage to croak out.

He doesn't hide the shock on his face. "Oh. Okay."

Class passes fast in a blur of *The Canterbury Tales*, and reading aloud, and essays. I wait for Colter after, pacing in front of my locker, clutching my book, ripping it at the edges. He finds me, and gestures for us to walk.

We make it a few steps before he looks expectantly down at me.

I twist the book's binding in my fingers. "I need you to leave me alone. Your . . . uh, girlfriend found me."

His forehead furrows. "Kirstyn?"

Her name sounds toxic on his lips. "The one and only."

"She's not my girlfriend anymore." He rolls his eyes. "What did she say to you?" There's that protective tone again.

"No." I grab his arm and yank him to the side of the hall. "Stop it. You don't get to have that tone with me."

Confusion sweeps across his face. "What tone?"

I realize I still have his arm in my grasp. I let go and grab onto my book again. "Like you want to protect me. I don't need your protection."

"What are you talking about?"

Maybe I misread his tone. For the first time in a long time, I'm embarrassed. I look anywhere but at him. The words I said echo in my head at max speed. I barely recognize that emotion. It means I . . . care about what he thinks.

Oh, God.

"Nothing. I have to go." I quickly duck out from in front of him, but he snags my arm like he did the night of the shotgun return debacle. "Wait. Stop leaving so fast."

My arm sears with nervous heat where his hand touched. I slide it from his grip. "I'm sorry. I can't . . . I just." Oh, God I sound like a lovesick girl. What's wrong with me? *A guy pays attention to you and you become a stuttering zombie.*

He grins slightly. "Are you nervous?"

I close my eyes. He's not here. *You will die soon and you'll never have to deal with him again.* An ache grips my chest and moves up. It's unfamiliar to me.

I peek out and he's still standing there.

"You're so strange. But I have to admit I'm fascinated by what's going on in that brain of yours," he says.

Compose yourself.

"I have class, so can we, uh, finish this later. I mean, not later. I hate you. I have to go." I run away from him into the classroom and bury my face in my hands thankful he doesn't have this class with me.

What the hell was that?

The bell rings in my last class of the day, so I shuffle my way to detention. Detention's so strange. It's mostly students staring out into nothing and it's so damn quiet. My shoes squeak on the linoleum as I walk into the room. There's only one other person today—Dean Prescott. He sees me and his expression says the words he doesn't utter: *Great. Now I'll never get away from her.* I take a seat beside him.

How did he get detention if he never talks? Or maybe he just doesn't talk to me.

Dean, Jackson, and I were friends until junior high, when Dean decided that we were just baggage in his life and he didn't need us. He's always been a quiet guy, surly, kind of crusty around the edges, like burnt toast.

Mrs. Benton is seated at the front of the room, her fingers clicking the keys on her laptop, not paying attention to anyone else.

"Hey," I say to Dean.

He rolls his eyes. I can feel the words crawling up my throat like vomit. "I saw your scars." He looks at me but doesn't say anything so I continue. "Does your dad know?" I know it's nosy of me. He and his dad have never exactly gotten along. I want to feel bad for asking, but my obsession with him and his attempted suicide trumps regular human decency, apparently. He doesn't react, just sits there. I fold my arms across my chest. "Come on, Dean. Just talk to me. I was your friend once. Remember? The time when you and Jackson tried to shut me out of your Boys Only club?"

He glances sideways toward me with his crooked smile. "You never could take no for an answer." He looks back down to the desk.

"Well, you guys always wanted to play without me. Was I really that bad?"

He doesn't say anything for a moment. I'm looking at him, waiting. My breath is sporadic. I don't know what I'm going to do if he says I was.

"No," he says quietly. "Jackson didn't like it because I liked you and he thought if you played with us that you would ruin the vibe."

No way.

"You liked me?" I push his arm a little.

He gives me a look like I've changed into a hideous creature with ten heads. "We were eight years old."

"Still." I smile at him. "I'm just glad you're talking to me."

He sighs. "What do you want, Ellery?"

"Why do you have cuts on your arm?"

He runs his hand through his hair. "Jesus, subtle much?"

"Come on. Level with me."

"There's nothing to level with. This is none of your business. We're not friends anymore. I know what you're trying to do, but just don't. It's too late. Okay?"

"Too late for what, Dean?"

"Nothing."

Mrs. Benton is still typing away on her laptop, oblivious to anything we've said.

I lean over, curling my lips around my teeth, hungry to know more. Excited that there's someone else who feels the way I do about life. "I *know*."

He curls his fingers around the front of his desk. "You know what?" he snaps.

"I know you want to do it again. I can tell."

"Do what again?"

I move in close to him, hoping I guessed right. "You want to die," I whisper.

He shifts in his seat, trying to avoid my gaze. "Wh . . . what are you talking about?"

Sliding my arm across his desk, I yank up on his shirt, exposing his scars. He tries to push his sleeve down and quickly glances up at Mrs. Benton, then his gaze finds mine. He looks as if he's seen a ghost or something he never thought he'd witness. I pull up my sleeve and show him my matching scars.

His eyes widen and for the first time since we were kids I think he actually sees me. It's like he's never noticed me before this moment. He darts out of the seat so fast I almost fall over my chair. His shoes squeak on the floor as he runs out of the room.

❀

I'm wired when I get home from detention. I want to know more about Dean and how he tried to kill himself—what methods and how they failed. I can hear how all that sounds in my head, and I know I'm doing the right thing by dying. Anyone who has that many morbid thoughts should just be snuffed out. I search online, Twitter, anything I can find and there's nothing. I suppose it's a medical thing. I should be grateful, since I don't really want the Internet to have my suicide details either. I'd rather it just say that "she was found dead" and leave it at that, and then name all my non-accomplishments when I was alive. Like I won a lame softball trophy when I was seven or shit like that. As if people really care.

I close my laptop and tap my fingers on the lid. I glance around the room and stare at the books scattered on the floor, my guitar in the corner I don't play anymore, the light blue heels I bought for the dance last year where Jackson and I took the Johnson twins. I grab my nail polish to paint my nails but change my mind when I realize it wouldn't dry fast enough. I click through every channel on the TV and stop on a random Food Network show. I wish Mom could cook like them. All the smiles when they try their food. That must be what it looks like when you taste something good. I've never seen that smile on anyone my Mom's cooked for. I get bored after about five minutes and call Jackson.

"Talk," he says.

"God, I hate when you answer like that, you know you sound like a complete douche."

"Is that you, Mom?" He laughs.

"Ha ha. Why'd you give my number to Colter?"

He pauses and I can almost hear the churning of his brain.

"He wanted it."

"What if he was dangerous and you gave him access to my personal information."

"He was pretty convincing. He *is* a security guard."

"Yes, which means he has access to . . . I don't know, a baton?"

He laughs again, this time harder. "A baton. Really? Are you scared of Colter?"

I sigh. "No."

"Exactly. He's a good guy. Plays soccer, is nice to old people. I didn't see the harm. Next time I'll have him fill out the Ellery-approved pre-number form."

"I would appreciate that, thank you. I have copies here if you need 'em."

"So, I have to know something," he says, with a serious tone.

I take a breath in, ready to hear something important. He knows. He can feel my desperation. "Okay."

"What are you wearing?" He laughs again. He does this to me every time. He thinks it's so funny, and I fall for it every time.

"I'm hanging up now."

"Night, Ellery Bellery."

"Night, Jackson Douchebag."

"Hey, that doesn't rhyme."

I hang up before he can say anything else and toss my phone onto the bed. I open my laptop to torture myself in a different way and Google my dad, crying myself to sleep.

9

26 Days

I clutch my stomach as I near the choir room. I have no idea why I agreed to this. Trying to be *Happy Ellery* is exhausting. I was in choir my freshman year and loved it. The sound of my voice mixing with everyone else's, the movement of the chord progressions. It was the only thing I could do well. I just didn't want to be part of it after Tate died.

A cacophony of voices singing different notes materializes in the air as I near the room. They're warming up. I turn around to run, but remember what my mom said about Dr. Lamboni. He'd see right through me if I visit him. He'd ruin my plan.

You only have to do this for another twenty-six days.

I take a deep breath and pull on the door. The tones continue to crescendo into a thunderous wake, the room shaking underneath me. It's amazing how something inside all of us can do that—literally move you. I don't recognize anyone but Janie Reynolds at first. Aunt Sue is in front, plunking on the piano, guiding her fingers across the keys, looking up at the four rows of singers. I stare up the sloped stairs of the room and spot someone at the top I never expected to be in choir. His eyes are squinting as he laughs with the grinning girl next to him. Colter looks different when he's smiling, lighter, but there's something more to his smile, something I've never seen in my interactions with him. He's never smiled around me. I guess that's my fault.

I take a step in and it's like a knife cut everyone's vocal cords in half. I swallow in the silence as Aunt Sue halts playing, leans around the piano, and winks at me.

"Come in, Ellery. Don't be shy."

My aunt has always been outgoing. Always picked first in everything. She married right out of college and my cousins are the most beautiful people on the planet. If karma had a lucky bucket, it would reside below Aunt Sue.

I flinch at her voice and take tentative steps toward the piano. I dare a glance up at Colter. He has his head cocked to the side and his confused, surprised gaze could pierce me.

"Guys, this is my niece. Be nice to her." She turns to me. "You can take a seat over by the tenors and look on Joe's sheet music."

Everyone's eyes are looking down on me like I've invaded their space and they need to protect it from outsiders. My breath is shallow as I maneuver my way past the chairs at the front and step up onto the highest landing. I try to avoid Colter as I near an empty spot two guys down from him. I glance over at who I think is Joe and look at the song we're singing. I know the song— "Somewhere," from *West Side Story*.

Aunt Sue doesn't waste any more time on me, thankfully.

She looks up at the ceiling as if searching for some meaning she can physically grab while curling her hands into fists. "This time, I want you to imagine what it's like for Tony and Maria while you sing this." She centers her gaze on us. "Imagine the pain and anguish they feel with the knowledge that two people they both loved dearly are gone." With emotion in her eyes, she lifts her hands up and we take a collective deep breath in.

I swallow the bile fighting to come up at the notion of hearing my voice, and push the air out of my lungs. The note vibrates in my throat. It's scratchy and off, but I sing it and the other ones, losing myself in the music and letting it all wash over my body.

As quick as the good feeling comes, it leaves and gets replaced by betrayal. Tate can't hear my voice sing to her ever again. I stop singing and have to sit down so I don't collapse. Thankfully no one notices but Joe, who looks concerned for about a second then returns to singing.

When class is over Aunt Sue gestures for me to come see her. She gets close and hugs me tight, just like Mom. "Thank you. I owe you. The soprano section lost so many graduating seniors, I needed one more to make it perfect."

"It's fine."

She lets me go and nods her head toward the door. "Friend of yours?"

I crane my neck around and see Colter leaning against the doorway. "Not really."

She gives me that same look Mom does. The teacher in her is trying hard to think of a lesson I can learn. The aunt in her wants to find out why a boy is waiting for me at the door.

"Be careful with that one," she says. She grins and looks younger than her thirty-five years.

"I gotta go."

I make my way to the door with sweaty palms and nerves bouncing around in my stomach. Why is he waiting for me?

He kicks off the doorframe. "I didn't know you sang."

"I could say the same for you," I say, keeping pace with him as we walk down the hall.

"You assumed I was some jock."

"You're not?"

"Well, I play soccer."

"Jocks play soccer."

"Maybe, but that's not all they do." He grins and raises his eyebrows as if he knows something I don't, like he knows me somehow.

I stop walking. "What do you want from me, Tom Sawyer?"

He scrunches up his hair and leans against a nearby locker. He's always leaning on something. "I'm trying to figure you out, but I can't."

I clutch my calculus book that's never far from me and rip at the edge. "Stop trying." I glance down the hallway. "I gotta go."

"Wait."

I turn around and shrug. "What? Kirstyn isn't interesting enough for you? Why are you talking to me?"

"You remind me of someone."

I pause and readjust my fumbling feet. "So?"

"So, I'm curious."

"I'm not a specimen in a jar for you to figure out. I have class and I'm sure you do too."

He stares at me for a moment and his expression changes from fascination to frustration before he nods and takes off without saying another word.

I try to ignore the empty feeling that descends on me.

10

Dean isn't in Sociology class today. He's been gone all week. Normally I wouldn't even have thought twice about it, but after what I know now, I have to see him. Mr. Fellows is talking about labeling theory and all I'm thinking about is whether Dean's dead body is rotting somewhere. I clutch onto my notebook and take a deep breath. Images of Dean's sixth-grade smile flash through my mind. I shake my head to get them out.

He's fine. He's just sick or something.

After class I try and remember where he lives, but my sixth-grade brain has no idea. I drive around his neighborhood for about ten minutes before giving up and Googling his name. His dad has that ice cream shop, Tasty's. The last time I was there was—no. I shake my head to erase the memory of my last day there, of what happened the day after, of what I would do differently if I could have those twenty-four hours back. I've tried to forget everything about that place, but I need to make sure Dean is okay. If he's okay, then I'm okay, and everyone's okay. I type Dean's name into the search bar and the address to Tasty's shows up.

Are you really going to stalk him? He doesn't want anything to do with you. I close the browser and toss my phone into the passenger seat like it will burn my fingers, like somehow Dean will know what I'm doing.

What's wrong with you?

I start to drive home instead of to the ice cream shop. What the hell would I say to him? Why weren't you at class this week?

Why should I care? Before I know what I'm doing I'm in front of Tasty's, staring at the scoop of ice cream on the roof.

I'm just making sure he's okay. That's it.

I stroll up to the store and open the door. A scent that can only be described as cold wafts over to me as the bell above the door rings. I immediately see Dean's dad. He looks exactly the same as sixth-grade dad. Long face, dark brown hair that's pulled back in a ponytail, and the same deep green eyes as his son. His face lights up behind the glass doors that house a thousand flavors.

"Is that Ellery Stevens? I haven't seen you since . . . ." He scratches his head.

"Last year."

His eyes get that glossed-over sheen to them like he's remembering a memory. "Yes. It's been a year? Wow. Time flies."

"It sure does," I say, trying to make my fake tone sound real.

Dean sneaks in behind his dad and I heave a sigh of relief. His shoulders are slumped as he scoops an older lady's ice cream. She looks like one of those grandmas who has extra candy in her purse and tissues shoved into the sleeves of her pink sweater. I smile at her as she retrieves her ice cream from Dean. She grins as she walks by me out the door, causing the bell to ring again.

"Strawberry Cheesecake with chocolate chips and sprinkles, right?" Dean's dad says, causing Dean to look up at me.

Dean's gaze centers on me for a second before he looks away quickly.

"I'm glad you're back." He turns to his son. "Dean, get Ellery anything she wants. I need to make some Rocky Road in the back." He slaps Dean on the back, and Dean cringes and drops the ice cream scoop.

He starts to scoop the Strawberry Cheesecake. "Rainbow sprinkles, right?" he says, glaring at me.

"Right." I drum my fingers on the glass and he gives me an annoyed look. "Sorry," I say. "Hey, you haven't been at school."

He grunts as he goes for the last scoop, holding the cup in his other hand. "You noticed."

"Of course, I noticed."

He snorts. "Right."

"You don't believe me? I'm here, aren't I?"

He finishes scooping my ice cream and tosses chocolate chips on the top. "Ellery, we haven't talked since . . . what? Sixth grade? If this is about your show-and-tell the other day, then I'll save you time. I'm still here." He finishes with the sprinkles and shoves the cup in my hand.

I dig in my pocket for a few bucks and hand it to him. "I just want to make sure you're . . . okay. I guess."

Why am I trying to talk to him?

He gives me the annoyed look again. "I'm fine," he says, then quickly adds, "You can leave now."

I start to go but turn around to finish what I came to do. "Listen. I know we're not close, but I thought that since . . . I don't know. I want you to know you're not alone. I want to do it, too." I have no idea why I'm talking to him about this. I know I sound like a crazy stalker. But knowing he's in the same boat as me makes me want to be around him. I don't want to stop him. I just want to join him, I guess.

He darts out from behind the counter and confronts me, getting inches from my face. His eyelids are creased and his glare makes it obvious I hit a nerve. "Stay out of it," he growls. He shoves me out the door and follows behind.

A car goes by and the tires screech a little as it makes a turn. My hand is freezing from holding the ice cream. "I don't want to."

He pushes me farther away from the door and my ice cream slips from my hand. I watch it fall to the ground in a pink and white heap. "Thanks for *that.*"

"I'm sorry about your ice cream, but . . . ." He sighs loudly. "You don't know me anymore."

"I know." I have no idea why I care. I mean, we were friends once. "I just think if we—"

"There is no *we*," he says in a dark tone. "It's not going to matter soon anyway," he says under his breath as he walks away.

※

Later that night, I walk out on the porch and stare up at the black sky. Everything feels eerily familiar. It wasn't that long ago that this was *our* porch. Tate and I would spend almost every night counting the stars outside before bed.

※

"Why are there stars, Sissy?" Tate whispers, like she thinks we'll get in trouble.

We're rocking slowly in the glider on the porch. The sky is dark and there are only a few stars in the sky. It's March, which normally would be cold, but it's in the sixties. Of course, next week it'll be in the thirties.

"Well, they're burning balls of gas that were produced back in . . . ." I start to waver on my answer, realizing I don't really know the rest of the story.

I can make it up.

"Gas?" she laughs. "Like Daddy's?"

I laugh too. "Not quite the same, I don't think," I say. "See, the stars are really old. Sometimes they even burn up. Did you know the sun is a star?"

Her brown eyes light up and she hikes herself up on her knees to look closer at the sky. I'm afraid she's going to fall off the swing, so I stop swaying it. "Really?"

"Yep. And someday it's going to burn out . . . I probably shouldn't say that."

Her face drops and she curls up into herself. "You mean there won't be a sun anymore?" her voice squeaks.

I struggle to come up with an answer that won't scare her. "Yeah, but it won't happen for a while. You won't be alive for it. I don't think."

God, I'm terrible at this.

"It's okay," she says placing her tiny hand on my arm. "You tried."

I laugh at her. "You're too smart," I say, still laughing. "You know, there've been people who have walked on the moon. They're called astronauts."

She sits up higher and lifts her chin. "I know. I learnt about them at school."

"Hey, you two. It's past *someone's* bedtime," Mom says in her sing-song voice.

"Guess she means me," I say.

Tate lets out a giggle that quickly turns into a groan. "I wanna stay up with you."

I lean over and whisper in her ear, "I'll sneak you in some lemonade before you go to sleep."

She grins up at me, hops down from the swing, and runs up to Mom and gives her a hug. "The sun's going to burn up, but hopefully it'll happen when we're dead. *NightIloveyou.*" She lets Mom go and runs inside.

Mom looks over at me, shaking her head.

"What? She asked what stars were."

"For the love of God, just lie to her next time. I'm still fixing the whole boogeyman fiasco you caused." She gives me her patented Mom-glare and laughs.

I laugh with her.

✿

It's cold again. It's not in the sixties anymore. The laughter builds up in me like a scream. I grab hold of the porch railing and watch my breath make smoke in the air. I almost wish the sun would burn up; then we all could die and I wouldn't have to do it myself. I close my eyes and see Tate's little brown eyes staring up at me and her smile with her one crooked tooth, and Mom trying every night to get her to go to bed, not knowing I sneak in there after she tucks her in and we talk until she sleeps.

I lower my head and watch my tears drip onto the white wood.

11

25 Days

I open my history book to study the War of 1812. I don't remember anything I've learned in the last couple days. Colter hasn't talked to me again, and Jackson keeps asking me why Colter wanted my number. I have to keep lying. Dean's ignoring me worse than before. I haven't even gotten my customary nod in Sociology class. I've become obsessed with wanting to talk to him.

My phone beeps. My heart freezes until I realize it's a text. Jackson.

J: We're going out tonight

E: Busy, find someone else

J: No I'm at your door

E: Then leave

J: Listen chica, you're going

I laugh. No matter what I do, I can't get rid of Jackson. That pang of guilt tumbles inside me again. I brush it away. I just have to humor him.

E: Be down in five

J: Make it ten. Brush your hair and put on some lipstick

E: Five

J: TEN

E: FIVE.

I run a brush through my hair and slap some of my mom's mascara and lipstick on.

Jackson's waiting in his car, a beat-up silver Ford Taurus, otherwise known as the ugliest car on the planet. I slide into the front seat and turn the radio station from country to my favorite eighties station. "Where we going?"

He turns it back to some twangy country song. "A party."

I shove the door open a crack and try to slither away. He grabs my arm and pulls me back in. "Stop it. You're going. We need to get you out of that house. You're alone too much."

He puts the car in drive and we head down Capital Avenue.

"So?" I say.

"So. I just . . . I don't think you should be alone tonight."

"Why?"

He groans. "I just don't. Listen, Janie's having a party."

"No fuckin' way. The three slutketeers are not going to welcome me into their party."

"Stop. They don't give a shit about you. Remember?"

"I'm on their radar now, Jackson Gray."

"What? Why?"

"Long story."

He gives me that look—the one only someone who knows everything about you can give you. It's loaded full of memories and almosts and disappointments.

"Fucking Colter."

"Ah, Kirstyn-with-a-Y?" He grins. "Are you and Colter . . . ."

"That's funny. I still can't believe you gave him my number, asshole." I smack him in the arm.

"Hey. Stop," he says, avoiding my next smack. "He's a nice guy, Ell. I mean, if you forget about his whack-job mom and bitchy ex. You could use a nice guy in your life." He gives me his goofy, toothy grin, the one that makes me forgive anything he does.

"But I already have you." I lick my finger and stick it in his ear.

He wipes my spit away, groaning as the car swerves to the right. The jolt smashes him into me and he corrects and straightens out the wheel. "Thanks for *that*."

I laugh at the phrase he utters so often that I've started to use it myself. "Why a party? Can't we go . . . I don't know, to a shooting range and pretend the clays are our fathers?"

He contemplates it for a second, then he must decide it's too late at night. Jackson never turns down an opportunity to shoot something. He's been trying to drag me to his dad's gun club for months. "Janie invited me. She likes me. We're dating."

I turn to face him. Saying I'm surprised is an understatement. "What?" I shake my head. "Get me out of here. Now."

"She doesn't hate you. She knows we're friends. She wants to get to know you," he says in clipped sentences. He always talks in short phrases when he tells me information he knows I don't want to hear.

I clap my hands together. "Oh, a playdate? You're so thoughtful." I glare at him.

"Just give her a chance." He smiles mischievously over at me. "She says you joined choir?"

I groan. "Yeah. Aunt Sue to the rescue. Mom made me join. She used a damn shrink attack against me."

"Shrink, huh. Might not be a bad—"

"Jackson Gray. I'm not in the mood."

Jackson's done a million things for me and I've done none for him. Because I'm selfish and I deserve to die. But tonight, I can do this for him. "Fine, I'll go. Just don't expect me to be friends with any of them." His face lights up and I smile. It feels good to make him happy. I switch the subject before I can change my mind again about going. "Hey, do you remember Dean Prescott?"

Jackson tilts his head to look behind him, flipping on the turn signal. He darts the car into the left lane. The clicking sounds like a metronome and quickly lulls me with its hypnotic rhythm. "Um, yeah," he says knowingly. The whole school talked about Dean and what happened to him last year. Of course he remembers him. What a stupid question for me to ask. "Why?"

"I've started trying to talk to him again."

He turns to me and gives me a strange look. "He still goes to McKinley?"

"Jackson Gray," I tease.

"What?" He grins. "Okay, yeah, he's in my Biology class."

"He won't talk to me and I have no idea how to get through . . . ." I almost give away Dean's secret. "How to get him to talk to me."

"Why in the hell would you want that?" he says through a laugh, turning down Janie's street.

I chuckle a little too, but it's fake. "I don't know. Maybe you're right. I'll just leave it alone."

I don't need to worry about anyone but myself. I have my plan, and I'm not going to let anything or anyone derail it.

Janie's house sits on a humungous hill in the middle of nowhere, staring down to the street like Janie and her friends do to everyone else in the school. The pillars on the front rise into the sky and the huge backyard is the span of a football field, which right now is filled with people I go to school with.

My stomach jerks with the loud music and my head spins at the muffled voices and bass jammed together. I clutch onto the seat belt strap. "I don't know if I can do this."

"Since when do you care about what other people think?" He turns the car into the yard and parks beside a blue SUV. "Don't change that. It's one of the many things I love about you," he adds, jerking the keys out of the ignition.

He gets out and slams the door, causing me to jump at the sound. He walks around to my side and leans against the SUV parked next to us, waiting and probably wishing for a more normal best friend. After about a minute, he throws his hands up in the air and opens my door. "Come on, Janie's waiting for us."

I take a large breath and follow him to the backyard. Bass booms through at least five huge speakers, and a DJ sits in front with a laptop, pushing on the keyboard, his tongue hanging out of his mouth. Several groups of people (some I recognize, some I don't) are gathered in the center of the yard, laughing and drinking out of red plastic cups. A group of guys are huddled near a silver car, passing a joint around.

I huddle close to Jackson. He wraps his arm around my shoulder, like he always does when I'm nervous. It makes my insides settle, but only slightly.

"Jackson! Over here!" Janie's unmistakable, high-pitched voice barrels over to us.

We follow her voice to a circle of Janie, Dee, Kirstyn, Colter, the dude from English that Colter fist-bumps every day, and a few other people I don't know. Jackson removes his arm from me and gives Janie a hug. I avoid Colter's gaze.

"Ellery, I'm so glad you could come." Janie eyes Kirstyn. "Aren't we, Kirstyn?"

"Thrilled," Kirstyn says in a tone that proves she's obviously not.

"What did you have to do to get her out, Gray?" Colter asks, eyeing me suspiciously.

I feel the blush surface on my cheeks and I'm thankful no one can see it in the dark.

"Unlike some people, Ellery actually likes me," Jackson teases.

Colter laughs. "She doesn't like anyone."

"She's standing right here," I say.

Janie eyes me carefully then walks over and weaves her arm through mine. "Let's talk." She glances back at a confused Jackson. "We'll be back."

I shove down the fear manifesting in my body and walk with Janie. We stop near a large tree with a tire swing attached to it, swaying in the breeze. Janie grabs the rope as Justin from Sociology class scoots by us and grabs a beer out of the cooler nearby before leaving to meet up with his girlfriend. "I heard you singing in choir. Your voice is really beautiful," she says, sounding sincere.

I turn my head slowly, leaning against the bark. "Really? But yours is so dark and haunting. I'd rather have that any day."

She laughs and it fills the yard. "I'd give anything to be a soprano, you guys get the melodies." She sticks her foot into the tire swing and stands, holding the rope at the top. "I wish I could still fit in this thing like I did when I was little."

I smile and remember how sad I was when I outgrew my stuffed puppy, Maynard. Mom had given him to Tate when she was little. I barely noticed it was gone until I saw Tate holding him against her chest like it was hers. The amount of anger that built up in my chest surprised me. Why did I care? She was my sister and I loved her. Even though I couldn't remember the last time I'd actually held Maynard, I didn't want *her* to have it. It was *mine*. It sucks to outgrow stuff sometimes. "We never had a tire swing. Not enough big trees in our yard. It looks fun though."

She hops down and wobbles a little, hanging onto the rope to keep balanced. "Yeah, it just made me dizzy. Come to think of it, I really don't miss it all that much." She laughs and hands me the rope with an expectant expression like she's trying to make peace with me, and giving me permission to climb her tire swing would accomplish that. I shake my head, but smile so she knows it's not personal.

For some reason Janie isn't that bad. She was there when Kirstyn confronted me about Colter, but if I remember correctly she didn't say anything. This could all be a cruel trick. She's never talked to me before tonight.

She walks us to the cooler, submerges her hand in the ice, and yanks out a beer. She holds it out to me.

I take it, but I don't open it.

She grabs one for herself, pops the tab, and takes a long drink. "I know we don't know each other, but I really like Jackson and you're . . . well, you know him better than anyone. I just thought we should get to know each other, ya know?"

I nod, and I'm sure I look confused at why she's talking to me.

"Don't give me that look. I have no ulterior motive. I promise."

If Jackson trusts her, I guess I can. "Okay."

"All right. I'll take you back so you don't have to hang out with me any more." She winks at me. "I want to kiss Jackson anyway."

I groan.

She laughs again. Even her laugh is a beautiful song.

We make it back to the group and Jackson whispers in my ear, "What was that about?"

"Girl talk," I tease.

Jackson grins at me. "I'm going to get a drink."

"I'll come too," Janie says, leaving me alone with a bunch of people I don't know and a few I wished I didn't.

I start biting my lip and casually try to move toward the DJ table, away from the group. I didn't want to admit it, but I wanted to talk to Janie more. Find out what songs she likes. If they're the same as mine.

You don't need any friends.

You're right.

The wind blows my long hair into my mouth. I yank it away and look up at the stars. Even with all this music and people, the stars are still glowing. I've always thought the stars were a lot more beautiful than the sun. The sun just sits alone in the sky, but the stars all have each other to form constellations with. Also, the stars only come out at night, my favorite time of the day.

"Where you going?" Colter says from behind me. "And don't say, *why do you care?*"

I dig another strand of my hair out of my mouth and try to think of a witty retort. But I forget it when I meet his eyes. They're looking at me with something. Interest? Before my next blink his words echo in my mind.

You remind me of someone.

I attempt to recover and snap back into the moment. Why can't I act like a semi-normal human around him? "I wanted to see what the DJ had to play other than this pseudo hipster shit that isn't good enough to be made into elevator music."

He smiles wide. "Not a fan, huh?" He rocks back on his heels, biting his lip a little.

I look away from him. "Remind me again, why are you talking to me? I thought we had an understanding. I said I wasn't a petri dish and you agreed."

"Maybe I like talking to you."

No, no, no. This is bad.

I glance back at him and he still has that stupid grin on his face. "That's weird."

He laughs. "Not really. You're kind of interesting."

"Interesting? You just don't hear that enough."

He leans on the DJ's table and the DJ, a guy with spiked purple hair and a hundred tattoos on his arm, glares at him. I envy the DJ. He wasn't scared to do that to his arms. I want a tattoo. A haircut too.

No, you want to die.

12

Jackson finds me at the DJ booth and saves me from the awkward conversation with Colter. "Having fun?" he says.

Janie smiles at me then looks at Colter. "I didn't know you two knew each other."

Colter runs a hand through his hair. "Yeah. She's in my English class."

"And now choir," she says, eyeing me like she knows a secret about me that no one else knows.

I smile nervously and say nothing.

She gives Jackson a conspiratorial look. "They're playing spin the bottle in there." She turns to me. "I mean, are we twelve?"

My gaze turns toward the house. Maybe she thinks I want to play. She'd be wrong, but she doesn't know me. Most girls probably want to kiss guys. Why am I here? I should just leave.

"Spin the bottle?" Colter says, grinning. He looks over at me. "Let's go play."

My heart starts pounding out an uncomfortable rhythm. It's not real. I don't belong here. I can feel it in their gazes. The way everyone looks at me like I'm an elephant in the middle of a gaggle of geese.

Jackson chimes in. "Uh, let's not. I have my own personal spin the bottle and it's in Janie's room." He squeezes Janie to him and whispers something in her ear.

She giggles.

I roll my eyes as Janie leans up and gives Jackson a kiss. They get really into it and Colter and I sneak uncomfortable glances at each other.

"Get a room, dude," I say.

Colter laughs.

Jackson lets her go, but Janie is still kissing his neck as Jackson cranes his neck toward me. "I'm gonna go upstairs. Colter?"

Colter perks up at his name.

"Can you take Ell home?" Jackson grins deviously at me.

Hell, no.

I glare at Jackson and squeeze my hands into fists. "I can find another—"

"Sure," Colter says.

Janie and Jackson leave, her stuck on him like a leech, him groaning in pleasure.

Colter turns toward me. "Let's go get something to eat. I'm starving."

He doesn't wait for me to answer and starts walking toward the front of the house. He looks back once and gestures his neck toward the cars. Without another choice, I follow him.

We stop at a white Escalade. I should have known it was his SUV I saw at Kmart. He opens the passenger door and waits for me to get in. There are so many things wrong with this. I glance at him like he's nuts and hesitate for a moment.

He gives me an impatient, exasperated look and rolls his eyes.

Taking a deep breath, I get in. The seats are leather and plush, and the interior smells like his cologne. I sink into the seat and feel it enclose all around me, the trapped feeling hovering in the foreground of my mind waiting to manifest into echoing noises and slams of car doors in my head. I try to think of anything else.

Why is he a security guard at Kmart if he can afford a car like this?

That moment between him closing my door and walking to his side is palpable—it feels like a surreal dream. My heartbeat magnifies and the scent of his cologne brings me back to the night when he stopped me from getting arrested. I can't believe I was that stupid. I wouldn't be able to kill myself in juvie as easy as I could out here. I can't make any mistakes like that again.

He slides into the driver's seat and starts the car.

I stare at him closely, examining him. His dark hair is a little too perfect for me. I like it more disheveled. He's wearing a fucking button-down shirt. He's not my type at all. He's not rough around the edges. He's a goody-goody. Probably spends his extra time volunteering for shit. So why is he talking to me? I'm not that good-looking. I'm certainly not popular. Is he trying to save me? Is there a bet I don't know about?

"Why are you staring at me like that?" he says, arching his arm around the back of my seat, backing out of the driveway.

"Why didn't you turn me in that night?"

He shifts into drive and takes off down Janie's 500-mile-long driveway. "I didn't want you to get in trouble."

"Why do you care, again?"

He turns the corner and gets on the road. The ride is smooth, like we're riding on piles of money. He shakes his head. "I knew who you were. I'm not really into making people suffer needlessly."

Who is this guy?

"But what did you get out of it?"

He grips the leather wheel tighter, grinding his fingers around it. "Can't I just do something nice for you and just have you accept it?"

"No. There's always a motive."

He lets go of the wheel and runs a hand through his too-perfect hair, messing it up. It looks better now. "I felt bad. I saw this cute girl and she seemed desperate and unstable. And I don't know why, but for some reason, which is becoming lost to me the further into this conversation we get, I wanted to help her."

Desperate. I was desperate. Could he have known what I tried to do?

"I didn't want to kill myself with the gun," I blurt out.

His hands grip the wheel tight again. "What?" His voice is shaky and uneven.

"I mean, if that's what you thought."

We jolt to a stop. I jerk forward, but the seat belt catches me.

"What are you saying?" he says suspiciously, turning toward me slowly, tentatively like he's afraid any words he says will break me.

Shit.

I search for a way out of the car. I unhook the seat belt, fling the door open, and start running. I was trying to get him off my trail and I led him right to it. He'll have me committed or worse. He'll tell Jackson and then I'll never be alone and I'll never be able to leave. God, he could tell his lawyer mom, then I'd really go to jail. I need to get him off my trail so I can make it to Halloween. Tate's dead and it's my fault. It will always be my fault that she's not here.

I run hard and fast, but I hear his footsteps and quick breaths behind me.

"Ell, come on. It's freezing. Come back."

I shake my head while trying to keep myself steady. My steps on the cement echo in my head like I'm stepping on steel drums. The wind whips my hair in circles and the breeze cuts into my face like it is made of something sharp and tangible.

He catches me quickly and turns me around. I'm putty. I'm gum. I'm taffy, like Jackson. Tears roll out of my eyes. Stupid betraying tears.

"Hey, it's okay." He pulls me into his arms. I resist and try to push him away, but he begins to stroke my hair. His touch is honest and pure, but it feels like flames are slowly devouring my body.

"It's not okay. You're wrong. Whatever you think, you're wrong," I say, his shirt muffling my words.

"Ellery," he says in a serious tone. "My brother committed suicide. I know what it looks like."

I jerk away from him and wipe my eyes. I remember hearing that a couple of years ago. How could I not have remembered?

"You're wrong." I say it out loud, but it echoes in my head a few more times.

He wipes a piece of hair out of my face. "Am I?"

I slap his hand away. "Yes."

His forehead creases in concern and his posture changes to something less stiff. "Jackson doesn't know, does he?"

I don't say anything, but I slowly move away from him.

He moves closer to me. "I thought so. I'm the only one who knows."

Again, I don't say anything. I'm not sure what wouldn't incriminate me.

"Please," I say and I'm not sure what will follow.

"You need to get—"

"Don't say it. Don't you dare say I need to get help. This is none of your business and you're guessing things you don't know. I'm not your brother. I'm me, and you don't know me. At all."

"How can I? How can anyone? I saw it with Ryan too. He pushed me away, everyone, before he did it. Stopped talking to people." He scrutinizes me again, like he did that night at Kmart. "How close were you? You said the gun was broken. Did you use it and it didn't work?" His eyes widen.

I look down at the street, knowing he's had me figured out for a while. "I need to go home."

"I . . . I want to help you. Let me."

"No, I'm not a fucking charity case. Just go back to ignoring me like before."

"I never ignored you."

I give him a *duh* look.

"Okay, maybe I didn't know you, but you never let me. Or anyone, other than Jackson."

"Look at me, *Colter*. Why would anyone want to be near me, why would they want to *see* me? I'm a mess. I'm a loser. I'm the girl who killed her sister."

He looks at me and it's like he's seeing me for the first time. He tilts his head to the side and his eyes crease sympathetically. "Everyone knows that was an accident. *I* believe it was an accident." He moves forward and before I can think of anything else to say, he reaches for my hand. Needles. It feels like needles are coming out of his fingers, piercing my skin. His skin is on fire.

I slip away from his grip. "It doesn't matter what you think. It won't change anything."

He stares at me for what seems like hours, then drops his hands and sighs. "You have to tell someone, Ellery," he says, with his serious security-guard tone.

"It's not that serious."

He laughs, but it's an annoyed, exasperated kind. "I'd say almost doing it is pretty serious. I didn't turn you in about the gun, but . . . ."

I grab his hands and clutch them tight, my skin igniting with his. "Please don't say anything to anyone."

"Ellery."

"They'd lock me up in a hospital. I can't be locked up." I backtrack. I have to lie. "The gun didn't break when I tried to do it, okay? I was testing it out. I . . . wasn't even that close to doing it." I paste a fake nonchalant expression on my face. "Really. It's no big deal. I've just been kind of depressed."

"You bought a gun, though."

"I know. It was so stupid of me. I regretted it immediately and then thought maybe I could just learn to shoot it with Jackson instead. He loves guns and shooting things." I shrug.

"Have you changed your mind then?" he asks, his voice relieved, but still suspicious.

There's this point in a conversation that you have a decision to make. You can either follow it down the rabbit hole, or stay on the surface and face reality. I prefer the rabbit hole. It's really dark and easy to hide in. "Yeah, of course," I lie.

He smiles, but his eyes are still suspicious of me. I'm not sure if my lie worked. I smile back.

"I'll get you home. Come on."

I walk past him and get in the car. He's not the type of guy that would let me go where I need to go right now. "Can you drop me off somewhere?" I ask when we get settled in the car.

He nods.

13

The air is cool and clouds have overtaken the sky, blocking out the stars and leaving a gray hue behind. I hated lying to Colter about where I was going, but I got the feeling he wouldn't have left me alone in a cemetery.

He's going to be a problem.

The carving on Tate's headstone glints in what's left of the moonlight. It's really not that different from the other graves here, except for the carving of a teddy bear in the upper right-hand corner. Mom thought we should have something on it to show she was a little girl. I would have picked a carving of the moon or the stars. They were her favorite. Her teddy bear sat in the corner of her room collecting dust most of her life. The inscription gives away that she was young anyway. *Here lies Tatiana Stevens, beloved daughter and sister. Our precious girl who was taken too soon. May she be with God for eternity.* The carved letters blur, transforming into muddled shapes. I look away and stare up at the sky, trying to make constellations out of the stars left.

I remember hearing somewhere that the day before your life changes is just like any other day. It was so . . . normal the day before Tate died. We went to Tasty's and got ice cream. It was so cold inside. I remember shivering as Dean handed me my cup.

Tate grabs her cone of Mint Chocolate-Chip and squeals so loud the birthday party of seven-year-olds in the corner look up from their sundaes.

"It's just ice cream, Tate," I say, handing her a napkin. "You act like we never get it. We were just here three days ago."

"I know. I just like embarrassing you." She grins like someone who just won a competition.

I grab her arms and start tickling her as we walk to our seats. She almost drops her cone and glares at me with a smile on her face.

"You're too smart. I know you didn't get that from Mom and Dad. Are you sure you're not an alien? That would explain your love of the stars."

She licks her cone and shrugs.

"You were born on the moon, weren't you?" I add.

"Am I green like an alien, Sissy?" she says, her tone matter-of-fact, like how dare I suggest she's from another planet. She peeks at me from the side of the bright green scoop, ice cream on the sides of her mouth.

"Well, you do have green on the side of your mouth."

Her eyes grow large and she quickly grabs a napkin and wipes it off. She takes a bite of her cone. "Can we go to the zoo today?"

I take a spoonful of my Strawberry Cheesecake. "I've got a lot of homework. This weekend, though. Okay?"

Her smile drops a little and she sucks in her ice cream–coated bottom lip. She doesn't say anything for a moment and I think she's going to get mad or try to manipulate me, but she simply says, "Okay," with a sweet smile.

❀

Had I known it would be the last time I was going to talk to her, I'd have taken her to the damn zoo, maybe imparted some sisterly wisdom. Given her more hugs.

Something inside me tells me *Let go*. It whispers memories into the night while I sleep. It claws at my insides, begs me to surrender to the words. I don't know if it's *Happy Ellery* trying to prepare me for the end, or if it's an angel, or my own subconscious. But it's always there, calling to me.

"I know I told you I would try to forget, but I can't get over what happened. So I'm going to do the one thing that's still in my control." My voice is carried on a gust of wind.

I wait to see if her spirit will appear and tell me not to do it. I'm not sure if I want her to or not. She's the only one that can set me free.

Mom hasn't visited Tate's grave in months. Sometimes when I look in her eyes I see it. The pain she's trying to hide. The shameful thoughts she denies. *Why wasn't it you? Why is my precious girl in the ground and you're here taking up space?*

Jackson was there after she died, holding my hand, telling me it wasn't my fault.

He has no idea what the real story is. No one does.

It was raining hard that night and my tires kept slipping on the wet pavement. The bridge loomed in the distance, mocking me with its height.

I close my eyes and I'm there. Driving on the bridge. Then I'm floating, floating down.

My phone's shrill ring echoes in the cemetery. It's a call again, not a text.

I groan and push the button to ignore it.

It rings again. I put it on speaker. "What?"

"Ell?" Colter says, sounding panicked.

"Yeah?"

He clears his throat. "Just wanted to make sure you got home okay."

I told him I had to go to the store to meet a friend and that they would make sure I got home. "I'm fine, Tom Sawyer. I can take care of myself. Just leave me alone."

"Believe me. I wish I could, but I can't. If I have to ride your ass, I will."

I laugh. "I have to go," I say, hanging up on him, still laughing until tears come again and then I'm crying, weeping, and screaming into the empty darkness.

This decision was supposed to be easy.

I crouch down in front of Tate's grave and stare at it. I can barely see a thing in the shadow of the hidden moon. Tate's laugh bubbles up in my mind, and her ice cream–covered mouth, and her big brown eyes as they looked up at the stars. Her tiny hands as they grasped mine when we visited the zoo. She pointed at the zebras and wanted to pet the goats. She told me she wished she could have a goat as a pet. She begged Mom, but Mom told her we didn't have a farm. So she begged for that too. She never gave up. She wanted to be an astronaut. She could have been one. She was so smart.

I sink deeper into the freezing grass. Guilt seeps into every thought, it colors every blink, every breath. It turns love into something ugly, something undeserving, wrong. It tackles my soul and demolishes it. I rip at the grass in front of her headstone and toss it to the side. I need something to hold in my hands, something to squeeze the life out of. I tear more grass and hit soil. I shove my fingers into the dirt and squish it in my hands. It's soft and cold and I toss it on her grave and it falls on me and turns me black. I dig. I dig down into the grave. I want to be there. I want to be there instead of her.

"It should've been me," I whisper. "This wasn't the way it was supposed to be."

I collapse onto the dirt and continue digging weakly, trying to get somewhere else. My fingers are so cold I can't get very far. My tears drip into the soil, absorbing instantly. I lay my head on the curb of her headstone; it's cold and the jagged edge hurts my face, but I don't care. I want it to hurt. I want to feel the pain. I want something to feel right. A trickle of blood flows down the gray stone. Wiping it away, I lie there, watching the clouds hurry past the moon, covering and uncovering it in a special dance that can only be seen at night.

My face is stiff from tears, and my nose won't stop running. I curl my feet up into me, scraping the soil with my shoes. I grab my knees and lie next to my sister, wishing for once she could tell me what to do.

I close my eyes and listen to the animals scurrying, the slight wind rustling the leaves, my own heartbeat.

Maybe tonight I can die. Out here among the trees and the moon and stars. Where I belong.

"I'm so sorry."

I feel a hand shake me. "Ell."

Chills run through my body from the cold. My toes and hands are numb. I curl more into myself, trying to get warm. For a moment I forget where I am, but it comes back like a dagger to my skin. The dread is back, circulating through my body like it's in my blood.

"Ell, come on. Get up," Jackson says.

"I'm f-fine where I am, J-J-Jackson Gray," I say through chattering teeth.

The chill feels good. I deserve to be cold. It doesn't even bother me.

It feels right.

"It's freezing, and you're bleeding and covered in soil." He grabs me under my shoulders and yanks me off Tate's grave. I struggle in his grip, but he holds on.

I pull away from him. "Leave me alone."

Jackson holds tight and pulls me into him. I push at his chest, trying to keep him at arm's length. He rolls his eyes and then I'm being lifted in the air. He has me in his arms and he's carrying me out of the graveyard.

I pound my fists on his back. "Put me down. Have you lost your mind?"

"Have you? Anything could have happened to you out here. How many times am I going to have to come rescue you from this cemetery?"

"I never asked you to."

"Jesus, Ell. Let me help you. It's obvious you aren't over what happened with Ta—"

"Don't you fucking say her name."

We near his car and he sets me down, never letting go of me, and opens the door. He lifts me into the front seat and folds my legs into the space under the dashboard. I lean my head back on the headrest and stare at the graves. The sky is dark, but with shades of morning pinks. I have no idea what time it is and I have no energy to look.

A whoosh of cold air comes into the car and I shiver again. Jackson turns the heat on high and looks over at me with a worried, frustrated expression on his face. "Are you trying to kill yourself?"

My breath stops. Colter told him. He didn't believe my lies. I knew I couldn't trust him.

"It's thirty degrees out there. You'll get pneumonia."

At least it would be over.

I let out a sigh of relief. He's just talking about tonight. "I wanted to see her."

"You have to stop blaming yourself."

I nod like I agree. He doesn't know. It's all my fault.

"You should have just left me there."

He pulls out of the cemetery and onto the road. "Don't be so dramatic. Besides I told you I would never leave you. Just like you never left me."

"I think you've repaid that debt, Jackson Gray."

He shakes his head. "So quickly you forget our pact."

I put my foot on his dash and hold my hands in front of the vents. I still can't believe he's still rescuing me, years later. "Who could forget that. You were cowering on the floor of the library."

"I wasn't cowering."

"Okay. You were leaning down to get a book when large bullies materialized in front of you." I glance at him. "Is that better?"

He rolls his eyes. "No one's ever done something like that for me before. Even though I'd never admit a girl fought one of my battles."

I adjust the seat belt so it's tighter. "Get over it, Jackson Gray. I did what anyone would do."

"No one else would have stuck up for the new kid." He shrugs. "Is that the type of person you'd leave freezing in a cemetery?"

"You mean, you'd leave other people freezing in a cemetery?"

He sighs and nudges me in the shoulder. "Just shut up."

14

23 Days

"Sing from your gut. Suck it in and hold out those notes," Aunt Sue says from the front of the class.

I hold my breath and hold out the high C for as long as I can. I have to stop and take a breath and decide to just fake the rest of the note. I can't bring myself to care about choir. Janie's in the front row really belting it out. It must be nice to be so confident in your voice that you can belt it out in a room of thirty other people. She and Jackson are together now, and he hasn't found an excuse to leave her yet. I sneak a glance at Colter two seats down. Something unfamiliar roils through my body. It feels like butterfl—Shit.

Impossible.

I've been staring at him for too long. I quickly jerk my head back to the front and watch Aunt Sue and her animated gestures. She notices me and gives me a glare. She can tell I'm not singing. I don't start.

She waves her hands in the air to stop the music, then folds her arms across her chest. "There's someone in this room who isn't singing."

"Shit," I say under my breath.

She centers her gaze on me. "Ellery, care to share why you aren't singing?"

Fuming, I curl my hands into fists. I don't like caring about what other people think, but Colter's here and Janie, and all of a sudden, I don't want to look stupid. I hate them for that.

"I ran out of breath and couldn't get back into it." Sort of the truth.

"How about you sing the note right now."

I glance around me at the expressions all facing me. They're curious, but my mind quickly starts to picture all their faces contorting to angry, vengeful stares.

I close my eyes. "How about I don't," I say.

Aunt Sue and I have been here before. A stalemate. She's as stubborn as me and these standoffs always end in her getting her way because my mom always tells me to concede.

"Okay, how about this. Pick someone to sing with you," she says, surprising me.

Suddenly all the faces grimaced at the same time. No one wants to sing with just one other person. Everyone but Janie, who's giving me a conspiratorial look.

"Janie."

Aunt Sue smiles. "Okay, girls. Let's hear it."

Janie smiles at me and starts first. Her note is low and her voice is bluesy and beautiful. I join in and my voice is high and pitchy. I can hear it, but soon it transforms. I'm matching her voice. It's different, but it sounds . . . .

"Gorgeous," Aunt Sue says as she signals us to stop. "We need to find a duet for you two."

Janie smiles up at me and I can't help smiling back.

The bell rings and Janie makes her way up to me. "God, Ell. Your voice is so gorgeous. That was amazing. What kind of duet do you think we'll do?"

I shrug and feel someone behind me. Janie glances over my shoulder and rolls her eyes through a smile. "I've gotta go meet Jackson. I'll see you later?" she asks.

"Sure."

I turn around and Colter is standing way too close. I back up a little almost tripping down the step. "Tom Sawyer."

"That sounded . . . nice." He rubs his neck and looks toward the door. "Look. Can we . . . I mean, do you want to . . . ." He looks uncomfortable and it seems so foreign on him. Nerves don't work for him. He doesn't need them.

"I want to get a tattoo," I blurt out. Not sure why. It seems as though anything goes around him. My mind is full of jerky, unplanned outbursts and they are manifesting in front of him for some reason.

We walk out of the room, my aunt watching us carefully.

"That was random," he says.

"I'm not old enough to get one. But you are, right?"

He eyes me suspiciously. "You want a tattoo."

"Yeah. Can you help me?"

"Are you sure you know what you're doing? You know those are permanent, right?" He grins, then a shroud of darkness washes over his face like a trigger has been switched. "Maybe you shouldn't get one just yet. Wait a bit before making up your mind." He looks at me expectantly.

"Can you help me or not?"

He glances at the ceiling and lets out a breath that blows his hair out of his eyes. "You're gonna get it anyway, aren't you?" he says, glancing down to me.

I don't answer, I just wait for him to make up his mind.

"Yeah, I know someone. We can meet after school and I'll take you."

"You won't regret this."

"I already do," he says, walking away.

After school, Colter and I drive out of town. Far out of town.

"Rick lives in Evansville. We have to go to his house, but he's not going to care that you're seventeen. I've known him for a while. He gave me mine."

"You have tattoos?"

He lifts up his sleeve and a gothic-looking music note in black stares back at me. I reach out and touch it with the tip of my finger. He flinches and I retreat quickly. He pulls down his sleeve. "Your hands are cold, sorry."

"Is that your only one?"

He grins to himself and something in his expression fuses into my brain. It's a look I'll never forget. It holds a crazy memory, or a story I won't hear. "I have another one."

"Can I see it?"

He bites down on one of his lips. "Maybe."

"Oh. So it's in a place that . . . I get it. Uh, never mind."

He laughs and pulls into someone's driveway.

Rick Thatcher looks like someone who could be a hacker for the government. Not what I expected at all. He has surfer blond hair and no visible tattoos.

"Are you sure we're at the right house?" I whisper to Colter as we take a seat in the living room.

The air smells like lemons and there are doilies everywhere—on the tables, on the counters, there's even framed ones hanging on the wall.

"My grandma lets me stay with her. I lost my job a couple months ago," Rick says.

"And she lets you turn this place into a tattoo parlor?"

He lets out a throaty chuckle. "My grandma's my biggest customer."

Colter and Rick exchange a look that I don't understand. "This is her, huh?" He raises his eyebrows and looks me up and down.

I cover myself as nonchalantly as I can while Colter smacks Rick in the chest, with a warning glare.

Rick gives him a look. "What?"

"You know what."

Rick laughs and slaps a hand on Colter's shoulder, gesturing for me to go in the basement. A stab of fear slips through me and I pause at the top of the stairs.

Rick goes down first, leaving Colter just below me. He turns around and looks up at me. "You don't have to do this. You can change your mind."

I snap out of the fear. What am I afraid of? I want to die. And for some reason, I trust Colter. As long as he's around, I really believe I'm safe. "No, I want to do this."

He lets out a sigh. "Okay, come on."

The basement is filled with dark colors and photos of a pilot that looks my great-grandpa's age. One picture has the pilot standing beside his plane, his helmet propped at his waist, squinting in the sunlight.

"My grandpa was a war vet," Rick says from across the room.

I run my finger over another photo with the pilot. He's smoking a cigar beside the same plane in the other photo, grinning at whoever was taking the picture. "My great-grandpa has some like this too." I turn to see the rest of the basement.

Rick slaps his hands on a black leather chair. "Sit."

I glance back at Colter. He places his hand on my back and gently pushes me toward the chair. "He's a little rough around the edges, but you can trust him," he whispers in my ear.

My body shivers involuntarily. It doesn't go unnoticed by Colter or Rick. Colter chuckles behind me, and Rick shakes his head. I sit in the chair and take a deep breath. I know it will hurt. I want it to. The more pain the better.

"It stings a little, feels like a lot of pressure pushing down on your skin, but your body gets used to it," Rick says.

I nod.

"Where do you want it? Colter didn't say."

"My shoulder blades."

"So what do you want?" he says, screwing a needle on what looks like a small gear.

I glare at the contraption he built and the needle at the end of it, and gulp. "I've gotten shots before, but it never looked like that."

"Relax. It only stings. I can tell you're tough."

He brings out a folder of fonts. I pick a beautiful loopy one, but make sure it's legible. I raise my chin, reach into my pocket, and hold out the paper with the lyrics. "I know it's a lot."

Rick shrugs and takes the paper. "I can do words. In this font?" he says pointing to the one I chose.

I nod and point to my left shoulder blade. "I want the first lyrics here. They're from one of my favorite bands, Pearl Jam. *'Now my bitter hands cradle broken glass of what was everything.'* Then a space, then, *'All the love gone bad turned my world to black.'*" I point to my other shoulder blade. "Here's where I want, *'I know someday you'll have a beautiful life, I know you'll be a star in somebody else's sky.'* Then, *'As the curtain comes down I feel that this is just goodbye for now.'*"

I thought about picking lyrics from an eighties song, but none had the right feel. I needed them to be perfect for this. Rick sets the sheet of paper down on the wood end table and smooths out the wrinkles. "Deep. What made you pick these?"

It's my suicide note. But I don't say that. "Just some lyrics and verses I like."

Colter gives me a weird look. "Wait."

I glance at Rick. "Do it, please."

Colter grabs my arm and yanks me out of the chair. "What the hell are you doing?" His tone is threatening and his voice shakes like it did in his car when he figured out what I was really doing the night I tried to return the gun.

"I told you I wanted a tattoo."

"That's not a tattoo, that's a fucking letter."

I jerk my arm out of his grip. "So, maybe it is."

"But, I thought . . . ."

I lift my head so it's as even with his as I can get. I'm still a couple of inches shorter. "You're either with me or against me."

"Jesus, Ell. It doesn't have to be like that."

I get back in the chair, making it rock to the side.

Rick steps back and holds the machine in the air. "Everything okay?"

"Yeah, just a difference of opinion."

Colter folds his arms across his chest and glares at me. "Rick, don't do this. Can't you see what she's doing?"

"It's not my decision, man." He turns toward me. "Do you want this tattoo?"

"Yes, I do."

"She's not even eighteen yet," Colter blurts out.

I glare at him and shake my head in warning.

Colter won't look me in the eye.

Rick sighs behind me, sits back in his chair and sets the machine down. "Look, I don't know what you two have going on here, but I need you to make up your mind."

"I want the tattoo. I paid you already and my parents know I'm doing this. I can have them sign something but we'd have to go back to Grand Creek and I'd really rather just get it done now if I can."

Colter slouches in defeat.

Rick ponders my dilemma for a moment then asks, "What color?"

I lift up my shirt and gaze at Colter. "Black. All of it needs to be black."

The grind of the machine comforts me. The pain is coming.

15

22 Days

My back is on fire and no amount of lotion is easing the burn. On the way to my last day of detention, I try to rush past Colter as he's shoving books inside his locker. At this point I'd do anything to avoid the awkward dance we've been doing since I got my tattoo. I'm almost past him when he looks up and our gazes meet. At first I think he's going to say something, but he stays quiet, opting to glare at me instead. He slams the locker door and shoves past me, making a point to graze my arm with his. The needles come back where he's touched. I still don't know what it means. Are needles a good or a bad thing?

I ignore the feeling and head to detention.

Mrs. Benton isn't here; instead Mr. Chandler is asleep in the chair in front. There are a few other kids in the room, but they are all on their phones, playing a game, texting, or tweeting from the looks of it. Dean is sitting next to me and he's said a few words to me today. But mostly he's still quiet and moody.

I try to remember the last time I was around him. It was summer, I think. "Hey, have you been back to the park where we built our fort?"

I watch his face for a reaction. He lets a small smile slip. "No, but I always wanted to go back."

"Things were so much easier when we were little."

"Yeah, they were."

Something clicks in me, like every moment in my life is a puzzle piece and I have to snap each piece together for things to make sense.

He searches my face, a confused expression building in his features.

"It was easier, wasn't it?" I glance at him and try to read his possible reaction to what I'm about to suggest. I can't. It's either going to be good or he's going to push me away more. "Let's go."

"Go where?"

"To the park."

"You're deranged."

"He won't even know we're gone," I whisper.

He gives me a look like I've grown a third arm.

"Come on. It may be the last time we can."

Contemplation then acceptance and then I have him. "Fine. It's better than being here," he says, indulging my craziness.

He gets up, slings his backpack over his shoulder, and walks out the door. Mr. Chandler doesn't make a move. I follow Dean out the door, garnering stares from the others in the room, but only for a second before their heads tilt back to their phones.

The park's only a mile from the school so we walk. I keep glancing over at him, and he is at me. It's a weird sort of lost friendship feeling bubbling up inside me. Dean had always been a good friend when we were kids. He'd been there when I needed someone. I'd always had more guy friends than girls. Girls just didn't get me, I guess, or maybe I pushed them away. I don't know. I wanted to climb trees instead of play house or with dolls, and I liked playing violent video games—the more blood and gore the better.

"The swings are still that same hideous yellow. Do they ever change it?" I say, squeezing into one of them, letting my feet drag on the sand.

Dean sits in the one next to me and twists in it, making the chains cross. "I think they just keep repainting it the same color over and over."

"That's so depressing."

He lets out a laugh that doesn't sound funny. It sounds sad. "Yeah, well. A lot of things are depressing these days."

"True."

"You know, Jackson liked you too. It wasn't just me."

I glanced over at him. "I know. He told me."

"But he never told you about me?"

"No. That was new information."

"You had this bike. It was the worst color pink I'd ever seen," he says, twisting in the swing, avoiding my gaze. "I remember when you left it at Walmart and someone stole it. You cried on my shoulder."

"It had rainbow streamers. I loved that damn bike."

"I wanted to make you stop crying. That's all I could think of."

"I remember. You told that horrible joke about ketchup."

"It made you laugh."

"I was nine years old. I laughed at my feet."

He laughs again, but this time it sounds real. "What happened to those kids?"

I sigh and look toward the sun. Half of it is hidden behind red and orange clouds. That crazy dance again, but this time during the day. "They grew up. And got jaded."

"Except for Jackson."

"Except Jackson."

Just then my phone rang out. "Speak of the devil," I say, answering my phone.

"Ellery Stevens. Did you skip out on detention, young lady?" he says in a low voice that's supposed to sound authoritative.

"How do you know I'm not sitting in there right now?" I stare at Dean and roll my eyes.

"Because I'm staring into the room."

"Busted." I glance over at Dean. "Dean's with me. We're at the park."

Jackson pauses. "*The* park?"

"Yes, *the* park."

"Okay. I'm going to pretend that isn't weird. Except it really is," Jackson says.

"Okay, I gotta go."

"Wait. I called you for a reason."

"What?" I say.

"What are you wearing?"

I groan at being caught off-guard again with his lame joke. "I'm hanging up now."

"No, no. Okay. Listen, Janie is giving me shit. She wants me to tell you that she really wants to be your friend." He pauses. "Shit, this is stupid. I sound like I'm ten years old. Just be her damn friend, Ell."

"I'm not sure how to answer that. Okay?"

"Good. Okay. Well. Have fun with Dean, weirdo."

"Bye," I say.

Dean looks over at me. "He's confused, isn't he? He doesn't know why you're here with me."

"It doesn't take much to confuse Jackson Gray." We're silent for a moment, the squeak of the chains on the swings the only sound. "I got a tattoo yesterday," I say. The squeaking stops. "Actually it's four. Wanna see?" I start to pull up my shirt in the back.

"What the hell are you doing?"

I finish pulling up my shirt in the back and try to point to my back.

He sways closer and is silent for thirty seconds. I count it in my mind. "It's beautiful."

"I thought it would be cool to make my suicide note permanent." He swings away from me while I pull my shirt back down. He doesn't say anything. "Have you written yours yet?"

"I keep tweaking it over and over. I just can't seem to get it—"

"Perfect," I finish for him.

"Yeah," he says with a sigh. "You never struck me as someone who'd want to kill herself."

I look at the horizon. The burden of this guilt is killing me, eating me up, and he's the only one who would understand. "I killed her."

He leans in closer to me. "What?"

"You know what I'm talking about."

His eyebrows crease like he's trying to remember it.

"Last year?"

Recognition appears on his face. He nods somberly.

I take in a breath and let it out slowly, letting my words glide on the air. "My sister was almost seven."

"Oh, man."

"Sometimes I talk to her. I know that's morbid, but . . . I don't know. I can't let her go."

He moves closer, appearing intent on my words.

"I always wondered what she would have grown up to be. If she would have made it to the moon like she dreamed."

"That would be really hard to live with."

I nod. "I tried to kill myself after the accident. I couldn't take it anymore. The pain, fighting my own life for breath." I grip the chains tighter. "I was just so tired. I just wanted to sleep forever. I mean, that's what you do. You sleep. You don't even know. When you die. That's it. You don't even know that you're dead. It just . . . happens. And then you're gone. And all the pain has disappeared. All the memories that are trapped in your mind, all the almosts and too closes, and pressure to be perfect."

He doesn't say anything but there's understanding painted all over his face along with another emotion—sympathy.

"I mean, we didn't choose to be born. I didn't go out in the world and say, 'I choose to be born to these parents.' I sure as hell wouldn't have picked to have a dad like mine."

"I hear ya," he says.

"You know the last words he said to me before he left us?"

He shakes his head.

"He said he'd never forgive me for taking away his little girl. Not 'goodbye.' Not 'I love you.' Not 'I'm sorry about what happened.'"

I look over at Dean to make sure he's still there. The sun's oranges and reds are reflected in his eyes as he stares into the horizon.

"Why do they do that? Put us down and make us feel like shit?"

I shrug.

"I wouldn't have picked my dad either," he says with a distant tone. "He said if I don't get into Harvard he would send me into the military." He sighs. "I asked him why it mattered so much. What the hell he wanted from me."

"What did he say?" I ask.

He rolls his eyes. "He said he wants for me what he didn't have and that I would understand when I had a son someday." He chuckles, but it's empty, void of any humor. "He just doesn't get it. I don't care about that. About Harvard or homework, or scooping fucking ice cream."

"What do you care about?"

He shrugs. "Maybe that's the problem—nothing."

I don't say anything back.

He shifts on the swing and makes the chains squeak. "When I do it, then he'll know. Maybe he'll finally listen to me for once. Too bad I won't be around to say 'I told you so.'"

Something burrows into the pit of my stomach at his words, and I realize I don't want him to die just to show up his dad. But I can't say anything. Who am I to judge him? He's accepted that I want to die too. We have an understanding. A silent pact he probably never meant to enter into.

Dean stands up from his swing and glances over me, his expression melancholy. "I should get home. I have to work tonight."

"Thanks."

"For what?" he says.

"This. It was nice to be a kid again for a second."

He glances off toward the road. "Yeah, it was."

16

21 Days

My greasy butter-coated fingers slip down the side of my drink and I lose my grip, almost dropping it. "Whoa. That was close."

The girl in front of me turns around as the ice jostles in my cup. She must have sensed the impending explosion of Coke I just avoided. She flicks her hair behind her shoulders and attempts to cover up that she was worried.

"Sorry," I say, replacing my cup in the holder beside me.

The girl smiles. "They should put grips on those things."

"Right?" I agree, holding up my cup.

She turns back around.

Janie laughs and pops a Skittle in her mouth. "You said you wanted butter on your popcorn."

"Is there any left in the theatre?" I ask, wiping my fingers on a napkin.

She rolls her eyes and giggles, then glances up at the ad for the mall on the screen. "I can't believe they're actually playing *Sixteen Candles* and *The Breakfast Club* on the same night, and on a Thursday too."

"I had no idea you liked eighties movies too."

She gives me a sly look. "There's a lot you don't know about me." She plays with her straw for a moment and appears to want to say something else. I wait but try not to stare at her and make her uncomfortable. This feels like a date for some reason. Is this how all girls' night outs feel?

She lowers her chin like she's embarrassed. "Thanks for coming out tonight."

"Thanks for inviting me." I mean it too.

Jackson's my best friend, and if he's into her and wants me to be, I can figure out how to hang with her. I just have to make sure not to get too close. Keep my distance. The last thing I need are more eyes watching me.

"So you've known Jackson for how many years?" she asks, taking a sip of her iced tea.

"Since second grade. I don't know how it's lasted this long or why our friendship works, but it just does."

She giggles a little. "Yeah, he's kind of infectious isn't he?"

"Like taffy."

Her eyes widen in agreement. "Yes, exactly." She nods, dipping her fingers into her bag of Skittles to get a handful. "I can't believe you just joined choir this year. We've needed you."

"I couldn't. I don't really want to be there now, but my aunt . . . ." I debate whether I should tell her the real truth or be *Happy Ellery*. "It's just after my sister died, I didn't want to sing any more. Every time a note came out of my mouth it tasted like acid."

"I'm so sorry. Why was it so hard?" she asks but then quickly adds with a surprised expression, "Oh God, I'm sorry. That's seriously none of my business. Forget I asked."

I grin at her and decide right then I'll answer her question and let her in a little. "No, it's okay. I would sing to her at night before she went to bed. We would play this game where I would tell her she has to go to sleep and she would keep asking for *one more song, Sissy.* She'd keep repeating the same thing over and over. She was so persistent that I would eventually cave. She would have made a great lawyer."

I have no idea why I just told her that. She's so easy to talk to.

She gives me a grim smile, her eyebrows dipping down to form that sympathetic look I remember getting from everyone after the accident. "When my grandma died, I didn't even want to look at a piano. It's been a few years but now I can play a song and not cry." She lets out a sigh and appears to be staring at something on the red crushed-velvet wall. "It gets easier . . . and harder, the more time goes by."

I don't know what to say back to that. She has no idea about the guilt I feel. But at least she's trying. "Thanks."

She grins and tosses another Skittle in her mouth. "Okay, confession."

"Oh . . . kay?" I say, slowly.

"I've never seen *The Breakfast Club*," she says, ducking her head down like I'm going to slap her.

"Seriously?"

She nods. "I've seen *Sixteen Candles* and *Pretty in Pink*. Even *Better Off Dead*."

"*Better Off Dead*?"

"Yeah, John Cusack plays Lane Meyer, this nerd skier who's suicidal, but in a funny way."

A funny way? Is that possible? "Sounds like an . . . interesting movie."

"We're totally going to watch it."

I've avoided making future plans with anyone past Halloween, but maybe it wouldn't hurt to see a movie about funny suicide. "Sounds like a plan, Stan."

She laughs as the lights dim. I've made a mistake and made another friend.

My list of goodbyes keeps growing.

17

The movie theatre parking lot is dark, so I grip my keys tighter and watch Janie drive off. I can still feel the awkward hug we had before she got in her car. I slip into my car, lock the doors, and check my phone for messages. I have no idea why. The only people who contact me these days are Jackson and my mom, and, in the past couple days, Colter. But he's the last person I want to talk to right now.

I look down at my phone's display. Of course, there's three missed calls from him. I'd finally broke down and programmed his name. Better to know who it is when I ignore his calls. He's called me every day since Janie's party—so determined, like he's trying to save his own life instead of mine. Even with all that, I'm unexpectedly drawn to him. I've tried to lock the doors around my guilt and pain, but pieces of me keep falling and he's the only one who can catch them. I know nothing I'm feeling is real—it can't be. It wouldn't matter anyway. He's only trying to save me.

I sigh and call him back to make sure it wasn't anything important—knowing it's not, but I also know he'll keep calling me if I ignore him for too long.

The patron saint of lost causes. Damn, the boy has issues.

"Ellery?" He sounds groggy like I woke him up.

"Yep. You raaang," I say, with an accent like an old butler.

"What's up?" he says through a yawn that sounds kind of adorable.

I need to hang up.

"You called me first. Also, I'd like to introduce you to this thing called texting—it's quite state of the art."

He lets out a breezy laugh, like he has no worries in the world but to be amused by others. "I like hearing people's voices. Call me old-fashioned."

"Well, that's not the first thing I would think to call you." I grin, but I know he can't see it. Maybe he can hear it. "I'm alive. You can call off the search party."

"I knew where you were."

"How?" I say realizing once I've said the words I know exactly how. "Fucking Jackson," I grumble under my breath.

"He's a pretty cool guy."

"Yeah, he's a damn angel."

"Are you okay?"

"You mean, have I blown my brains out?" He stays silent like I've offended him somehow. I suppose it was kind of offensive. Dr. Lamboni would call that a defense mechanism. "Okay, that was a little harsh." Why does silence turn me into a truth-telling moron?

"I know what you're doing."

"Oh yeah, what?"

"You're trying to make me uncomfortable."

"Trying?"

"Succeeding."

"Good," I say.

"I'm just trying to help," he snaps.

"I don't need help, Tom Sawyer."

"Fine." His tone has gotten continually impatient and growly. I groan. "What do you want from me?"

"Nothing. Just . . . ." I hear him sigh. "Can you just humor me for a second."

"Just a second?" He pauses again. Then I start to feel bad. I adjust my phone so I can hear him more clearly. He's not Jackson, so I know he's not going to ask what I'm wearing. He's trying to be serious, which I hate. "Okay. You have my undivided attention."

"My brother, he . . . ." He pauses again. I wait for him to finish. "You're going to do it again, aren't you? That's why you got those tattoos."

I thought he'd understood that at the time and that's why he'd been calling me. But I haven't told him my plan. I haven't told anyone the date or what I'm doing—and I'm not going to. "It's complicated."

"It really isn't," he snaps.

I climb up out of the rabbit hole. He didn't believe my lies, it's obvious. "What did you think I was doing? You knew or you wouldn't have given me a hard time."

"I can't have this conversation over the phone. Shit. This is . . . ." He sounds like Jackson, the way he won't finish a thought. I must do that to the people around me. "Can you meet me?"

"It's late." I glance at my phone's display. 10:43 P.M.

"Please."

"Fine. Meet me at The Beanery."

"Done."

❀

A few minutes later I'm sipping coffee across from Colter, and if I thought the hug with Janie was awkward, it has nothing on this moment. He steeples his fingers and I let out a nervous laugh at the sight. He notices and quickly moves his hands to the table, tapping his fingers instead. We stare at each other, not saying anything as the folk music plays softly in the background and the smell of chocolate circulates in the warm air. I glance up at the menu over the counter before surveying the room. A guy in his twenties is sipping his coffee while typing with his free hand, his eyes wide, mouthing the words on his screen between sips. A girl is plunking on her computer keys like she's writing the next break-out novel. A couple in the corner are in a heated discussion about this year's election.

I turn back to Colter. He's looking down at the table, turning his mug. "Okay, this is ridiculous. Did you just meet me here to watch me drink coffee?"

"Yes, is that okay?" He grins.

I can't help but smile back. He delivered his line perfectly with no change in facial expression. Maybe he really is funny underneath all that martyr swagger. Like the same guy who said Shakespeare was a pervert in English.

He stops tapping his fingers on the table as a somber look covers his face. We'll have to talk about it again—the pink elephant in the room. "Are you going to do it soon?"

"Define soon."

"Tomorrow, the next day? Do you have a plan?" His voice is even, like he's trying too hard to sound like this isn't bothering him.

My breath accelerates with my heartbeats. "If I did, I wouldn't tell you." His posture drops and he locks his jaw. "No, I'm not going to do it tomorrow or the next day."

"So you have a plan, then."

I take a deep breath. "Why does it matter, Tom Sawyer?"

"Because I'm in this," he says with conviction.

I arch an eyebrow and drag my finger around the rim of my mug. "In what?"

"I have to help you now."

"Help me what? Live?"

He takes a sip of his chai. "Yes."

"Thanks, but I'm good." I give him two thumbs up.

He smiles, but his expression is tense. "It's either that or I have to . . . ." He doesn't finish the sentence again.

"Have to what?" I snap. "Are you threatening me?"

"No, just stop. You're hearing me wrong."

Flames start shooting around my body, burning up my bones. "I don't think I am," I say, breathing hard. "I'm relieved. I thought for a second you were going to be a bossy asshole, glad to see that's not the case." I scoot my chair out and stand, taking a huge gulp of my coffee, scalding my throat. "Fuck, that's hot." I push the chair in and walk to the door.

"Ellery, wait." Colter catches up to me at the door and leans on the doorframe, his expression painful and guilty, like he just swore in front of his grandma. "I'm sorry. That all came out wrong."

"I appreciate the sentiment, really. But I don't need any help."

He looks at his shoes and shakes his head before turning his gaze on me. "I'm pushing you, aren't I?" he says, clutching the back of his neck. "I do that."

I want to melt into the ground when I look at the damage behind his smile. "Just—I mean, I get it."

"I keep thinking that's the reason my brother finally did it. I just pushed too hard." He shrugs and his voice sounds so sad and hopeless that I want to kick myself for caring so much.

You've got to get out of here.

I can't.

Flexing my fingers a few times, I move to pat him a couple times on his shoulder. God, I'm so monumentally bad at being a human. I want to say something to make him feel better, something that will bring his breezy laugh back, but that's not the person I am. I jerk my hand away before I make it worse. "I'm sure that's not what happened."

He clears his throat and his eyes brighten like he's trying to cover the moment with a blanket. "Yeah, maybe."

I nod my head toward my car. "I've got that English paper to do before tomorrow, so . . . ."

He stands up straight and pushes the door wider. "Me too. Last minute." He chuckles.

"I'll see you in class?"

He nods, but his expression has slipped back into somber, like he's thinking about his brother, like he blames himself for his death. If I remind him of his brother, then why does he keep hanging around me? It's only making it worse on both of us.

I hesitate at the door, but only for a moment before I snap back into plan mode.

He's not going to stop you.

18

20 Days

I drive by Tasty's on the way home from school. I've been doing that, without even thinking about it, like it's just something I have to do. I duck down so Dean can't see me, but I make sure he's in there, alive, and "scooping fucking ice cream for people," as he put it.

I rifle through Mom's medicine cabinet and pull out the leftover pain pills from her knee surgery. I shake the bottle. It's full. I open the orange container and pour all the pills out onto my palm. They're white and huge. I hate swallowing pills, it always feels like they're stuck there for hours afterward, like a cough that won't disappear. I shake the pills around in my hand. There's a dozen or so.

Could that kill me?

No. Pills are for cop-outs. Anyway, they would take too long and there's no guarantee in the end. I grab the bottle and shove all but one of the pills into the container. I take one, then dunk my head under the faucet and swallow it down. I lie on the bed, and before I even have a chance to close my eyes another memory slips through the drug's haze. All the scenes from the night Tate died flow in and out of me like I'm a conductor.

✿

I hold on to the railing and lean over. Mom's at the bottom of the stairs with that stern parental look, holding an empty laundry basket. "I know you have dirty clothes. I saw them on your floor."

"Those were clean. You need glasses."

She laughs. "Just gather them up and put them in the hamper. I'll do the rest," she says, setting the basket down. "It's like magic, isn't it? How they just show up folded on your bed."

"Magic's awesome," I say.

"I'm going out to get some milk for dinner; your sister drinks more than a high school wrestler."

"We need more Halloween candy, too," I say, sheepishly.

"You didn't."

"I may have partaken of some. You need to find a better hiding place." I cower down, and hang my head in mock shame. "Tate gave me some, what was I supposed to do?" I smile.

"Bringing your little sister into your lies; you are shameful." She grins up at me. "I may have had some, too."

I laugh. "See, and you're my role model. Who's the shameful one now?"

"I'll be back. If the kids come early, just give them the shitty candy from Easter."

"Gross. Okay."

Her keys jingle as she leaves and closes the door behind her. I'm heading to my room when I hear a whisper floating on the air. I move closer to the voice.

"I know. My wife just left, so I can meet up with you. I've been thinking about you all day."

It's my dad's voice. He's talking to *her*.

"I love you too. Can't wait to see you."

Bile churns in my throat. I catch myself on the wall, flattening my hands against it and sink to the floor. Rage builds in my heart.

He promised he'd stop seeing her if I didn't tell.

You have tell her.

The memory slinks away as the drug washes over me. Everything feels cozy and warm. A fuzzy haze surrounds every object I look at. The light bends and my feet feel like they're not touching the ground. Then I check my phone for the time and see the texts from Jackson.

J: Be there soon

J: Don't try to get out of this. You said

J: ARE YOU IGNORING ME ELLERY STEVENS?

J: Ok ok. But I'm still picking you up at seven

J: I'm outside your house. It's raining

It's 6:45.

Jackson and Janie have roped me into a double date with, of all people, Colter's friend Phillip, the guy in my History class.

Shoot me now.

I glance at the mirror long enough to make sure I don't look like a prostitute with haphazard lipstick. The pill's made it hard to put anything on straight. But I don't care. I shove on my skinny jeans and T-shirt that Jackson said I should wear and walk out into the rainy dark, shielding my head with my purse as I run to Jackson's car. He gestures to the back and I shove in next to Phillip.

He smiles at me. I smile my fake *Happy Ellery* smile at him.

His short blond hair is wet and droplets drip onto Jackson's seats; his shirt is soaked and stuck to his body so you can see the contours of his muscles.

I only have one thought looking at him: He's not Colter.

Why am I thinking that? It's true that I feel bad for him, but there's no way I actually *feel* something for him. That can't be what's happening. No, I'm still reeling from his vulnerability last night, that's all this is. I search my heart for an answer, but find it hollow and empty, like a glass that has remnants of liquid on the sides. There was something once there, something that filled it, but it's all gone.

Jackson pulls out of my driveway, heads down the street, and enters the highway. I listen to Janie and Jackson fight about the music selection for at least ten minutes.

Phillip texts something to someone, then looks over at me. "Thanks for coming out. Wasn't sure you'd want to."

"No problem. It sounded fun," I lie.

He gives me a sideways glance. "I'll admit, when Jackson said you were coming I was surprised."

"Oh yeah?" I was, too.

"Yeah, I just didn't think you'd want to."

"Why not?" I'm genuinely curious.

"Colter told me . . . I mean—"

"What did he tell you?" I fight not to sound so desperate but when someone holds a secret of yours, anything that person says about you makes you on edge.

Phillip shifts in his seat and doesn't answer. "It's nothing."

I want to scream, *It's not nothing. I need to know all the words!* But I don't say anything until Jackson pulls into the drive-in parking lot.

"We're heeeeere," Jackson jokes in a high-pitched voice.

I laugh and kick his seat.

We park next to a rusted-looking speaker that's really only for looks—everything is digital, but we love it because the drive-in keeps it authentic. Jackson and I have been coming here for years, watching old movies in black and white and even a few of the new ones. There's something really comforting about sitting in your car with the windows rolled down, watching an old movie. Tonight's isn't old; it's the new horror reboot about clowns in space.

The movie starts and I realize quickly we're not here to see the actual movie. Janie and Jackson are smothering each other in the front seat, steaming up the windows.

"This isn't why I came. Hello?" I say.

Phillip laughs beside me. "They can't hear you," he whispers in my ear. Goosebumps break out on my skin. Everything feels hazy and something hot builds in me as I listen to them moan.

I have an urge to kiss someone.

I look over at Phillip. He's gone back to watching the movie, and his eyes are wide as he tries to avoid what's going on in the front seat. I stare at him for a moment. His silhouette blurs and I can't tell if it's really him for a second. I shake my head.

God, what was in that pill?

"Are you okay?" he asks.

"I think . . . I think I want to kiss you."

Did I really just say that?

His grin widens and he leans over and then his mouth is on mine and we're kissing and his hands are everywhere and the urges in me are raw and real, and I'm numb. He could do anything to me right now. Suddenly a flash of something snaps into my mind like one of the puzzle pieces to my life. I don't want to be doing this. I can't do this. I push him off me. He resists a little, thinking I'm playing with him, until I shove him into the door on the other side of Jackson's car.

"What the fuck?" he says, giving me a confused glare.

Sweat pours off my forehead. I have no idea why I just did that. I'd said I wanted to kiss him. I wanted to kiss him, right?

I panic, grasping at the handle and missing it twice before opening the door. I run hard and fast. Jackson calls my name but I ignore him and keep going. The wind whips against my face as I dart out of the drive-in.

The streets are empty and a dog is barking in the background. A couple argues with each other. I watch the orange ashes from their cigarettes bob up and down as they flick them at each other. Then a door slams and I cover my ears 'cause it sounds like a bomb going off.

I run until I'm gasping for air and my legs are cramped. The freezing chill makes my throat burn, and my eyes are watering like I have sieves implanted in my tear ducts. I grab my knees and cough, not realizing where I am. I lift my head and look up at the red Kmart sign.

19

I glance at the door and contemplate what to do. My hair is damp when I push it away from my face. The bridge is only a few miles from here. I could run. Screw Halloween. I'll just go now. What am I waiting for anyway? It's not like anything's going to change before then. I'll always want to die.

Why do I need a plan?

No more thinking. I turn to run to the bridge and run right into an Escalade—Colter's Escalade. My knee throbs as I smack my palm onto the driver's-side window. "Fuck you!" I lean against the cold metal of the rear passenger door and look up at the moon. "You can't stop me."

An urge comes over me as quick as my decision to run to the bridge. I need to see Colter.

I run to the dilapidated building, open the door, and sneak past the guest service desk toward the back room. I search the security office, ignoring the memories of the last time I was here. He's nowhere, but the air smells like him. I breathe it in and savor the cologne mixed with boy. I can taste it in the back of my throat.

I fly out of the back room and search the aisles. I head past electronics, bump into an end cap of DVDs, make my way past the office supplies and run to automotive. My footsteps slap against the shiny linoleum. I pass a couple, laughing, holding on to each other's hands, coasting through the store like they have no worries.

I'm panting and sweating. My vision starts to blur and darken. My skin is on fire, my heartbeats fluttering and skipping around and they're so loud in my ears.

Closing my eyes, I take a deep breath and think of the states in alphabetical order to calm the storm inside. *Alabama.* I need to find him. He can make it all better. *Alaska.* I need to control this need for him—box it up and build walls around it.

My heart is going to stop. My sight is about to disappear. My legs are turning to gum.

"Ellery?"

His voice is the only thing that doesn't make me want to cover my ears. The ache for him is strong and familiar and scares the shit out of me. I turn around and stare at him—his ratty, stained baseball cap, his mess of hair hidden under it, the way he purses his lips, the way he looks at me like I'm the only thing that matters.

My body collapses under me and I have to lean against a kiosk of Posturepedic pillows next to me. He walks up to me and grabs my arms. I fall into him and the tears come savagely.

He strokes my hair again, like he did the night of Janie's party. "Shhh. It's okay. I'm here," he whispers, his breath speeding up under my cheek. I grasp onto him, clutching fistfuls of his T-shirt in my hands. I can't get far enough into him. His heart beats against me and I count the thumps. They're fast, faster than they should be.

Is it because I'm here? I must've freaked him out.

I pull away from him as he wipes a tear from my cheek with his thumb. "What happened?"

"Phillip. I . . . ."

He locks his jaw and I can hear his breath come out his nose. "What did he do to you?"

"Noth—nothing. He didn't do anything. It was me. We were on a date and then I just." *Pushed him against a door.* I pause. I can't tell him anything about what happened. He would think I'm crazy. He may already think that. I would, if I were him. "It's okay. I'm okay." I wipe the remaining tears from my face with the sleeve of my jacket. I don't even know why I'm crying. It has to be that damn pill.

"You're not okay."

"I am. I promise, I just haven't been on a date in a while. It—I wasn't prepared for it. Anyway."

We're the only ones in this section—half of us is in automotive and the other is in electronics. A squeaky wheel echoes nearby as I move us away from the pillow kiosk into an aisle full of windshield wipers and rows of blue fluid.

He bites down on his lip and looks toward the car mats with Tasmanian Devils on them. "Did you kiss?" he says through gritted teeth.

Should I lie?

"Yeah. It wasn't a big deal."

"I'll fuckin' kill him."

I grab the bottom of his jaw and turn his face toward me. "What's the big deal? I'm not dating anyone, and he was there."

He flares his nostrils again, similar to how Kirstyn did when she confronted me. People flare their nostrils a lot around me. "I told him if he laid a finger on you I'd kick his ass."

He knew about our date? I suppress a grin at the image. "He didn't do anything wrong. *I* kissed *him*. Don't blame him for anything." I let go of his jaw. "Why do you care, anyway? It's not like you and I are together."

He shuffles back a little like I've offended him again. Does he like me? Is this more than just trying to save me? Why would he like me? I'm trouble. I'm extra work. Do I like him?

"I know we're not. I just don't understand why you'd want to kiss him considering . . . ." He lowers his chin a little and gets a sheepish expression on his face like he said too much, like now *he's* offended *me* in some way.

I keep it as light as I can so he won't feel bad. "Considering I want to off myself?"

He glares at me, lifts up his cap, and runs a hand through his hair. "I keep hoping you'd just let me in so—"

"You can save me from myself?" I tease.

He doesn't find the humor I do in that statement.

"It's not funny. You're—"

"Fucked up? I know this."

"Quit finishing my sentences. I was gonna say lost."

"Unstable at best?" I say, using his words against him.

He stares at the mats, straightening a few of the plastic blue containers of wiper fluid. "I need to get you home. I'm off in five minutes." He moves his gaze back to me. "Can you wait in the front for me?"

A few minutes later we're in Colter's SUV watching the houses whip by, creating blurry colors in the windows. The drug is still there; I can feel it like a fog in my system, marring all my thoughts. He's quiet and I know he's thinking of how moody and strange I've been with him. I would be too. I'm supposed to be pushing him away, but he's become someone important. A safety net I need to get me through these last couple weeks. God, I'm not being fair to him. I'll just make sure to do something really horrible to him before Halloween so he can forget me and move on.

That's such a shitty thing to think.

I close my eyes and try to imagine another way. He knows. He's known I'm going to kill myself since after the party. There's an expiration date. He's going into whatever this is willingly. I don't have anything to feel bad about. He's already said he's only trying to help me. It doesn't matter that I like being around him.

He grips the steering wheel tight. I noticed it last time. He's always uneasy around me, like he's waiting for me to scream or run. I guess I don't blame him.

"Are you still mad at me about the tattoos?"

He gives me a look like I should know the answer to my questions already. "Yes, I'm still mad at you. But not just about the tattoos."

"Then why are you taking me home?"

"I don't know."

I can appreciate his honesty, but I feel the disappointment deep in me. I wanted him to say I was important, that I mattered. Which is so backwards. Why do I need him to validate me?

"I'm just gonna ask. 'Cause I don't know what else to do at this point."

I wait for him to ask his question, worried that it might be something I can't answer.

"Why do you want to kill yourself?" he asks quietly as if he didn't really want those words to leave his lips.

It's strange to hear the words out in the open like that. I want to burrow down into the seat to get away from them. Instead I answer as honestly as I can. "I'm tired."

"You're tired."

"Yeah, don't you ever just get . . . tired?"

"That's when I take a nap."

"I don't mean tired in your body. I mean tired in your heart, your soul."

It appears as if he's thinking about it. "I don't know. I guess I just think about the good things in my life and then it all goes away."

"What if you didn't have any good things? What if when you closed your eyes you only saw one thing, felt one thing. Over and over."

"What do you feel?"

"Guilt."

"And you think killing yourself will make it better?"

"I won't feel it anymore."

"Yeah, but you'll be gone. You couldn't feel *anything* anymore."

"That's the point."

"It's scary how much you remind me of my brother." He shudders like he just thought of a memory of him. "He didn't want to feel anymore either. Well, according to the letter he left me." He choked out those last few words. "I mean, why? Such a waste."

I'm sure he feels destroyed. I know Jackson will be so angry at me when I do it. But that's not something I can change—how someone else feels. I have to do this. This is the only answer. It may demolish everything around me, and I want to do something to stop that. I do. I want to make it easier for everyone. I wish I could just accept life and grasp it in my fingers and play with it, and move it around to a place where I can live with *Happy Ellery*. Be her. I've tried.

I clutch onto the seat belt and squeeze it in my hand. "Nothing I say will make you feel any better."

He takes a breath in and twists his hands around the wheel again. "You do the same things Ryan did. The strange moody shit, the changes in how he looked at me. The tattoos. The fakeness he tried to hide. I see all that in you. You don't have to answer me, Ell. I know the answers. I've watched them happen."

We pull up in front of my house and he turns off the car. We sit in silence for a moment, both of us staring at the front windshield.

He turns to look at me and lowers his head to get to my line of sight. "You need help, Ellery, and I can't just keep something like this inside. Not this time."

Shit.

"Please. I'm just confused. I need time. If you turn me in, that's it. I'm stuck in a hospital and no one looks at me the same. My mom. She'll be destroyed. And Jackson." He cringes when I say each name. I know I'm being cruel, but I have to convince him.

There's sincere concern in his eyes. In this moment I want to say whatever I can to get that expression off his face. "I can't live with myself if something happens to you. I've already lived that life, and I almost didn't make it out." He pauses and his face displays the scars of the memories he tries to forget. "You should talk to someone. Another perspective can help. It helped me after . . . you saw someone after what happened, right?"

"Yeah. It helped a little. At times. But I think I left there more confused than I started," I say. "I know you said I remind you of your brother, but I'm not like him. You know me, at least a little by now. I can . . . ." *Wait.* "I'll try. Just please don't say anything."

He stares above him and shakes his head. I let the air out of my lungs I've been holding in. He's not going to tell.

"Fine. I'll give you till . . . ." He pauses again and I can see the thought in his expression. He's thinking of an arbitrary date, so he can feel good for a certain amount of days and not worry. "Halloween. That's the next big holiday, right? It's in, what?"

"Twenty days," I whisper, knowing exactly how many because I think about it every day.

"If you give me twenty days, I promise I won't push you, or tell. But you have to promise me you'll try." I see it in the depth of his eyes, the conviction. The determination for his cause. His gaze is sure and his words are sincere and permanent. He won't say anything.

I place a hand on his cheek and pull him toward me so I can look him in the eyes. "I promise," I lie.

He looks slightly relieved, taking a breath like he's just recovered air for the first time after being deprived of it. I have to look away. He grabs my hand and squeezes it once.

I let him.

20

17 Days

Janie and I have started eating lunch together. She keeps mentioning Colter to me, like she knows something's up. She's coming over this Friday to watch *Better Off Dead*. I keep trying to find excuses to blow her off but she's persistent.

At the end of the day I'm fumbling with the key fob to my Escape when Colter comes up to my car, smiling like he has a secret. "I have somewhere I want to show you."

"No, I have a lot of—"

"Homework? Yeah, heard that already. Come on. Indulge me for once." He's practically bouncing in place.

"Colter, I can't."

"Ha." He points at me accusingly and I wonder what I said. "You said my real name."

Shit. I did.

He's all puppy dog excitement and it's hard to say no to him when he's like this. He's relentless in his pursuit of making me enjoy life, or whatever he's trying to do. I'm making secret deals all over the place—one to die with Dean, and the other with Colter to live.

"You drive," I say.

A few minutes later we're in the back of his Escalade on top of a hill looking out into the city. There's not much here, but what is, is beautiful. It spans for miles. The lights, the windmill shadows in the distance, the trees covering every part. The wind whips my hair into my mouth; I have to keep yanking it out.

I swing my feet under the bumper. "This is gorgeous. I can't believe this is here in the middle of all this flatness."

"I know." He's next to me, rocking his legs under the back of the trunk hatch. "I come up here to think sometimes."

I've never asked him about his family and I don't really know anything about him other than his brother killed himself and his mom's a royal bitch. She worked with my dad and even though I've never met her, I've heard about her. I've been too caught up in myself. It isn't fair. Maybe I shouldn't find out more. If I get to know him too much . . . . "What was it like when Ryan died? I mean, for you?"

I hear him suck a breath in. "Hard. As you'd expect. I couldn't believe he actually did it. I was so shocked. At first I couldn't even cry. I just stared at the wall for days." He grabs a soccer ball from the trunk, tosses it up in the air, and catches it. "You see someone every day and then they're just gone. It's such a weird feeling. When we lost my uncle to cancer, we watched it happen. He got thin, his skin grayed. We knew it was coming. But with Ryan? Once I started to realize he was depressed, I never really thought he'd go through with it. I was in denial for a long time. When I realized he was serious, I threatened to turn him in. He said, *No one's going to lock me up* and I told him at least he'd be alive." He drops the soccer ball and kicks it. It flies through the air and drops into a roll, crunching on the dirt. "He told me to stop pushing him. That he would do it if I didn't stop." He looks over at me, a film of tears forming in his eyes. "I never thought—if I'd known." A determined expression falls over his face as he blinks the tears back into his eyes before they have a chance to fall.

My insides try to rebel and I fight not to touch him, to make him feel better in some way. "I'm so sorry."

He gives me a knowing glance, shakes his head, and a puzzle piece snaps into place. He doesn't have to say the words. He wants to save me, because he thinks if he does, he'd be saving Ryan.

"That had to be hard on your parents too."

"Yeah, it wasn't easy, but they stayed married," he says, looking down at his shoes. "They pretty much have the perfect marriage now."

"I'm glad for you." My parents didn't make it after Tate died.

"You know, I think they love each other more now. It's kinda sick, really."

"It's not sick at all. It's beautiful. I want that." I can't believe those words came out of my mouth. I want to take them back and shove them down my throat.

He glances sidelong at me. "You'll get it someday."

He sounds so sure of himself. Everything he says sounds like he has no doubt. His words are gospel. They never waver like mine. I let out a sigh. The sky is pinkish orange and the sun is huge, setting in the distance. The moon is peeking out the side of the sky, as if telling the sun to quit being a sky-hog.

"I'm not so sure I'll be around to enjoy it if it does happen."

His posture deflates. Nothing I say is ever right with him.

"I wish you knew how beautiful you were. If you believed it, I think you could be happier."

"I don't care about looks."

"Yeah, I kind of figured that. But I was talking more about what's inside you."

"You can't be serious. You're one of those annoying glass-half-full people, aren't you?"

He smiles, but doesn't say anything. "I have something to ask you." He looks nervous, running his hands in and out of his hair. "There's this thing. My little brother, Atticus—"

"You have another brother?"

"Yeah, and a sister who lives in California. She and the twins are up for a visit," he says. "Anyway, I told my brother I'd plan this dance for his class. He's in eighth grade. They're having this competition with the seventh graders. There's judges and everything, and whoever puts on the best dance wins a trip to Disney World for the class. Atticus is a huge Disney freak. He wants to be an animator. Anyway, I need people to help. We only have a couple weeks left to get it going and their class picked an eighties theme, which I know nothing about. Jackson mentioned you like the eighties, so I thought that maybe . . . ." He's looking at me like I could give him the directions to the fountain of youth. Hopeful, naive. He's trying to get me to join something, something that will keep me alive. Or maybe he really needs my help.

Of course Jackson told him I love the eighties. When will that boy stop interfering in my life?

When you're dead.

"What would I have to do?"

His eyes light up and I feel it in my gut.

"Just help with the music, the decorations, the setup, maybe help find a DJ?"

"So, basically everything?"

He laughs. "Well, I'll be helping, and Jackson and Janie offered to help too. They said something about getting volunteer hours for it. You could, too, if you want."

I swing my feet under me, thinking about what type of decorations they would have in the eighties. Lots of pink and bright colors. Maybe there could be a booth for pictures and the kids could put on sunglasses and leg warmers.

He gives me that sidelong glance that turns my insides to mushy pea soup. "You're already thinking about it, aren't you?"

I am. I can't tell if I'm happy about that. I seem to be.

He claps his hands and hops off the back of the Escalade, then holds his hand out for me.

I grab it, and smile up at him. I almost forgot what it felt like to really smile. It's not *Happy Ellery* smiling either. It's me.

"I should get you home," he says, dragging us to the front of the car. He opens the door for me and I slip in.

"When's the dance?" I ask, buckling my seat belt.

He starts the car. "Oh, huh. Halloween," he says with a tone that says he's thinking about the deadline he gave me. It must be a full moon on that day or something. There's way too many events that fall on that date for there not to be some cosmic meeting or a planet in retrograde or some bullshit.

It doesn't matter.

Only one thing is happening on Halloween.

21

16 Days

Mom used to take Tate and me to the train tracks when we were mad. We would wait until a train went by and then she would tell us to scream like you wanted God to hear you in heaven. It's not as cold as yesterday, but there's a chill in the air that makes me want to sit by a fire, not in the middle of the woods waiting for a train to pass by.

"I thought you were kidding when you said to meet you at the tracks," Dean says from behind me.

"Then why'd you come?"

He sits down beside me on the tracks. "I was curious."

The cold air rustles the sleeve of my coat. I pull my arms deeper inside. "Make sure to get close enough to feel the wind from the train. Do you know what you're going to yell?"

"I can think of a few things, but this isn't really what I thought you meant," he says, standing up and moving beside the tracks. I glance down the abyss of train tracks and see faint lights before the tracks begin to rumble under me.

"Just try it," I say.

It would be so easy to jump in front of it. Or even just stay where I am and let it run over me.

"Come on, Ellery. Get up," he says as the train moves closer.

I stand up and slide into the middle of the tracks, the gravel kicking up from my shoes. So much should be going through my head, but I search for memories and scenes and find emptiness.

"Ellery, I'm serious. I don't want to see you die."

At his voice, a memory finally slips into the vast emptiness of my mind—the day my dad left.

❀

"Fine. Go!" Mom yells, pacing in the living room while my dad lugs his bags to the front near the door.

I'd try to avoid their conversation, but I can't get up from the couch. My leg is in a cast and my arm's in a sling. I'm a shell—empty and vast. It doesn't even feel like I'm here anymore. I try to breathe but the air gets stuck in my throat. Anger doesn't build in me anymore. It lies dormant, with every other emotion.

My dad slams his suitcases on the floor. "I can't live in this crypt anymore."

"Our daughter died, what did you expect around here? A party?" Mom says.

"I can't be here anymore."

"You still have another daughter and she needs our help. Dr. Lamboni—"

"That quack will never get us back to normal."

"Can't we talk about this?" she asks with sympathetic eyes, wringing her fingers through a towel.

"There's nothing to talk about." He turns to me and his eyes narrow.

"I'll never forgive you for taking away my—" He chokes up, tears streaking his face as he stutters out, "m-my little girl."

I don't say anything.

He grabs his bags and heads out the door.

I lean my head back and start counting the cracks in the ceiling while Mom throws plates against the wall in the kitchen.

❀

I scream at the train and spew everything I wanted to say that day out of me. I've relived that day in my mind so many times. I just sat there. "You fucking piece of shit asshole!"

The train barrels toward me. It's still a few miles away. I have plenty of time to move. It starts blowing its horn as it sways on the tracks. The squealing of the wheels pierces through the night air. I keep screaming. "I didn't want her to die!"

I raise my arms into the air and let everything out of my lungs until the train gets close enough that the headlights are two beams on my chest.

"Ellery!" Dean yells.

I move out of the way as the train rolls by and honks its horn. "Scream, now," I tell Dean as loud as I can, my breath sputtering out of my lungs. My voice is practically hoarse after yelling.

He shakes his head and backs away from me as the train continues to rumble by. "You're crazy."

I laugh. "Well, yeah? I thought we knew that about each other already."

He creases his eyebrows and scrutinizes me. "You have a good life. A mom who loves you. Jackson. Why give that up?"

Irrational anger threatens to pour out of me. "You have a good life, too," I snap.

He laughs. "Not really. It gets old having to prove your worth every second of your life."

"It's not about who gets left behind. You know that. I want to get rid of the pain. I thought, of all people, you'd understand that."

"I do. More than I can say. But I keep picturing that little girl and her pink bike and it makes me wonder if . . . ." He shrugs, avoiding the rest of his sentence. Maybe he realizes the same thing

I do about him—that we don't want each other to die, just to die ourselves.

"Well, the boy who made that joke about ketchup just to make me stop crying makes me wonder if, too."

"I gotta go," he says abruptly, backing farther away from the tracks. "Bye, Ellery."

"Bye," I whisper. My voice is gone.

I hope Dean doesn't kill himself tonight, is my last thought before going to bed.

22

15 Days

Janie and I pick a booth at the back of The Beanery, the same place Colter and I were last week. It's Grand Creek's best coffee place that isn't that other place that's on every corner. I grab a white mocha and Janie comes back with her coffee, a huge piece of apple pie, and two plates.

She sets out the plates in front of us. "This is an intervention."

"A what?" I ask, getting up to grab forks.

I hand her one and she scrutinizes me. "Inter-ven-tion," she says slowly.

I take a bite of pie and try to ignore her.

She cuts into her piece and starts sawing at the crust. "I just don't get you."

I chew the chunks of cinnamon apple and crust, and they are the best thing I've tasted in my life. I forgot how much I loved pie. "What's to get? And what is this an intervention for?"

"You know, Colter and I are good friends. He lives down the street from me." She gives me a knowing eye, while scooping out a bite.

"Oh, yeah?" I take a bite of my pie and try to stop my fingers from shaking the fork.

"Come on, Ell. Talk to me."

The pit in my stomach grows to apple-pie size. What if he told her what I wanted to do? What if he sent her to me to stop me? "Look, I don't know what he told you, but it's not true."

"How do you know?"

"What?" Now, I'm confused.

"He likes you."

I stop my fork halfway to my mouth. "He doesn't know what he's doing."

Janie flashes a smile. "I think he does."

"Did he tell you that?"

She looks to the side and bites her bottom lip. "Not exactly."

She has no idea. He's only trying to save me. We have a deal and it doesn't include feelings for each other. Although the more I hang out with him, the harder it gets for me to separate my feelings from the truth.

"I'm going to tell you a story," she announces, breaking my thoughts.

"Oh, boy."

She glares at me, but it's playful. "In second grade, this girl ... Cara, I think her name was. She had these shiny black shoes and a bright red dress that she wore almost every day. She got picked on. All the time. They called her Orphan Annie and some other names. One day she was cornered by a group of girls. They were being so mean to her, pushing her around and stuff. Colter stepped in front of Cara and told those girls off. I watched it happen."

"Does this story have a point?"

She flicks her fork at me and I cower as pieces of apple mush fly off the tines. "He's protective. It's kind of in his nature. You know he's told Kirstyn to back off you a few times now? Which means he's protective of you." She narrows her eyes at me, like she's trying to look through me for something. "It's more than that with you, though."

"Why are you telling me this?"

Has Janie said anything to Kirstyn about me?

"I just thought you should know." She scrapes the last of the crust off her plate. "Anyway, I don't want to talk about him anymore. We need to go shopping."

"That's okay."

"No, it's not." She scrutinizes my outfit of jeans and a T-shirt that I suddenly realize has a hole in the shoulder.

I shrug. "Okay, yeah. Maybe."

She laughs.

I get home and lay on my soft comforter. After two hours at the mall, my feet are sore and I feel like I walked across hot coals, if the hot coals were needles the size of hot dogs. Janie loves to shop, and she has three iguanas, and two tarantulas. She bought *Better Off Dead* and she's bringing it over tomorrow, but I really just want to sleep for a few days. All this faking is tiring. I'm about to close my eyes when my mom's voice echoes in the hallway.

"Dinner!"

I scramble from my room and slip into my chair at the table. The smell of onions and burnt meat wafts into my nose. I cringe. "Mom, what did you make?"

She sets the steaming plate in front of me. "Try it, you'll like it."

I nod and stick a fork into the green beans, the only thing I will be consuming. I place it on my tongue and take a bite, crunching down on the barely cooked bean.

"Honey . . ." she starts, pausing to look at the wall. "I'm worried about you."

She knows. Oh, God. She knows. I freeze. I'm a statue. I want to be a chameleon. "I'm fine."

She places her hand on mine. Her skin feels like smoldering ashes. "You just look so pale and tired. Are you getting enough sleep?"

"All teenagers look like this without makeup."

She gives me the mom-eye, the look that knows everything about you at the same time as knowing nothing at all. Conversations with her have become stilted and strained since I decided to kill myself. But silence is uncomfortable. Silence means questions from her. I can appreciate that she wants to ask them, but I get tired of lying so much. I need to throw her off track. "I met a guy," I blurt out.

Her eyebrows raise in a surprised expression. I try not to get offended by that. "Tell me about him."

"He's . . . ." I smile before I know what I'm doing. "He's nice."

"Nice."

"Yeah, I picture him rescuing cats out of trees and helping old ladies cross the street."

"Well, nice isn't bad. What's the problem?"

"It's complicated."

She sighs. "It always is." A concerned expression falls over her. "This boy, you haven't . . . you know."

"Mom. Really? We've had this conversation already, when I was, like, twelve. I was grossed out then, please don't make me go through it again."

She grabs a napkin and wrings it out like it's soaked and she's trying to make it dry. "I know, but . . . ." She glances in the air as a small smile grows on her face. Mom hardly ever gets nervous, but when she does she smiles the whole time. She could never play poker.

Before I realize it, I'm wringing my napkin, too. I place it back on the table and start to get up.

"Hold on," she said in a serious tone, still smiling, because she's still nervous.

I sit back down and set my hands in my lap.

"I'm just going to say one thing. If you . . . ." She cringes. "Decide to . . . ." She takes off her sweater and drapes it on the back of the chair. "Is it hot in here? What's the thermostat at?" She laughs. "Okay, I can do this. Just be safe. I mean, don't do it. For the love of God, just wait until you're married." She shakes her head. "No, that's not realistic, is it?"

"Mom, are you okay?"

"It can't be a hot flash, I'm too young." She fans herself and glances around the room, a smile still on her face. She places her palms on the table. "Please, if you're going to do it, just make sure it's with someone you trust and love. It's so much better that way. When you meet someone it can seem like it's love, but it's really not sometimes. But when you know, you know." She pauses and I think she's done, but she's not. "But always be safe." She heaves a breath out and starts laughing again. "Whew. I'm glad that's over." She gets up from her chair, opens the fridge, grabs a beer, and takes a huge gulp.

"You know what?" I say, rising from my chair. "I actually think that was harder on you than it was on me."

She lowers the bottle and leans on the counter. "I think you're right."

23

Later that night I search for Dean's Facebook page to see if he's posted anything since it's too late to drive by his house. I friend him expecting him to ignore it.

But he doesn't.

A pop-up of Dean's face comes up shortly after we become friends.

D: Hey

E: Hey what's up? You talking to me now?

D: I want to do it tonight

I lift my shaking fingers from the keys slowly, my heart thumping like bongos on my chest, my breath uneven with each thought. Oh, God. No. No, no, no. Not tonight.

E: Really?

D: Yes

E: What's your number?

There's a pause, then his number streaks across the chat window. I grab my cell and call him.

"Hey," he says.

"I'm not sure tonight's good. For that," I say, knowing how stupid it sounds. "Um, we should meet."

"Okay," he says. If a voice could sound like an emotion, his would be defeated.

I sneak out of the house and make it to the park in ten minutes. I run the entire way.

Dean's sitting on the swing, looking up at the sky. I stare at him for a moment, wondering what I can do, if anything, to stop this. I don't want him to die.

You could tell someone.

He'd hate me.

The air has cooled to ice cubes and the swings are rocking in the wind, squeaking every few seconds. I slip into the swing next to him. He doesn't look away from the sky.

"I'm sorry I've been so cold to you all these years," he says.

The sand is hard as I try to bury my shoes into it. "It's okay. We all changed."

"Except Jackson."

I let out a clipped chuckle. "Except Jackson."

"Do you think we'll go up there by the stars?"

I glance up at the sky and start looking for the constellations I know. It wasn't that long ago I looked up with Tate and told her what the stars were made of. I thought we'd be able to gaze at the stars forever, that we'd swing on that old glider when we were older and reminisce about those moments. She wouldn't remember 'cause she was so young and I'd have to tell her again, and then I'd remember it through her eyes. Every day I mourn that feeling.

"Never really thought about what happens after. I just thought of the end being the end, ya know?"

"Yeah," he says softly.

I search my mind for something else to say. Something to get him to stop, or at least wait. I'm such a damn hypocrite. "Do you really think dying is the answer? I mean, for you? What if you told your dad . . . ." I pull my hood over my head to stop the wind from burning my skin.

He lowers his head and turns to me. "I can't go to the military, Ellery. I wouldn't survive with all those rules. I failed another test last week. I'm not getting into Harvard."

"There's gotta be something you can—"

"Whose side are you on?" he yells, cutting me off. "What about you? Do you think dying is the answer? Do you think that will bring your sister back?"

I open my mouth but say nothing, grasping the swing's chains tighter in my hands. The urge to run spreads in my bones.

"What did you think? That your death is somehow more warranted than mine?"

"No, I just thought. I hoped."

"No, I know what you thought. I'm sorry I let you in." He storms off, the swing thrashing against the metal pole in his wake.

"Dean! Dean! Wait," I say, running after him.

He runs faster. I follow him, dodging trees and cars on the sidewalk. He finally stops and leans against a large oak tree. I come up next to him out of breath. He pants. "You're unbelievable."

"Look, I'm sorry. Okay? I'm a hypocrite."

He glances up at me, still panting like a marathon runner. "I'm not going to do it tonight. Not anymore. I'm too tired." He pushes off the tree.

"Okay," I say relieved. I don't say anything else, just in case it will make him change his mind.

He walks backward, his sneakers awkwardly catching on the asphalt. "Don't worry about me."

I nod and apologize again.

He quickly turns around and jogs to his house.

He's not going to tell me when. I'm just going to wake up one morning and he won't be in school. And it will be over. I imagine the world without him, without his crooked smile and dreamer's mind. My stomach drops as a thought snakes around my body.

This must be how Colter feels.

24

14 Days

I start to regret agreeing to help plan Colter's brother's dance when it starts pouring and thundering.

Jackson's car isn't as nice as Colter's Escalade, and apparently Colter lives on the bumpiest street in all of Grand Creek. Janie is sitting in the front seat and she can't stop looking over at Jackson, smiling. He's doing the same. They're enough to make me want to bash my head against the window, but I have to admit to being happy for Jackson. He should have someone who adores him like she does. And now that Janie and I have become friends, I'm happy for her, too.

They will have each other when I die. Something about that comforts me. They have each other. I can finally start to let Jackson go.

Colter's house sits on a hill facing a lake. It's not huge, but it's big enough to have a three-car garage. A rusty-looking boat sits in the driveway with a grease-stained tarp thrown over it. Pumpkins sit on the porch (some carved, some not), rain-soaked ghosts hang on the trees, and Halloween decorations are plastered to the windows.

Halloween. It echoes in my mind. *Halloween, Halloween.* The notes go down an octave each time, ending with a tone so low, it resembles something unearthly.

We get out of the car and pass the soggy ghosts hanging from the large oak tree in the front yard. Orange and black lights are strung from the roof, dripping down in streams. Five cars are parked in front of the house already. We run, trying to avoid the slamming of the rain. I toss my hood over my head, but the rain is coming down so hard my left contact has moved to the back of my eyeball.

Nerves build in my body at the thought of so many people in one house. I really hope his mom isn't here—the bitchy, take-no-prisoners district attorney who worked with my dad. The last thing I want to do is talk about him. Colter said she was away on a work trip, but that she was due home sometime today.

We make it to the front door. I work to dislodge my contact as Jackson knocks once. The door opens and a little brown-haired girl runs out, laughing, followed by another girl who looks exactly like her, but with blonde hair.

They look like drowned rodents within seconds.

"Retta, give them back!" the girl with the blonde ringlets says, chasing the brunette.

The blonde girl takes a leap and knocks Retta to the ground and their laughter echoes in the yard. I've always loved the sound of kids laughing. It never makes me want to cover my ears.

I turn back around, and Jackson and Janie have already gone inside. Colter's standing in the doorway, watching me stare at the girls with a goofy smile on his face. I imagine it's the same smile I had when Tate was running around the yard, chasing the neighbor's dog, calling him Floofy even though his name was Max.

Colter cocks his head to the side, then yells, "Greta. Loretta. Get out of the rain, unless you want me to tell your mom that you both ate extra candy."

Their little heads perk up and their eyes go wide. Their hair is stuck to their faces, and Loretta's face is full of dark mud.

"Noooo!" Greta screams, running through the door. She hugs Colter around the legs and looks up at him. "You won't do that will you, Uncle Cole?"

He looks as if he's considering it when Loretta walks up to his side.

Loretta wipes a piece of wet hair out of her face and folds her arms across her chest. "He won't tell, Greta. Because then we'll have to tell her that he's the one who gave it to us." She gets this determined look on her face and I can't help but smile.

"She's got ya there," I say.

He mouths *Shut up* to me with a smile building on his lips.

. "You drive a hard bargain, Miss Loretta, but I'll concede."

"What does that mean?" Greta asks, unhooking her arms from him.

"It means he's giving up," Loretta says, confidently.

The girls run into the kitchen and I'm left staring after them, mouth agape.

"Wow, that Loretta's going to be trouble."

Colter attempts to wipe off Greta's muddy handprints and turns to me. "No shit." He shakes his head as if trying to get a memory dislodged. "Come on, we're starting."

I shake off the raindrops, finally get my damn contact in place, and follow him into the living room. It's filled with people. I recognize a few from school. Dee, Kirstyn, a girl with red hair from their group.

I freeze when I see Phillip. I didn't know he would be here. I try to slink out of the room unnoticed, but Colter grabs my arm before I can make an escape. A boy who looks suspiciously like Colter is sitting in the corner on a recliner, his legs folded under him. A younger woman is chasing Greta and Loretta through the living room, momentarily distracting Colter. An older golden retriever is curled up on the floor, oblivious to any of the commotion in the room.

"It's okay. It's not an execution," Colter says, letting me go with a sweet smile.

"It feels like one," I say under my breath.

I sit down on the floor in the corner. Jackson looks down at me and gestures to the chair beside him. I quickly hop into the chair and try desperately not to stare at Phillip.

I'm admiring the intricate paintings on the wall when I see his mom. She's dressed in perfectly ironed slacks and a flowy blouse that looks like it cost more than my house. I don't think she's seen me yet. I stop moving, afraid any movement will attract her gaze. She smiles at Greta and Loretta, and for a moment I think that maybe I can do this. I can see her and maybe she won't talk about the accident or my dad leaving.

Her eyes narrow in curiosity at the sight of me and her jaw locks tight. She stares like that at me for at least thirty seconds before I avert my gaze from her. I take a deep breath and have the desire to check my pulse to make sure my heart's still beating.

Has Colter told her about me? Does she recognize me?

Colter moves into the middle of the room. He has a rolled piece of paper sticking out of his back pocket. He commands the room just with his stance. I envy that about him.

"Okay, so we only have a couple of weeks to plan this thing. I have Janie and Jackson on the logistics committee." He pulls the rolled piece of paper from his pocket and spreads it open. "Phillip and I will take care of the band and music selections. Kirstyn? You and Ellery will be on decorations, if that's okay?" He nods toward me.

I shrug.

Kirstyn isn't looking at me, she's staring up at Colter like he's reciting the meaning of life. It doesn't surprise me that out of everyone, she and I get paired together. Is he trying to punish me? I thought we were past that. Maybe he wants Kirstyn and I to be friends. Wow, he's pretty delusional if he thinks that.

Kirstyn looks over at me and rolls her eyes, then gazes back up at Colter. "We're getting credit for this, right? I still need a few hours to graduate."

"Yes," he says with an annoyed expression. He clears his throat. "Dee and Riley offered to take care of marketing. We need every student to come to it."

The redhead girl that came with Kirstyn and Dee must be Riley.

"Just because you're on a committee doesn't mean you have to only do what that committee does. If you have any ideas about anything else, feel free to say something," he says, edging back toward me. "That's it. Enjoy the refreshments."

The room is a clatter of voices and moving chairs scraping on the wood floor. I stand up to get the hell out, but Colter turns around and cocks his head at me like he wants to say something. Before I can get out of the room, he's beside me with his dopey eyes and pouty mouth. His expression turns sympathetic when it reaches my eyes.

I roll back on my heels. "Kirstyn, really?" I whisper.

He gently touches my arm and it sparks with unrelenting warmth. "I'm sorry. Every other spot had enough people. I thought it may be good for you two to try and get to know each other. You don't have to if you don't want."

He really is delusional.

I let out a sigh. "It's fine. It's not like you and I are going out. She shouldn't care about me."

He gives me a confused, sympathetic expression again. "Right. Right, okay."

Does he want us to be going out? Why can't I figure him out? Why am I thinking any of this when I should be darting out the front door?

We stand there in a nervous haze. The twins run past. Greta slams into Colter's legs and he goes flying into me. I try to brace him, but we topple over the chair I was just sitting in. We tumble to the ground and his weight is heavy on me. I can't move. Our faces are so close I can feel his small stubbly hairs on my cheek. If he turns his head our lips would be too close. I need to get out of this position. He starts to turn his head and I panic, squirming. I scoot out, trying to wiggle my body out from under him. He braces his arms on the carpet and pushes off me with a strange look on his face.

"I wasn't going to do anything to you."

"I know." I look toward the door, wishing I could just run out.

He nods, but it's obvious he doesn't believe me. He shakes off whatever disappointment he has in me and smiles again. "We're going to the game tomorrow to watch Jackson and Phillip. You should come."

I haven't been to a football game in three years. I think I went to one my freshman year, realized they were boring and I didn't understand a thing, so I stopped going.

"Who's we?" I ask.

"Just some friends."

"You mean Kirstyn and Dee?"

"Yeah, they'll be there."

I don't know why, but I'm hurt to hear he's still friends with Kirstyn. I know he can be friends with whoever he wants, but I just wish it wasn't her.

"I don't know. I have a lot of homework and a calculus test on Monday."

He eyes me. "I got the night off work. I think you can spare some time. Plus, you get the pleasure of my company for a whole night."

I love those words on his lips, even though I shouldn't. "I don't even know anything about football."

"I'll teach you. I'm a good teacher." He waggles his eyebrows.

I roll my eyes.

He grins and I smile back until I see his mother come up beside him. My breath starts stuttering. I should have run earlier. Why did I stay and talk to him?

She's holding a glass of wine. She sips it and regards me suspiciously, scrutinizing my appearance. I wish I'd worn something other than my ripped jeans and concert T-shirt. "Ellery Stevens, right? How nice of you to help out with Atticus's dance."

"Thanks," I squeak out, looking down at my shoes. I don't know why she makes me nervous, but she does.

"You're Trent Stevens's daughter, right? The one who . . . well, never mind."

I jerk my gaze from my shoes as rage swirls in my chest. I knew she'd bring it up. It's no secret she blames me for him leaving. She made it clear last year that she blamed me for the accident, too, that I deserved to rot in jail for killing my sister, an example of what not to do when driving in *inclement weather*, she had said. Luckily the cops didn't agree. They deemed it an accident, but that doesn't mean I'm not in my own kind of prison anyway. "Yes, ma'am."

She chuckles, but it sounds forced. "Oh, don't call me ma'am, you make me sound old." She lifts the corners of her mouth in a smile that looks more like a sneer. "Trent was one of our best attorneys. I'm sorry we lost him to Atlanta. Is he enjoying it there?"

"I'm sure he is," I say with an attitude I didn't know would come out.

She narrows her eyes at me. "Well, good," she says, clipped. "How do you know my son, Ellery?" she asks, tipping her head to the side, sounding innocent, but again it's fake. It's clear she doesn't want me anywhere around him.

"We . . . uh . . . ."

I feel like I'm naked in a nightmare.

"We have English together, Mom," Colter finishes for me.

"How nice," she says in a masked tone. She takes a small sip of wine. I watch the red liquid tip and flow into her gulping mouth.

I cringe. Colter hasn't picked up on her venom toward me. She's grasping her wine glass like it's my head and she wants to shatter it.

Colter looks at me so thoughtfully, so sincere. "Actually, the first time we met was at work." He smiles.

I know my cheeks are reddening and I'm mortified. Her expression changes to shock. She can see the attraction between us. She knows.

She nods slowly and gulps down the rest of her wine. "How nice," she repeats like before, then walks away without another word.

A shudder snakes up my back.

Colter leans down and comes closer. "She's a little uptight," he whispers in my ear. He leans back and gives me a thoughtful look. "So, the football game?"

I can't look into his innocent eyes, his gentle face, and say no. I know I'm going to regret this decision, but I'll worry about that later. I let *Happy Ellery* win this one.

"Okay, Tom Sawyer."

25

13 Days

Janie and I decide to watch *Better Off Dead* after school before the football game. She's been talking about this movie non-stop since we went to see the *Sixteen Candles* and *The Breakfast Club* double feature.

"I didn't even think about streaming it, that was stupid," she says, holding up the DVD.

"If it makes you feel better," I say, shoving a handful of popcorn in my mouth, "I didn't see it available to stream."

She hops onto my bed. "That does make me feel better." She pops the DVD in the player and we settle to watch.

There's a knock on the door, then my mom peeks in. "You girls need anything else? I don't see chocolate anywhere."

I wave Mom in and she plops onto my bed, setting a huge Hershey bar beside the popcorn bowl. She grabs a handful of popcorn. "Is this *Better Off Dead*?"

Janie laughs. "You wanna watch with us?"

Mom looks at me like she's asking permission.

I nod and smile at her.

She settles into a spot by the wall and hoards the popcorn while Janie and I snarf the chocolate.

"So what are the kids up to these days?" Mom asks.

"Not a lot. What are the moms up to these days?" I ask.

"Touché."

Janie laughs. "You guys are hilarious."

"We're available on days that end with a Y," Mom says, laughing.

"It's not as cool when you laugh at your own jokes."

"Says the girl who taught me how to do it," she says, slapping an unsuspecting Janie in a spontaneous high-five.

Janie smiles at my mom and I know that look. The *where did you find this one* expression.

"All right, you win this rib-off, but only 'cause I want to actually hear what John Cusack is saying."

"Owned," Mom says, in her continuing attempt at being the cool mom.

Janie's right. The movie ends up being pretty funny and although I don't really identify with Lane, I still like watching him try to kill himself. The fact that Janie wanted to show me this proves she's more than just a shopping trip in heels, more than just a wavering piece of fabric, more than just a girl. She's my friend and she cares. Even worse. I care about her.

Shit.

Mom sits up with a groan. "That's just about enough for me. I'm getting too old to sit like this for too long. I need a nice comfortable recliner and a book." She scoots down the bed and heads to the door. "Don't you have a football game tonight?"

Janie glances at her phone. "In an hour."

"Oh, how I wish I could go to a football game instead of my shift," she says and closes the door behind her.

I run out the door and find Mom in the hallway. "Hey."

She turns around. "Yeah, sweetie?"

"Thanks for watching the movie with us."

She leans over and hugs me tight. "Thanks for letting me. It was a nice trip back to the eighties. I was a little girl when I first saw it, but I remember that movie." She lets me go and nudges her head toward my door. "That one's a keeper."

"Yeah, I guess I'll keep her around."

"I need to get to work. I'll see you in the morning. I assume you're going to eat after the game? I have some leftovers in the fridge."

"Mom, I'll be fine."

She reaches over and moves a piece of hair that had fallen in front of my face and tucks it behind my ear. "I know. You always could take care of yourself."

I head back into the room and plop on the bed, glance at the floor, and arch an eyebrow at Janie. It looks like my closet threw up. "Uh, whatcha doing?"

"We need to find you the perfect outfit for the game." I scan the piles of black shirts and jeans. The only differences are the designs on each of them. "Did I ever tell you your taste in clothes is depressing?" she says, folding up a pair of my jeans and setting them on my bed.

"I believe you inferred that when you said I had to go shopping with you the other day."

"We need to get more color on you. This is like a serial killer's wardrobe." She grabs the black shirt with a silver design and the newest jeans I bought with her at the mall. "Here," she says handing them to me.

I grab them from her. "You know I'll have my coat on, right? No one will see it. So it really doesn't matter what you choose."

She puts her hand on her hip and purses her lips. "Humor me, then."

"Clothes aren't going to instantly make me likable, Jane."

"Do you think that's what I'm trying to do?"

"I don't know."

"Colter's going to be there."

I groan and lay back on the bed, hugging the clothes close to me. "Come on. The horse is dead. You've killed it. Quit dragging it around."

She flops down beside me and gets in my face. "Ha ha. Get ready. We're leaving in ten minutes."

151

26

I pull out a strand of hair caught in my mouth and adjust myself on the bleacher. The ridges are already hurting my ass. Colter's late and I'm sitting behind a guy in a hat with one of those fuzzy balls on the top. Jackson's stretching on the field, stopping in between reps to give Janie slobbery kisses. His lips are attached to hers when the coach yells at him to pay attention, and they both laugh. They're so damn cute it makes me want to puke.

I've thought about Dean a lot. He's gone back to ignoring me, but he's still alive. I drove by his house on the way here, but his car wasn't in the driveway. I have no idea what to say to him anymore. I feel helpless, watching him get further away. He's like a painting that from a distance is beautiful, but when you get up close it distorts and melds into something ugly, something dark. Maybe that's what I look like too. I close my eyes to will his image away as the piercing wind blows my hair around. Wrapping my arms around me, I try to quell the chatter of my teeth.

Janie finally separates from Jackson and heads up the stairs to the bleachers. She sees me and her face lights up. "I thought maybe I'd have to chase you down in the parking lot."

"I thought about it. Why didn't anyone tell me how cold it got out here?" I say, shifting to the right so she can sit.

She plops down next to me, propping her legs on the spot in front of us. The guy with the ball hat half turns and gives her a glare for invading his space. "Hey, Ell?"

"What?"

"It's cold out here," she teases.

"Yeah, a little too late," I say.

She nudges my side. "Where's Colt?"

"I'm not his keeper today."

She rolls her eyes. "Yoooou want him. You want him bad," she sings, like we're in fourth grade.

"I don't want anyone, Janie. You're reaching."

She grins wide, like she knows my secrets. Guilt seeps into the moment. I can't tell her my secrets or this friendship will fade. She would never understand, just like Jackson. I want to tell her, though. I don't want to keep anything from her, but I have to. Add it to the pile of guilt and shame I have buried in my soul.

"Jackson's amazing. How have you been friends with him for so long and never tried anything?" She eyes me carefully. "Or have you?"

I chuckle at the insinuation. "He's like a brother to me. It would be like kissing a dead frog."

She laughs. "He said something similar. Not the dead frog bit, though. You guys are so cute."

Happy Ellery can play this game. "Not as cute as you guys. Do you two ever come up for air?"

Her cheeks darken. "Oh, Ellery. I love him." She covers her mouth like she let out a secret of her own, then her eyes go wide. She clamps onto my arm with a desperate look on her face. "Don't tell him."

"Like I would do that."

"I know. I just . . . what am I going to do?"

"Nothing. Just act the same. He's happy, even I can see it."

Her smile fades as she turns back to the field. "There's Colt. Ugh, he's with Kirstyn."

I glance over to her. "Are you not friends with her anymore?"

"Hell no. Not after the shit she's said about you. She's no friend of mine."

My insides warm slightly at her declaration. Wait, what has Kirstyn said about me? No, I'm not going to care about that. I'm not.

"She's such a bitch, I'd be surprised if anyone—hey." She looks up at Kirstyn and Dee. Colter's behind them.

A sliver of what feels like jealousy sweeps through me when I see the three of them walk up together.

Kirstyn sits next to me and sandwiches me into Janie. Janie turns and glares at Kirstyn. I do my best not to glare at her myself. I'm not supposed to care what she did or didn't say about me. Colter passes by and shrugs, taking a seat next to Kirstyn, leaving me wondering if she did this on purpose. Dee slides next to Colter. I can't learn about football when he's one seat over.

Janie gives me a conspiratorial look and stands up. "Colt? I can't see Jackson as well over here, switch seats with me?" She winks at me as she squeezes by.

Colter stands and they do an awkward dance in front of us, then he sits down next to me. His knee touches mine and my leg feels like it's a thousand degrees.

This has to stop.

Get control, Ellery. You need to be pushing him away.

I move my knee nonchalantly away from his.

"Vast improvement," he says, giving me a sidelong glance through his thick eyelashes. "Thanks, Janie. The view here is much better," he says, never taking his gaze off me. I shiver and for the first time tonight, it's not from the cold. He turns back to the field. "Okay, lesson one. Teams have to get touchdowns. Those are six points, and—"

I laugh. "I know that part. It's the downs and stuff I don't get."

"Well, the offense gets four chances, or downs, to get ten yards or more toward the opponent's end zone. When you get those ten yards you've gotten the first down, and you're given four more chances to get ten more yards." He leans closer to me, and his cheek is so close to mine I can feel the heat radiating off of his skin. "See those bright orange numbers?" He points to the sidelines, but all I can visualize are his lips on me.

I swallow. "Uh huh," I squeak out.

He turns slightly and his lips graze my cheek. I jerk away, surprised to feel his lips on me anywhere. "Those signs mark the downs," he says in a strained voice.

What's a down? What's football?

"Cool."

"Does that make sense?"

I nod, unable to speak, afraid it would come out as manic gibberish.

"We'll go over the penalties when they get them. And they *will* get them."

"Are you trying to bore her to death, Colt?" Janie says, leaning over Kirstyn, who seems to be in a deep conversation with Dee. Janie eyes Kirstyn. "Can you move over so I can sit next to Ell?" she says, dripping with attitude.

Kirstyn looks appalled, but gets up and moves closer to Dee.

Janie plops back down next to me, putting her feet on the bleacher in front of us. She lets out a sigh. "Thank God. That guy was taking up all my leg room over there."

Hat-with-a-ball-guy looks back again and glares at Janie. She matches his narrowed eyes. "You're taking up three seats, just so you know." He turns around with a huff as her gaze moves to the field. "Is Jackson up yet?"

I squint toward the field. "I think so. Isn't that him? Thirteen?"

She grins. "Lucky Thirteen. Or at least, it will be tonight."

I groan. "Seriously, stop."

She giggles. "Sorry, I forgot. So, Colt. You and Ellery have plans after the game?"

I glare at her and she just grins at me. She smacks the gum that I didn't know she was chewing.

Waiting for him to answer is like waiting for test results. I should say something. He should. Someone should.

He shrugs. "I hadn't thought about it."

I swear that guy can't tell a lie. We are so different.

"I have a lot of homework," I say.

Janie play-frowns. "Do you guys want to get us some drinks? I'll buy."

"The game hasn't even started yet, Jane," Colter says.

"Pleeeeeease, I need my hot chocolate."

"I'll go," I say, waving away the cash she holds out. "On me."

Colter stands to let me by but doesn't follow. Did I want him to follow?

I make my way down the stairs to the bottom and pass by a lot of people wearing funny hats with balls on the top of their heads. The concession stand is next to the bleachers, so I place the order and stand around, waiting. I tap my fingers on the counter and the PTA Mom of the Year gives me a glare. I stop and search the field for Jackson and spot . . . Kirstyn heading my way.

"Hurry up, PTA lady," I growl under my breath.

Kirstyn comes up beside me. "You didn't tell me you were coming here. I would have asked for a Diet Coke."

That's because I wouldn't have gotten it for you. "Sorry, Janie wanted some hot chocolate."

"Oh, I see. You're her bitch now."

I face her. Oh, no she didn't. "I'm no one's bitch."

She licks her lips like a predator ready to devour their prey. "I see how you look at Colter. I can't believe that you'd think he'd want you."

"I don't look at him. You're delusional."

"See, I don't think I am. I know about you, Ellery. I know *all* about you."

There's no way she could know. What does she know? Did he tell her I want to kill myself? Can she see it on me?

"No, you don't. You don't know me at all."

"I live with my grandma on Mason Drive. Right in front of the cemetery. I've seen you."

My whole body feels like it drops.

"I saw when Jackson carried you out of the cemetery the other day. Grandma and I like to take walks early in the morning. I was surprised to see Jackson at the cemetery. And lo and behold, he's carrying you in his arms. Why is that, Ell?"

"Stop it."

She gets closer to me, corners me against the side of the bleachers. "Who's in that cemetery? Or were you and Jackson becoming more than friends? You know, I've always wondered why he stuck around you for so long."

The metal rod that holds up the bleachers is jamming into my back. I can feel the bruise coming. I search for a way out. Her voice sounds like a bird shrieking. "You need to go."

"Or maybe you were visiting your sister. Is she the one that made you this basket case?"

I need to fight it.

Don't let her get to you. Breathe.

The rage builds in my body like the engine to a rocket. I'm bursting behind my skin, exploding into shrapnel.

"You're batshit crazy, and you're never going to get Colter. So just give up."

I can feel my eyes start to tear up and I'm ashamed. I want to run, but she has me blocked. She's hovering over me and I'm cowering and I'm weak. This is all my fault. I thought I could fit in. I thought I could have friends, but clearly I can't.

"Does Colter know you hang out in cemeteries with Jackson at night?" she asks, her eyes widening, her body curving over my hunched one.

"Kirstyn? What the fuck are you doing?"

Kirstyn freezes at Colter's voice.

He comes up behind her and shoves her out of the way, then grabs my shoulders and lowers his head so it's in front of mine. "Are you okay?" he says, concern in his eyes.

He didn't hear what she said.

I shake him off. "I'm fine." I wipe my eyes quickly, hoping he won't notice I'd started to cry. "Did the game start?"

He eyes me carefully. "Yeah, why don't you go back up; I'll get Janie's cocoa. Do you need anything?"

I shake my head.

"Actually, I probably shouldn't leave you alone," he adds.

I try to give him a strong grin and straighten my posture. "It's fine. Just girl stuff. I'll be fine. Just go. I'll meet you in the bleachers."

He considers it for a moment then spins and heads toward the concession stand. Kirstyn is gone.

Instead of going back to the bleachers, I head out to the parking lot.

27

I'm almost to my car when I see Dean's disheveled hair in the distance. What's he doing here?

"Dean?" I yell.

He turns around and gets an annoyed look on his face. He glances side to side, then walks toward me.

I move closer to him. "What're you doing here?"

He shuffles his feet on the gravel of the parking lot. "I left my algebra book. Had to get it."

I study him. He's avoiding my eyes and acting guilty of something. "What's going on?"

He shakes his head, then shoves his hands in his pockets. He doesn't have an algebra book with him. "Nothing. I gotta go. See you in Soc tomorrow." He flashes a crooked smile and takes off.

"Wait. Hold on."

He doesn't turn back around.

I hold the steaming cup of coffee up to my mouth and sip it. The drive from Starbucks is short, and before I take the third sip I'm home. I pull my car into the driveway and get out. I'm almost to the door when I notice Colter sitting on the stairs of my house. He must have parked down the street.

He stands up when I get close. "You left."

"I told you. I didn't know anything about football."

He runs a hand through his hair. "Look, I don't know what Kirstyn said to you, but she's an idiot. Don't listen to her."

I take a sip of my coffee, the keys in my hand jingling every time I tip the cup. "It's fine."

"It's not fine," he growls. "Has she been harassing you like this the whole time?"

"It doesn't matter."

"It *does* matter. This is about me, not you. She needs to leave you the hell alone."

"She wants you back. I get it. She thinks I'm a threat somehow. Which is totally ridiculous."

"Is it?" He lowers his head and again runs his hand through his hair.

He wants me to be a threat?

"Well, yeah. Right?" I ask, tipping my coffee to take another sip. I want to live in this cardboard cup forever just to get away from this conversation.

He slides near me. Everything in me is heightened. My breath sounds like a storm, my heartbeats sound like a million drums. He cradles my face in his hands. I take a breath in and drop the cup on the grass, the coffee sloshing onto my shoes.

He leans down, inching closer, closer, and stops just before our lips touch. "You are a threat. A big one," he says, then takes a breath and there's desire in his eyes, they're asking permission, they're hoping that I feel the same way as him. Shocked and confused, but filled with something strong, I give him an almost imperceptible nod, then his lips are on mine.

I keep my eyes open and stare at his closed eyelids. He tastes like hot chocolate. He deepens the kiss and I close my eyes without will. His lips are soft and gentle with me. His tongue touches mine and I wince. He stiffens for a second, then separates us. His smile is so genuine, so sincere. We don't say anything. He looks like he's afraid he did something stupid.

That wasn't so bad. I could probably do that again, but better. I grab his shirt and press my mouth onto his and devour him. I touch his bottom lip to mine and nibble on it, not sure where that motion came from. He does it right back as he makes a soft sound and pulls me closer to him. Our bodies meld together, and I'm lost in desperation and pain and pleasure. He leaves my mouth and slides his lips down to my neck, dotting my skin with tiny kisses.

Then like a beautiful dream turned nightmare, I remember my plan.

Halloween.

I'm trapped. The heat, the searing flames penetrate my skin. I'm on fire.

"No!" I scream, pushing Colter off me. He stumbles back with a surprised face.

"Did I do something wrong?" he says in the most beautiful, pitiful voice I've heard.

"No. You? You're perfect. I'm just fucked in the head." My voice sounds choked, raspy. I can't get my words to form right.

He slowly inches back in front of me and leans down to look me in the eyes. "I'm sorry I did that. I just . . . you were looking at me like you wanted to. Please talk to me."

I shake my head. "We can't do this."

He runs his hand down my cheek, cupping my jaw. "God, you're so stubborn. I wish you'd just let me in."

"Is that what this is about? Helping me?"

"Not just. I mean at first, maybe. But . . . ."

"Look, you can't help me. No one can."

He lowers his head a little and lets his hand drop from my cheek. "Okay."

Shit.

28

"I keep screwing up with him."

The grass is cold on my legs as I sit in front of Tate's grave. The moon is just a slit tonight, like a sideways smile on the Cheshire Cat, mocking me, waiting to pop up to make my life more miserable.

"He kissed me and I pushed him away. He's a good guy. Perfect, actually. I mean not perfect, but perfect for me and I don't know what to do, 'cause I've made up my mind and I think if I let him in I'm going to regret it, and I don't want to change my mind." I take a breath. "What should I do?"

I try to think of what she would tell me if she were here. If she were seven years old and had one year more of experiences and smiles to share. She would ask a question. She always asked too many questions. We talked about it once. What kind of guy I'd end up with.

❧

Tate swings as high as the glider will go, her little legs pumping under the seat. "Do you think Mom and Dad will be together forever?"

My feet drag on the deck to slow us down. "I don't know. I guess, if they want to be."

Her face contorts from curiosity to worry before I can blink. "They yell."

I lift my head toward the black sky. The moon is half full, hiding its other side like it's ashamed of it. I learned in Astronomy that it's in a waxing gibbous phase. "Sometimes people who love each other fight."

That's such a cop-out, she'll see right through it.

"Maybe. Do you yell at your boyfriend—wait. Do you even have a boyfriend?" she asks. "'Cause I've never seen you with one, but you're sixteen and Krissy Turner's sister has a boyfriend and she's sixteen."

"Emma Turner? Um, yeah she's had a few boyfriends; in fact she's what we call a slu—you know, not the right age for this conversation."

"Huh?" she says with her eyes narrowed and her big lower lip stuck out.

"There's no magical age you get a boyfriend. I just haven't found anyone I really care about like that."

She starts pumping her legs again, moving us higher in the air. "Oh, but maybe someday?"

"Sure, but they'd have to be pretty tolerant to stand me."

"What does that mean?"

"They'd have to be a friggin' saint, Tate."

She smiles up at me, then turns to the sky, gazing up at the stars. "A saint?" she says smiling, a knowing look on her face, like she got me this time. "Yep, you're right."

"Hey!" I say, grabbing her. She giggles, rolls off the swing, and runs around the yard, screaming that my boyfriend is a saint.

❧

"He's a saint, Tate. I found him. He's sweet and understanding."

He is. But you don't deserve him.

"I'm going to ruin it, I know I will. But I want to let go with him."

You can't.

I search my mind for anything else to talk about so I don't have to leave her, so I don't have to face the rest of the night with the guilt and shame. When I'm with her here, it subsides. It's like I have her again for a moment. "I actually went to a football game, and I made a friend. I know." I laugh. "Hard to believe."

You don't deserve her either.

I glance at my phone and groan at the time. Back to real life. "I should go before I end up in the soil again and Jackson has to save me." I place a kiss on my fingers and pat her grave softly. I stand up from the freezing grass, grab my coat off the ground, and slip it on, whispering the same words I say every time I see her: "I'm so sorry."

29

10 Days

It's our second committee meeting, and Colter's living room is decked out in orange and black. Streamers and ghosts hang from every available surface, and it smells like hot chocolate. Everywhere I go, Halloween keeps popping up. Whether it's decorations, or plans of costumes, or candy, it's everywhere. A constant reminder of my plan. I take a seat on the couch while his mom looks over at me with suspicion. I know she'd rather he spend his time with Kirstyn. It doesn't take a genius to know that. Colter's dog, Cooper, is asleep again on the floor. His ear twitches every few seconds while his snores fill our side of the room.

Colter clears his throat to quiet down the hum of voices. "So we may have a band. I've talked to Mrs. Green and she said the choir can perform a song at the dance, too," he says, excitement in his voice. "Also, Phillip has a friend of a friend that may get us a real band," he continues, scanning the room.

Wait. Mrs. Green is Aunt Sue. Which means . . . we're going to sing? "We want Atticus to win this thing, right? How can we do that with a high school choir singing at the dance?"

There's nothing I want less than to sing at this stupid dance.

"We're just a backup. Phillip's friends are the main band," Colter says, his jaw locked and business demeanor. "Dee, can you give me an update on marketing?"

Dee slides a freshly manicured fingernail up to her mouth and chews. "Ask Riley, she's been doing everything."

Colter rolls his eyes. "Riley?"

Riley glares at Dee. "We have posters up at the school, Twitter and Facebook posts, we even plastered all the hangouts. There shouldn't be anyone who doesn't know about this dance."

Colter looks at Janie. "How we doing on the event hall?"

Janie grins, but there's something annoying her. "My mom's country club offered their place up when we told them the mayor's daughter was involved." We share a knowing glance between us.

Sweet Kirstyn, the mayor's daughter. I roll my eyes. I haven't seen her since the football game. She isn't even here today. We haven't done anything decoration-wise. I just have to make something up when he comes to me.

Colter looks at me and smiles, his eyes creasing in sympathy. He's never going to kiss me again. Kirstyn's right. I'm batshit crazy.

"Ell? How about you and Kirstyn?"

"Nothing's bought yet, but we've, uh, scouted where we're getting everything. Party City has most everything we should need. I found a website called Eighties Night Life. By the way, make sure you don't Google 'Night Life in the Eighties,' not pretty. Anyway, that eighties site has everything else." It wasn't a lie. I'd bought a few posters off there before.

"Great. We have a little more than a week. Looks like we're close. Thanks everyone," he says. He sets his clipboard down and says something to Phillip.

Everyone bursts into conversations about what their favorite eighties music is and what they should wear. I glance at Colter. The awkwardness of what happened when he kissed me is all over me, like a shroud of embarrassment. I hate that. I hate that I did that to us.

Is there an *us*?

Colter finishes talking with Phillip and strolls over to me. He bites his lip and all I can think about is how those teeth have nibbled on my lip and how I want them to do it again. I tear my gaze away from his mouth.

"You doing okay? I feel like I haven't seen you in forever."

He's right. We haven't seen each other in a few days, because I've been avoiding him. I couldn't look him in the eye after the night we kissed.

"I'm fine. It's not like you haven't called to make sure I'm still alive," I tease.

He doesn't smile. He just gives me that pathetic, sincere concern expression he's perfected. "Sorry about Kirstyn. She's totally flaked on you, hasn't she?"

I want to ask him why he's still friends with her. Why he subjects himself to her. But I don't, 'cause I have no spine. "She's been busy. I just need her to be there to put up the decorations."

He smiles, and I swear he can solve any problem with that one expression. I melt into myself. "You don't have to work with her. I can move her to marketing or something."

"No, I'm good. Don't worry about me."

He reaches out and tucks a loose hair behind my ear. "I always worry about you."

My throat dries like I've eaten a thousand peanuts. I cough a little to get it wet. "Do you have to work tonight?"

He eyes me suspiciously. "Yeah, but I have a short shift. Why?"

"I need help buying all this shit for the dance."

"Oh, Party City's near Kmart. I'll meet you there after my shift tonight." His face lights up like a kid on his birthday.

"You're a dork, you know that right?" I say, gathering my coat to leave.

He grabs me and pulls me into him. "That's why you like being around me. Just admit it," he whispers in my ear.

An involuntary shiver wracks my body. "I admit nothing," I say into his shoulder. I see Mrs. Sawyer eyeing me, so I let him go.

He cups my cheek quickly, then he's off spreading his annoying cheer to the others in the room. I try to sneak out before anyone can remark on the display of affection he just showed me in front of everyone.

Jackson catches me sneaking out and gives me *that* look. I've seen it before many times. He thinks he's got me figured out.

"I wish you'd just admit you like him and put us all out of our misery," he says.

"Shhh, someone will hear."

"And that would be a bad thing?"

I grab his sleeve and pull him into the next room. It's full of fancy furniture and dark wood end tables. The framed photos of Colter's family stare at me in judgment. "Look, he's just a friend, okay?"

"Fine, don't admit it." He winks at me.

I sigh. "I'm surprised to see you without your other arm."

"Contrary to what you think, Janie and I can have separate activities. She left to go to the mall with her mom. The amount of time that girl shops is beyond me. What else could she possibly buy?"

I laugh. "More shoes?"

He grabs his coat from the closet and hands me mine. "I feel like shooting something, don't you?"

"Um."

"Perfect, let's put those gun skills to the test," Jackson says, opening the door, not giving me a choice or a word to edge into the conversation. "Don't think about it, just do it."

"Maybe we should just—"

He shoves me out the door and I stumble a little on the steps. "Nope, we're going. Get ready, Stevens. It's time you learn how to shoot."

Oh, boy.

30

The gun club on Washington Avenue is a boys' club. There's no other way to say it. When the guy tips his hat to Jackson and whistles at me, I know I'm in enemy territory. Jackson's dad has come with us to be my *accompanying adult* while I sign my life away and have a small lesson on how to hold a gun and why it's awesome to shoot things. I've been watching Jackson shoot for at least a half hour to see how it's done.

Now I'm crouched down on a wooden bench thing, facing a large field I can barely see through the plastic goggles I have to wear. Jackson is practically drooling on the wooden bench next to me and his dad is watching us both, his arms folded across his chest.

Jackson's eyes are glazed over with crazy, his gun propped under him. He glances at me once, then yells, "Pull!" I can barely hear the word through the earplugs, but I duck as the clay bursts out of one of the long pipes. Jackson shoots the clay and it breaks into tiny pieces above the empty field, like bits of solid rain. He looks over and smiles. "Your turn."

I must look like someone trying to walk for the first time as I fumble with the gun. His dad leans back against the wall with a tense look in his eyes, like he's afraid I'm going to shoot my foot off. Adrenaline is running through my veins and I'm fighting to not think of the last time I held a gun in my hand. Are they really going to let me just shoot something? I adjust the gun and turn my head to Jackson, gripping the gun so tight I'm afraid it's going to slip out of my fingers and kill him. "I don't think I can. . . . Am I holding this right?" I look up at his dad.

His dad nods. "Show the girl how it's done, son," he says.

Jackson laughs, comes over, and adjusts the gun to the correct position. He leaves me and stands on the other side and smiles. "Go ahead, say it."

I take a deep breath. "Pull!"

The clay flies out of an opposite tube that Jackson's clay did. I find it in the air and shoot. This sends me flying back into the wall as the gun topples onto the ground. The clay whistles in the air until it drops.

Jackson laughs as he holds out a hand for me. I grab it and dust myself off. I look down at the gun and the memories come back. Placing it in my mouth, pulling the trigger. I can still taste the metal on my tongue. An involuntary shudder passes through me. "I think I'm done shooting for now."

His dad walks by and places a hand on my shoulder. "I've seen worse, kid." Then he's gone faster than I can place the gun down.

Jackson gives me a crooked grin. "That's more than he's said to me." He laughs, then drags me inside to the bar. We take a seat at one of the tables and order our drinks. Jackson's dad glances over before turning back to the huge screen. As I look around I realize I'm the only girl other than a few of the servers.

"Where's all the girls?"

Jackson places his arm across the back of the booth and scans the room. "Huh, never noticed that, but yeah, you're right. It's pretty testosterone-filled."

"Have you brought Janie here?" I ask as our server brings our drinks and some chips and salsa.

He laughs again. "Uh, no. Not really her scene."

I grab a chip and dip it into the bowl of salsa. He scrutinizes me and I get paranoid, touching my face to make sure I don't have any salsa on it. "What?"

He folds his hands and weaves his fingers together. "What are you doing with Colter?"

I dip another chip into the salsa and take a bite. "I'm not going to talk about him with you."

"I *am* the one who gave him your number."

"So?"

He shifts in the booth and nudges my foot with his. "I never told you what he said when he asked for it."

My heart momentarily stops beating. I stir the salsa with a tortilla chip. "I don't care. It doesn't matter."

For once I can tell he sees through my lie.

"Sure, okay. If you don't want to know, I don't have to tell you." He smiles and takes a sip of his water.

I roll my eyes. I know he wants me to ask, but he can't know I'm actually starting to like Colter.

"He said he was curious about you. That he wanted to get to know you." He takes a drink of water and leaves me hanging on his words. He places the glass down carefully. "I told him you weren't interested."

"You said what?"

He laughs. "He wouldn't take no for an answer. I asked him what he saw in you, and you know what he said?"

I shake my head and clutch my fingers together under the table.

"He said he could help you. I asked him what with? But he didn't answer."

"Really?"

"So . . . has he helped you?"

I can feel the smile beginning to form on my lips, so I try to disguise it before Jackson can notice. "He's trying."

Jackson eyes me carefully, analyzing my expression like only someone who knows you can. "He must be a saint to put up with you."

I laugh for a few seconds before hearing Tate's voice slip into my brain, the memory of our conversation on the porch where she called my imaginary boyfriend a saint. Laughing feels like a betrayal, so I stop and try to recover before he can see tears form. I toss a chip at him. "What's your excuse?"

"Temporary insanity."

31

Party City is full of shit. Cool shit, but still, shit that can be thrown away or shoved into a closet and forgotten about until the next year. Most of the time it never makes it that long. I stare at the Party City sign through my smudged windshield and laugh. The sign has the R and the first Y burnt out, so it looks like it reads Pat City.

I'm turning my car off when Colter pulls up next to me. I lean my head back onto the headrest for a minute to compose myself. Is he going to try and kiss me again now that we're alone?

A knock sounds on my window and makes me jump, jamming my head into the ceiling. The wind whips the flaps of his coat around while he smiles at me under that dirty baseball cap. I roll my eyes, push open my door, and slide out of my seat. He moves closer to me and I'm afraid he's going to kiss me, but he just gives me a wry smile, grabs my hand and begins pulling me toward Pat City. It's so cold I regret not wearing gloves, but the feel of his hand in mine makes me forget I even wanted them in the first place.

"Do they have everything we need?" he asks, opening the door for me.

"Just the general stuff. I've already ordered the other stuff off that eighties website I told you about."

"Cool."

"So, this brother of yours . . . he hasn't said a word in those meetings we've had. Is he a wallflower like his big brother?" I tease.

"Yeah, he's a bit shy. Actually, there's this girl he likes. A lot. And he wants to ask her to the dance, but he's not sure how to do it."

"And his big brother can't coach him? I'm sure he's asked many a girl to many a dance in his day."

"His brother's shy when it comes to girls he *really* likes." He flips his hair in his face, like he doesn't want to look at me. He grabs a cart and begins pushing it down the aisle.

I feel the blush creep into my cheeks before I can figure out if he's talking about me. Is it arrogant to think I'm one of the girls he really likes? He did kiss me. But I'm still convinced it's because he wants to save me, not because he likes me. Why are boys so confusing?

I spot some hot pink plastic cups and pile fifty packs into the cart. "I can't ever imagine you shy. What do you mean, girls he *really* likes?"

"No, you don't; we're talking about Atticus." He grabs some white plates and holds them up to me. I shake my head, grab the neon blue ones and hold them up. He grabs fifty packs of the neon blue ones and shoves them into the cart. It's almost full.

"I have to get another cart. This is going to be filled before we're done." I grab another cart, thinking. Colter's kissed a lot of girls. A lot. It must be my imagination that he's talking about me. Why do I care? I shouldn't care about this. It's stupid of me to even entertain the notion of him. I roll the cart down the aisle of name-tag packs, goofy-looking glasses, and costumes. By the time I make it back to him, he's picked white silverware and napkins.

"Tom Sawyer. Color, not white." I roll my eyes and chuckle, then start to take the white packs out of the cart and replace them with neon ones.

"Dude, kids don't give a shit what color they are."

"Yes, they do. It's an eighties theme." I fling a package of white plates at his chest like a Frisbee. "White's boring."

He grabs the plates before they fall to the ground, giving me a playful evil glare. He raises the package in the air and fakes like he's throwing them at me. I duck in anticipation, giggling and hiding behind the cart. He moves to chase me around the cart, holding the white plates in the air like a weapon.

"Hey, guys," a female voice says from behind me. We freeze, my hands on the cart, and Colter holding the plates in the air. "I can make it after all, isn't that great?" It's Kirstyn.

I groan. I hate having to play nice with her, but the alternative is exhausting.

Colter replaces the package of plates on the shelf and gives me a sheepish look. "Hey, K. We're just getting plates and stuff."

"Great. I hope they have colors. I hate white."

I laugh a little. "They do *now*," I tease, looking right at Colter.

He grins at our inside joke and my body warms quickly in response.

Kirstyn giggles and shuts off all the warmth that entered my body. "Oh, Colt, you should leave this stuff up to us girls. We know colors better. Guys are more colorblind. It's a fact."

I cringe at her high-pitched voice. *Hey K, go away.* Ugh.

Colter shrugs it off and we continue filling the carts. We finish on a civil note on all parts and pay at the front.

The wind has picked up and I'm getting swept away with each step I take. Kirstyn, Colter, and I make it to our cars and stand awkwardly, each one of us waiting for someone to make a move.

I grab my keys out of my purse, shove the bags in the back seat, and start to get into my car when Colter grabs my arm lightly. "Don't go yet," he whispers out of earshot of Kirstyn. I crane my neck to look around the hood of my car at Kirstyn. She's searching the area, probably for Colter. He leaves me and finds her. I try to read their lips. Their heads are bowed together and he's pointing at something down the street. She smiles wide while he rocks back on his heels.

An intense anger and longing races through my body. I'm jealous? That's not good.

He comes back over to me and leans on the side of my Escape. "She's relentless." He laughs. "I swear, nothing I say will get through to her."

"Have you tried being honest?"

"Yes," he says in a playful tone. "She won't listen."

"Do you want me to beat her up?"

He chuckles and grabs my hand playfully, swinging it between us. "Yeah, could you? I'd like to see that."

"I bet you would," I say, letting go of his hand.

Pushing him away is going to be harder than I thought.

32

The wind whistles through the empty Pat City parking lot. The cold air carries memories of similar nights my sister and I shared, drinking hot chocolate. I get the sudden urge to see her again and for the first time ever, I want someone there with me. I want to share this with only one person.

"Are you doing anything right now?" I ask.

His eyebrows lift as he wraps his arms around my waist. "Why? Do you *want* to be doing something?"

I remove his arms from around me. "Probably not what you're thinking."

He feigns disappointment.

"I want to show you something."

He eyes me beneath the rim of his dirty cap. "I'm all yours, Ellery Stevens."

I feel a blush creep up into my cheeks. I love how that sounds a little too much. "Do you think my car will be okay here? I don't think we should leave yours, since it's a Escalade, and yeah. That sucker'd be gone in five minutes around here."

"We can drop off your car, then we can go. I don't trust this neighborhood with your car either."

I start to open my door when a question pops into my head. "Why do you work at Kmart when your parents have money?"

He takes off his cap and scrunches his hair. "Dad wanted me to have a good work ethic, and I've always wanted to be a cop. So this seemed the logical job choice."

"That actually makes sense. I didn't know you wanted to be a cop."

He leans in and kisses me quickly on the cheek. "There's a lot about me you don't know."

That seems to be a popular line for people around me.

I slip into my car and take off, grinning like I've been body-snatched by a lovesick girl. I keep glancing in the rearview mirror at his silhouette the rest of the trip.

Who the hell am I? *Happy Ellery?*

When we arrive at my house, I hop out of my car and get into his, feeling the familiar leather hug his seat gives me, and adjust the seat belt.

"Where are we going again?" he asks.

I flick the door handle back and forth. I'm sure I'm driving him crazy. "Mason Drive."

He glances over at me. "Kirstyn's? I highly doubt that."

"The cemetery."

"Oh," he says with a surprised tone. "Okay."

Gripping the wheel tight, he rings his hands around it as we make our way down Mason Drive, passing by the medium-sized houses with long driveways and Halloween signs in their yard telling the world to *Watch out! Ghost Crossing.* Colored leaves are scattered on the grass, filling holes and coating cars.

He parks the car outside the cemetery and we make our way inside. Crickets chirp a rhythm, and it echoes in my head like they've transformed into locusts. I resist the urge to cover my ears. Behind a canopy of trees, several headstones are bathed in blue-tinged moonlight. I cup my palms to my mouth and blow hot air into them before grabbing Colter's equally frozen hand. I lead him down the dirt path, our shoes crunching on the frozen leaves and branches. The trees rustle in the wind and I'm reminded of the last time Jackson had to rescue me. I'm determined not to have that happen again.

I feel him pull me back, so I stop and turn.

"Can we stop for a sec," he says, softly.

He's staring at another headstone. It reads, *Here lies Ryan Sawyer, beloved son, brother, and friend. Rock On!*

I hadn't considered that his brother might be buried here. I'm such an insensitive asshole. I squeeze his hand. "I'm sorry. I didn't even think about him being here, too."

He shakes his head a little and grabs my hand tighter, weaving our fingers together. "It's been too long since I was last here." He pulls me closer to him, squeezing us together, tighter.

I feel so safe in his arms.

"I'm so sorry. God. I wasn't even thinking. You must hate me."

"I could never hate you," he says quietly.

"What's with the *Rock On?*"

He chuckles a little. "He loved to play the guitar. He was in a band. He always wanted to be big, not for the fame or anything, he just wanted to share his songs. It's kind of weird and morbid, but he knew what he wanted on his headstone since we were kids. I think he might have been joking when he said it, but we put it on there anyway." A lost expression passes over his face. "You never think someone you're with every day is just going to disappear. I didn't see. If I had, maybe I could've—"

"Stop it. There's nothing you could have done. If he wanted to do it, he was going to do it. Nothing you would've said would've changed what he felt inside him—the hatred and the loathing, the pain."

I let go of his hand and feel myself start to come apart, so I compose myself. I can't make this moment about me. I can't.

He gives me a sidelong glance. "Don't do it."

"Colt."

"Please," he says.

We stand close to each other and stare into each other's eyes waiting, wishing—for the same thing, for something different.

He lowers his head. "I can't lose you, too," he whispers.

I stare back at his brother's headstone. "You're strong," I whisper and realize with every word, I'm admitting I haven't changed my mind and that I've broken my promise already. I'm not trying.

His breathing increases. I turn to watch his concern transform into something angry, desperate. "Why are you doing this?" he says, grabbing me by the shoulders, shaking me slightly.

I bite my lip hard and taste blood. I want to run. I want to hide. The heat starts to spread in my body again. It snakes around my veins, penetrates my bones, absorbs into my skin. "Please, I . . . I just have to," I admit. He makes me say words I don't want to.

"No, you don't," he says, pulling me into him. "I'm here," he whispers.

We hold each other for what seems like hours. The temperature rises in my body and I'm afraid I'm going to burn him. I gently move away, grab his hand, and lead him away from Ryan's grave and this conversation.

We stop in front of Tate's grave and the heat starts to dissipate a little.

"She was only six?" he asks.

The words are in my mouth. *Yes, six and a half,* I want to say, but instead I say, "I killed her."

He stiffens and it's like he's afraid if he moves a finger I'll know he's really here and alive and he'll have to respond. After a moment, he does. "I'm sorry, I didn't mean to bring anything up. It's just . . . I didn't know how old she was. You don't talk about her." He starts moving again, shifting his feet in the grass.

I sit down in front of her grave like I usually do and pull on his arm so he sits with me. He settles in beside me. "We had this obsession with the moon and stars. I think I'm the reason she had it." I smile at the memory of her face as she looked up into the sky. "I've always loved the night sky, there's just something about it." I let go of his hand and start picking at the grass. "She didn't like the night at first; she hated it. I think her mind changed when I brought her lemonade one night before bed. It was an accident, how it happened. I had gotten some for myself and I went to her room and her face lit up, like it did when she wanted something." I toss a pile of grass onto her gravestone. "She drank it all. Didn't even leave me any." I pause, trying to remember exactly what she said when I left. "She asked me to stay that night. I asked her why, and she said she had nightmares and woke up sometimes, and she'd see things in the corner. She told me later that when I stopped by with lemonade and sang to her she didn't have any nightmares. So it kind of became our thing, and she started loving the night as much as I did."

"Sounds like you were a good sister to her."

"I was. Up until the day she died."

He wraps an arm around my shoulder and pulls me into his chest.

"What about Ryan? You never talk about him, either."

"He was a pain in my ass." His voice rumbles in his chest and vibrates my skin. One word comes to mind at his voice. *Safe.*

"Oh yeah?"

He adjusts his chest so I'm tucked in closer to him. "He'd leave rotten food in my room, and unplug my PlayStation and hide the cord." He laughs and the sound vibrates deep in his body. "I used to listen to his band and he would tell everyone I was just a guy who was obsessed with them. He could be a dick, but he had his moments."

"Was he ever nice to you?"

Crickets chirp and the wind whistles in the cold air. A squirrel scurries out of the bushes behind us. We both look in that direction as he continues talking. "Yeah, he'd cover for me when I was out with friends. He'd help me study for classes he'd taken. He gave me his Escalade and never asked for anything in return. I guess I should've known it was for a reason." He smacks his hand on the ground. "Asshole."

He must have been giving away his stuff before he killed himself. What should I give away? I don't really have anything that's special. How can I think about this when he's grieving? "I'm sorry."

He stands up and shakes me off him. "Why? You want to do the same thing to me." He shakes his head then storms away, swearing, smacking each tree as he goes.

When I reach his SUV, he's leaning against the front passenger-side door. He sees me, lifts himself off the door, and opens it. I slide in without a word and he drives me home.

He pulls up in front of my house, the heat blaring in our faces, soft music playing in the background. I'm not sure what to do, so I open the door. He grasps my arm and pulls me back. He leans in and I think he's going to kiss me, but he switches at the last minute and kisses my forehead.

He lays his forehead against mine. "I care about you, and I don't want to see you hurt."

"Maybe it's better if you don't watch." I give him a quick peck on the cheek and close the door.

I need to stop hanging out with him. I need to push him away, but I just can't. As much as I don't want to, I care about him too.

And Halloween is only ten days away.

33

9 Days

The days are going by and in my mind I keep opening doors like an Advent calendar, ticking off my life in numbers. I hadn't realized when I made my deadline that it would be like this—a countdown. But that's what it's become. My room is my prison and the walls my bars. I'm in a jail of my own making and there is no parole—only the death penalty.

My phone rings and I don't even need to look to know it's Colter. It's his daily check-in to make sure I'm alive. I made fun of him for it at first, but I think he's starting to not believe everything I say anymore.

"Thank you for calling Papa John's, may I take your order?"

He's silent for a while and I picture him looking at the number on his phone to make sure he dialed the right one with an adorable, confused expression.

I put him out of his misery. "Before you ask, yes, I'm alive. No, I'm not a ghost answering from beyond the grave."

"Very funny."

"Unless there's something else? Can we—"

He always says, *No. I just wanted to hear your voice.* I know. I know. It's sweet. He's sweet. What the hell am I doing? Honestly? I have no idea anymore.

"Actually, there is."

I don't say anything. I almost hang up on him just to end it before he says something else. Something perfect, something that makes me think of things I shouldn't. Like if I should die or not.

"I want to see you."

"Why?"

"I need a reason?"

"I don't know?"

He laughs. "Just meet me."

"It's a school night."

"It's, like, seven right now, Ell."

I pause, but I already know I'm going to say yes. "Fine. Where?"

"I'll come get you."

"Is this a date?"

"Let's not label it, okay?"

"Okay, Tom Sawyer."

He hangs up, and I scramble to do my hair and get dressed and all the girl things you do before a date that's not a date. I don't know what I'm doing. I call Janie.

"Hey, he's coming over."

"Who?" she says, chewing on something.

"Shit. Did I interrupt dinner?"

"Yeah, but it's cool. Is Colter coming over?" she says, clearly excited.

"Yes. What do I wear?"

Did I really just ask that?

"Clothes."

"Janie."

"Or not." She laughs. "Sorry, okay. Wear the tight jeans and the black V-neck."

"Okay." I search my closet for the black shirt. "It's dirty."

"Hmm. I don't know. Ell, he likes you. Wear whatever you want."

My breath starts to come out rapidly and sweat breaks out on my skin. "I can't do this."

"It's not like you've never been alone with him before."

"Yeah, but I didn't really like him . . . I mean, I liked him. But now, I care . . . oh, God. I care about him."

"It's about damn time you admit it. It's fine. Just make sure to put mascara on and that sexy red lipstick. It brings out your dark hair."

"Okay."

"Seriously. Just be yourself."

"Hey, thanks."

"That's what friends are for."

I smile and get a little choked up at her words. "Have a good dinner."

We hang up, and I streak mascara on my eyelashes and paint bright red color on my lips. I pick out some random T-shirt and jeans, and hope he looks at my face, not my shirt.

A few minutes later, I see his SUV pull into the driveway. I run to the living room to fend off Mom before she goes to work.

"I want to meet him," she whines, adjusting the ties of her scrubs.

"Another time. I have to go." I lean over and hug her.

"Don't stay out all night."

I nod, slip my coat on, and head out the door. His SUV takes up half the driveway. I wave at him, then berate myself for it. I look like a deranged fangirl. I open the door and warm air blankets my body. I peek at what he's wearing and heave a breath of relief. He's in a T-shirt and jeans, too. He smiles at me as I scoot into the leather seat.

"Where are we going?" I ask.

"It's a surprise."

"Great, I just love surprises."

"It won't be that bad." He grins at me again and pulls out of the driveway.

We drive for at least an hour, passing cities with large buildings and houses, ending up in farm land with horses and no buildings. We're three towns over, I think.

"Seriously, where are we going?" I ask when I can't figure it out. He doesn't answer, so I start flipping his door handle back and forth. I'm about to lose it when we pull up to a little diner in the middle of a small two-lane highway. It's called simply The Diner. "Original name," I say as I get out of the SUV.

"Trust me," he says, grabbing my hand and pulling me toward the door.

It jingles as we go inside, and it reminds me of Tasty's. A familiar ache builds in my body as we sit down in a grungy booth with Formica tables. I'm betraying Dean. He's suffering, and I'm here on a date that's not a date. I try to picture what he would do if he saw me. He'd probably give me a contented smile, realize that I've decided to live even if for just a moment, then he'd run away and I'd never see him again. I may never see him again anyway. He could be dead now. A shudder passes over me, and I try to hide it.

Colter gives me a corny grin over the plastic menu. It has pictures of burgers and Coke floats, with people with fake smiles pointing to each item. "Everything's good here, but the pie's superior."

I eye him suspiciously. "How'd you know I liked pie?"

"Janie told me." He folds his menu up as the server comes our way.

Of course she did. I don't even need a voice, my friends will speak for me.

The server's perky and young and she glances a little too long at Colter. She has blunt-cut black hair with a streak of pink on the side, and skinny twig legs. But she's different in a really good way, in a way I wish I could be. Jealousy burns my skin and makes my hair stand up. I try to tamp it down but it's all-consuming. I hate that. I hate that he does that to me, makes me change my mood based on some other girl's actions.

"Hey, Colt. What brings your cute butt out here on a Thursday?" she says.

I glance at her name tag—Penelope. She even has a cool name.

"What always brings me in here. Oh, Pen, this is Ellery, my . . . uh, friend."

She gives me a genuine smile. "Nice to meet you." She turns back to Colter and shakes her head at him. "Bringing a girl to the diner your ex works at? Not cool."

Colter lowers his head a little.

"It's okay, we're just friends. Like he said," I say, directing the last part at Colter.

He lowers his head and creases his eyebrows, and I know I've screwed up again. Does he want more than that? Does he go around kissing his friends? I glance up at Penelope and try to see what Colter sees in her.

She laughs. "Oh, shit. Not me. Please; pretty boy is just too pretty for me," she says, smooshing his cheeks together with one hand.

Colter gently removes her hand from his face and adjusts his jaw like she knocked it out of place. "Are you going to take our order or just fondle my face all night?"

She giggles. "Ah, I see. Sore subject." She leans over to him. "She's more than a friend, isn't she?" She perks back up and gets out a small pad of paper and pen. "Don't answer that."

She takes our orders and we sit in silence when she leaves.

"Aly's not working today, if you were wondering." I must look confused cause he follows it with, "My ex."

"Oh. Well, if she was, it's no big deal."

He sighs, then grabs my hand unexpectedly. Flames build slowly at his touch. "Ellery. I don't want to just be friends with you anymore."

"What?" I say, slipping my hand out of his.

He sits up straighter in the booth and clasps his hands together. "I know you think I'm with you because I want to save you. But really, I think you're the one saving me."

I huff a little. "You sound like a Nicholas Sparks novel."

He grins, but it's reluctant, like he doesn't really want to. "I'm trying to be serious."

"Please don't."

"You only speak in sarcasm."

I shrug.

"Okay, I can work with that." He adjusts in his seat again and lifts his chin. "It's not like I want you to be more than a friend, it's just that I've always wanted to sound like I'm reciting a Nicholas Sparks novel. It's my dream," he says with a cock of his head at the end of his statement. His expression can only be described as cute.

I fight not to laugh, but it doesn't work and I end up giggling until I can feel sharp pains in my stomach.

"Is that better?" he says.

"I guess I can try. But no more Nicholas Sparks, okay? I want to keep my pie down."

He holds his hand out to me and I shake it. "Deal."

The pie comes, and it's huge, and it's a whole pie? "You ordered a whole pie? How much do you think I can eat?"

"The real question is how much *I* can eat. You don't get this figure by eating rice cakes." He gestures to his lean body and I can't help but look. "I'm taking the rest home, don't worry," he adds, slicing a piece out for me first.

We dig in and smile at each other over the crust and cherry-rhubarb filling, and it's one of the best moments of my life.

34

7 Days

Colter and I slip into a cruddy yellow booth that looks ten years old. My thighs burn as I slide them across the hard bench. A tear in the plastic scratches my leg before I settle in place across from him. I make the mistake of looking up at The Pizza Shoppe's fixtures. They have a mile of dirt packed on them. I shift in my seat to avoid getting any particles on my clothes. We're on a date again. This time to help his brother.

Colter unfolds the menu and huddles behind it, so I do the same.

I peek around my menu. "Where is your brother, and why are we hiding when this girl doesn't know who we are?" I whisper.

His head pops out the side of his menu. "She knows who I am. Atticus is coming. Act incognito."

I give him a wry look.

"You know what I mean."

I move back behind my menu and watch as Atticus slides in next to his brother. His hair looks like it's been slicked back with grease and he's biting his lip. His T-shirt has a picture of hipster glasses with no lenses and it says *DIE* in big red letters.

I suppress a laugh. I like this kid.

I lower my menu. "I don't think she can see me, guys."

Colter lowers his and looks at me like I'm ruining the big plan. He glances at Atticus's hair and musses it up a bit, causing the pieces to stick in different directions. One of the older servers, who looks like she lived when George Washington was president, takes our drink and breadstick order before we go into hiding again.

I notice a group of younger brunette girls a few tables over across the restaurant. One is giggling at something her friend said to the geriatric server. The giggling one has short-cropped hair and a smile that could freeze all of hell. Her friend has long, straight hair that's pushed back by a polka-dot headband. Polka Dot has a smirk on her face like she just said the funniest thing. The other girl is rolling her eyes, sticking her nose in the air. She's perfectly put together, not a hair out of place. I pray that's not the girl Atticus likes.

"She's over there, right? That's where you keep looking."

Atticus straightens his shirt and glances over and quickly back with a scared look on his face.

I grin at his cuteness. So innocent. "Which one is it?" I ask.

Please don't be the snobby one.

He cowers his head a little and I want to smoosh his cheeks, which is really strange 'cause he's in eighth grade and I'm a junior, but he's adorable the way he likes her and he's so nervous.

"She's the one with the head thing."

The waitress drops off our breadsticks and drinks. We each grab a breadstick and bite.

I breathe out; the smart-ass. I can work with that. "Polka Dot? Okay. Good. First we have to isolate her. She needs to be alone. Never, and I repeat, never ask her out in front of her friends."

He nods and I notice Colter looking at me with a proud smile on his face. My skin starts to heat a little at his stare. I'm in over my head here. Helping him with his brother? That's big time. Couples territory. I brush those thoughts out of my head in order to help Atticus. "I think it's a good idea for you to talk to her, though. In front of her friends. Show her you're not afraid."

His eyes go wide. "I . . . I have to talk to her?"

Colter and I laugh.

"Dude, how do you expect to hang out with her without talking?" Colter says, messing up Atticus's hair again.

"Talking is required for most date activities," I add.

I see Colter give me a seductive look then raise his eyebrows. "Well, not all of them." I throw a spoon at him; he ducks and it clatters to the ground. "It's true," he adds.

I roll my eyes. "Go on. Go say hello. Ask to borrow her Parmesan or something."

Atticus takes a few breaths in and puts his palms on the table. His face is a mixture of desperation and shock and fear.

I lean over a little. "You can do this," I say. "Wait." I grab three sticks of gum out of my purse, hand two to him and Colter, and take the last one myself. "Don't want to talk to her with garlic breath."

He shoves the stick of gum into his mouth, takes one last breath, and looks at his brother. The expression on Atticus's face, the look of pure admiration of his big brother, makes me melt a little in my cruddy booth.

Colter nods reassuringly, and Atticus leaves on his mission.

His brother looks at him like Tate looked at me. I close my eyes and fight the feeling that comes, the guilt-wrenching knife twisting my heart. Opening my eyes, I focus on where I am and what I'm doing, and see Colter's proud big brotherly expression as he watches his brother walk away. As quick as Tate's memory arrived it fades away, and I'm left feeling grateful for these moments with him in the present.

"What?" Colter says when he sees my expression.

"Nothing." I smile at him, then it feels like too much, too close to feeling. I switch gears. "You're such a pervert. Way to make him more nervous."

The edges of Colter's mouth turn up into a sheepish grin. "What? There's a lot you can do on a date without talking."

I shake my head.

"There he goes," Colter says, shoving his piece of gum into his mouth.

Atticus wipes his hands on his jeans obsessively, but he makes it to the table and from here it looks like his mouth is moving.

"How do you think it's going?" Colter asks with a worried look on his face.

It kills me how unselfish this guy is. I don't deserve to be breathing the same air as him.

"Good. He's still there, isn't he?"

He runs a hand through his hair and scrunches it in his hands. "I'm just worried. If he gets shot down. I don't know how to pick him up from that. I mean, I can only do so much."

I look at him. I'm starting to really like this guy too much. And for some reason he wants to be around me. Save me. "He has to do this himself. You can't help everyone. Even if you want to." I grab his hand across the table, not even realizing I'm doing it until it's done. "We need to make our own mistakes."

"You said *we*."

I let go of his hand and slide mine back into my lap. "I did. I meant him. He. He needs to make his own mistakes."

Atticus comes back and he's smiling. Good sign.

"How'd it go?" I ask.

His eyes are large. "She asked me to the dance."

Colt grabs his brother's shoulders and shakes them. "Dude, that's awesome."

Atticus turns to his big brother. "She asked *me*. How embarrassing is that?"

"Not embarrassing at all. Girls can ask boys out. Watch," I say. "Tom Sawyer, will you go to the Halloween dance with me?"

Colter smiles. "I thought you'd never ask."

Atticus beams, then gets a confused look on his face. "Why'd you call him Tom Sawyer?"

I giggle, but don't say anything.

"It's her code name for me. You should get one, too," Colter says, looking from Atticus to me. He claps his hands together. "Mission accomplished. Now, I need to take *my* girl, and we'll leave you to yours," Colter says, nudging Atticus out of the booth.

My breathing's sped up since he's said the words *my girl.*

Atticus looks at me and lowers his head a little. "Thanks for your help, Ellery. My brother's lucky to have you."

"I'm the lucky one." Shit. I sound like a Nicholas Sparks novel. But for that moment, I'm happy, and I know I'm falling for Colter. And it's scary and wrong, but I can't stop it. For the first time I'm wondering if I need to stick to my plan. Maybe this unexpected puzzle piece is the answer.

You can't change your plan for a boy.

It wouldn't be right.

Colter grabs my hand and drags me out of The Pizza Shoppe into the cold air. We sprint to his SUV. I stumble over a rock in the parking lot, but he keeps pulling me behind him.

"What's up with you? Is there a race I don't know about?"

He halts us before the passenger door and turns around. He gives me a seductive grin and wraps his arms around my waist. My heart is pumping hard and everything on me feels hot. I know the air is cold, it was freezing when we went inside, but I feel nothing but his arms around my waist.

"I think . . . ." He closes his eyes. "Fuck," he growls, and opens his eyes, his gaze strong and determined and a little confused mixed with surprised. "I think I'm falling in love with you?"

He says it like a question and that throws me off. I have trouble forming words. I can only stare into his deep eyes and get lost. "Is that a question or a statement?" I ask, finally recovering my voice.

"I'm in love with you," he answers firmly.

I freeze at his words. The finality of them, what they represent. I can't say it back. I feel it, but I can't say it, not when I don't know if I can keep the promises I keep making.

"Can I kiss you?" I back up a little, afraid of trying again, afraid of losing myself, afraid of changing. He walks toward me, moving his hands to my cheeks, and cradles my face. Concern flashes across his features.

I close my eyes and wait. I feel warm, but it's not the same. Somehow the warmth is good, different. For once, I don't want to be cold. I give him a firm nod this time.

A sly smile grows on his lips as he gently presses them to mine. The kiss is soft and sweet, tentative, careful. I open my mouth and press harder to his, telling him it's okay. I feel my strength pour from my lips to his. He moves his hands to my waist and his fingers trail under my shirt, touching my exposed skin. They're cold on my warm skin, and perfect. He spins me around and pushes me against the metal door. The handle wedges itself into my back, but I don't care because all I can feel, all I can think about are his safe warm kisses.

And for once. Nothing else.

35

6 Days

I used to take Tate to the zoo. We would watch the zebras roam in the savannah enclosure and she would chase the peacocks across the walkway to the train. Her little feet could barely keep up, and the peacocks looked scared shitless at her little legs moving toward them. It's these memories that keep me coming back here to relive those moments with her. It makes it feel like she's not so far away.

The sun's rays illuminate a group of toddlers with a Mommy and Me group who are running around the goats, touching them like they're playing tag. I crank the machine with the goat pellets and let them fall into my open hand. I lean against the fence of the goat corral and feed a black goat with white on his tail. He gobbles up the pellets quickly and I have to make another run to the pellet machine.

This was our place. Tate loved to feed the goats. She would tentatively go through the gate, and it would take her a few minutes to get up the courage to feed them. She always denied being scared. She never wanted me to see her weak. I would have to tell her that the zoo wouldn't let her in if they thought the goats would do anything to her. That always assured her. She believed everything I said.

One of the ruddy-looking goats is lying lazily in a plastic playhouse with an orange roof. He looks so out of place in that fake house. I glance around the wooden fence, then back to the goat in the playhouse. These goats are trapped, stuck in these

199

enclosures with hundreds of nameless zoo patrons feeding them awful-smelling pellets. They can't even piss without a kid pushing on its back or trying to mount it like a horse. Maybe they wanted something besides pellets. They didn't get to choose this life. Do they even want it? I have the urge to open the door and let the poor goats go, especially the black one with white on its tail. He looks like he wants to escape.

The sun blares down on me and I'm constantly amazed that it can be ice-cube cold overnight but sunny and sixty today. Tate and I mostly came to the zoo in the summer, so it was always hot and I would complain. She would grab my hand and tell me how much she loved the heat on her. I close my eyes and it's like I'm there, watching her.

"Sissy, come on. Pet the goats with me," Tate says in that little girl voice that drives me nuts.

She can be kind of annoying, always wanting me to show her everything.

"It's dirty and they stink." I point to a sandy-haired boy next to her. "Look, he's in there with you. You'll be fine." I look down at my phone and check my social media accounts for replies.

"I'm not scared," she says confidently.

I look up at her and smile. She's so different from me in so many ways. Someday she'll want that sandy-haired boy near her. I laugh at the thought. She never wants me to leave her side. Even when I go out with my friends, she wants to tag along. She even snuck in the car once and I didn't know until she popped up from the back seat during a movie at the drive-in.

That was embarrassing.

I look again, closer. The goat is chasing her in the corral and she's laughing and clapping. She stops, lets the goat catch her, and kneels down beside him, stroking his coat gently. She looks up and her big brown eyes find mine. She waves and grins so wide her cheeks dimple. I wave back. She's so small and fragile, like glass that can be broken with the poke of a needle. How do I keep her from shattering? How do I keep her smiling when I know our dad is going to ruin everything? She looks up to him. She doesn't see his flaws. She sees a protector and a bedtime-book reader, a monster capturer.

I wish I could live in her world, full of stars and moons shining in the night. I wish she could just chase goats instead of growing up.

The memory fades as the sun starts to set into the horizon, leaving me alone, staring at other people's sisters petting the same goats. The ache in my chest returns, but it's worse. I bite my lip hard, sinking my teeth deeper into my skin. It hurts so bad, but it feels good. It feels right. I leave the goats and make my way out to my car. It's the torture of her memories that keeps me focused. I think about last night. How amazing it was to kiss Colter. How for a moment I questioned my fate. I thought maybe I could stop and live. But the pain came back like a cancer this morning. I felt it deep in my soul. He's penetrated something in me, I can't deny that, but I can't let him change me, change what I need to do to make everything right.

I'm going to enjoy my time with him, then I'm going to leave.

He said he's in love with me. But is it just the idea of me he loves? What if he really is only trying to save me and he's confused? I know he said that wasn't it, but how could he know?

How could I have let this happen?

I slam my forehead into the steering wheel, pounding it over and over. I feel a bruise forming. It feels good again. Right.

How can I love him so much and hate myself? I do love him. I feel it. It's there hovering over my decisions, my plan. I lift my head and look in the mirror. My lip's bleeding and my forehead is full of steering wheel marks.

I spend the rest of the day driving by Dean's house and checking until I see his car in the driveway.

36

5 Days

My car's still running as I stare up at Colter's house. The hanging ghosts have multiplied and there are a hundred more decals on the windows. I don't want to go in, but Colter wants me to hang with him and his family. They're having a pre-Halloween scary movie marathon, complete with pizza, popcorn, and every kind of candy you can dream up. At least that's what Colter said.

I know his mom's going to be there, but if I'm going to be with him I have to accept her, at least until Halloween. I pull the flaps of my coat together and put my gloved hands in my coat pockets as I reach the front of the door. I stand staring at the door for at least a minute, contemplating running away and forgetting about all of this. As I'm about to raise my hand to knock, it swings open.

Loretta. The brunette twin's confused, suspicious eyes roam over me. "Are you dating my uncle?" she asks as Cooper strolls up beside her and cocks his head at me. I choke on a pile of saliva that formed during my walk to the door. Hearing her call him her uncle makes him sound old, and hearing that question spoken so honestly by a kid is something I wasn't prepared for. I should have been; Tate talked the same way.

She laughs and opens the door wider. "Don't worry about answering. I already know. I am eight and a half, after all."

I smile at her as Colter moves in behind her. "Is she giving you shit?"

Loretta's eyes go wide as she turns to face him. "You said a bad word." I suppress a giggle. Colter feigns like he's in trouble, but before he can say anything Loretta whispers, "I won't tell."

She sounds so much like Tate did. Sadness at their exchange is threatening to surface, but I glance at Colter and think about him instead. Try to remember what his lips feel like on mine, what his heartbeat sounds like, the words he said to me.

He crouches down and holds out his hand for a shake. Loretta puts her little fingers in his. "Thanks," Colter says.

"Are you letting that cold air in?" a woman's voice says from inside. It sounds like his mom.

My insides churn at her voice. I'm sure I'm the last person she wants to see. I wonder if he told her I was coming.

Colter ruffles Loretta's hair and she groans, slapping his hand away and leaving the entrance followed by Cooper.

He grabs my hand, yanks me inside, pushes me up against the hall closet and kisses me. I get momentarily lost in the wonderful heat his kisses produce. It's kind of amazing how he can make me forget about everything bad in my life, even if it is only when his lips touch mine.

Snapping out of my daze, I flatten my hands on his chest. "Stop that, hornball. Your family's in the other room."

He grins while removing my hands and moves closer. "So?"

I can't help but smile at him, at his complete lack of caring about what people think. I wish I had that in me. I used to have that. He kisses me once more and play-frowns when he lets me go. "Fine. You win. Come on, I have this great popcorn seasoning you have to try."

Orange and black decorations are spread throughout the living room, and his family is scattered around it. I recognize the twins and their mom. Mrs. Sawyer is sitting up straight in a seat by the corner with her laptop on her lap. Atticus is on the couch next to the girl from The Pizza Shoppe. I wink at him. He smiles back. The girl notices and I get a jealous glare from her that makes me smile. She really must like him.

Colter leaves me in the room to get the pizza. *The Exorcist* is blaring from the TV and I wonder why the twins are allowed to watch it. I take a seat on the floor.

"Ellery, I'm so glad you could come," Mrs. Sawyer says in a tone that contradicts her words.

I'm not sure if anyone else notices.

"So, do you like scary movies, Ellery?" the twins' mom asks. I realize I haven't learned her name and I suddenly feel stupid that she knows mine.

"I do." I look to the screen as Regan spider-walks down the stairs. I shudder. "*The Exorcist* is one of my favorites."

I shift on the ground to get more comfortable as a set of arms curl around me. Colter lays down a paper plate of pizza and scoots in behind me so I'm sitting between his legs. I feel the heat come to my cheeks as he leans in and lays his chin on my shoulder.

Cooper eyes our food from the side of the room. He makes a half-hearted attempt to move closer, but changes his mind, lays his head on his paws, and falls asleep.

"I didn't know you liked scary movies," Colter whispers, causing wonderful, awful things to happen to my body, things that his family shouldn't be around for. I want him to move, but I love hearing his soft, low voice in my ear.

"There's a lot about me you don't know," I say, using his words against him.

I feel the laugh vibrate in his chest before it bubbles up to his mouth. He grabs a piece of pizza and shoves the sagging bottom into his mouth.

I grab a piece, fold it in half, and take a small bite. I've never liked eating around people I don't know. I always worry about food spilling on me, or having something stuck in my teeth all night. But I'm starving.

A couple of hours later, I'm full of pizza, popcorn, and a pound of these scrumptious homemade chocolate-covered cranberries that are pretty much my crack. I groan. "The next time I come over, you're going to have to roll me out after all this food."

Colter laughs along with Atticus and his girlfriend, Grace. I learned her name during an impromptu quiz on horror movies Colter's sister, Alice, had. Colter's mom has left and retreated somewhere else and the twins have gone to bed. Alice is curled up on the couch with a multi-colored crocheted blanket covering her. Jamie Lee Curtis screams on the screen and Alice jerks, but stays asleep. Atticus looks nervous sitting next to Grace, like he wants to put his arm around her. I wonder if he's been thinking about it for hours.

I catch his eye and I mouth, *Do it,* gesturing toward her.

He wipes his hands on his jeans and takes a deep breath. Grace has no clue; she's leaning in watching the movie intently. He looks at me again and I give him an impatient glare.

He quickly moves his arm up like he's stretching.

I roll my eyes and shake my head.

He brings his arm down around her shoulders. He doesn't see her expression, but her eyes widen and the smallest hint of a smile spreads across her face. She leans into him, resting her head on his shoulder.

It's so cute I want to take a picture so I can remember it. Clueless Colter missed the whole thing. This is something Atticus and I have alone, and that makes me feel important, even if it's just for a moment.

I lean back and curve my head into Colter's neck. He places his chin on my shoulder and kisses it. He slowly raises his lips to my neck and trails kisses up to my ear. "I wish my brother and sister weren't in this room right now," he whispers.

Chills break out on my skin. He traps my ear in his mouth and sucks lightly. Cold heat pools everywhere. I lean into his kiss and the tension crescendos until I can't take it any more. I twist my body so I'm facing him and press my lips to his. The kiss ignites something in me I've never felt before. My hands are all over him and his are on me and I want him. Jamie Lee Curtis screams again on the screen and the light flicks on and it's like we're cockroaches scattering. Atticus moves away from Grace with a guilty expression that matches my own. Colter's the only one who looks unfazed. He's still staring at me like I'm the wind and the stars and the sun.

Mrs. Sawyer, on the other hand, is staring at me like I'm hellfire and brimstone and death. "I think it's time for you to go home," she says looking down at me.

Colter doesn't let me go. "We weren't doing anything wrong," he snaps.

"Atticus? Grace's mom is going to be here in ten minutes. Can you please find her things and get her on her way?"

A sleepy Alice has awoken from her nap. "What's going on?" she asks.

"Mom's being Mom," Colter says.

Alice rolls her eyes. "Mom, he's eighteen. Do you really think he's going to listen to you anymore?"

Mrs. Sawyer fumes, gritting her teeth hard. "Alice, this is none of your concern."

"You didn't care when his old girlfriend was here and you caught them more than once. Lighten up," Alice says.

I move slowly away from Colter. He's been caught before with Kirstyn. Of course he has. They dated. I'm out of my element here. He grabs for me, but I move away. He looks up at his sister. "Thank you for reminding me of that, and Ell, too. I'm sure she loves hearing about my old girlfriends."

Alice bites her lip. "Shit, I'm sorry, Colt." She looks at me and smiles. "He never looked at her like he looks at you, though."

Mrs. Sawyer is still standing with her arms folded across her chest. "That's enough. Ellery? I'll walk you to the door."

Colter stands up and faces his mom. "It amazes me how rude you can be." He grabs my hand and pulls me out of the room. I grab my coat and gloves and make a bee-line for the door. He places a hand on the door and twists me around toward him. "Don't listen to her. It's me that this is really about." He cradles my cheek in his hands. "Okay?"

I nod, but don't believe him. Not for a second. He gives me a quick kiss and I scoot out the door. I'm almost to my car when I feel an arm grab me.

"Colt, I . . . ." I turn around and it's not Colter, it's his mother, and she's glaring at me.

"Stay away from my son."

"I can't." It's true. If I could, I would have pushed him away a long time ago.

"You're not good for him. I'm sure you're a nice enough girl. But Colter needs to be with someone . . . ."

"Someone more like Kirstyn?" She's right, though. I'm not good for him, but her insult still stings.

"Just not someone like you. I'm sorry."

I recoil against the car. I'm not surprised she's saying the words. She's been wanting to. "I have to go."

"Look, it's nothing personal. I just want my son to be happy."

I glare at her. "No, you don't."

She opens her mouth like she's going to say something else, but closes it before words can come out. She stalks off in a huff as I get the hell out of there.

37

4 Days

"That's right, hold the note in place and . . . fade," Aunt Sue says as we let our voices go silent. "Great job. We'll pick it up next class." The bell rings. "Study your parts. See you tomorrow."

Colter grins at me as he walks out the door, and Janie comes up beside me. "You've got it bad."

"You're one to talk."

She giggles. "You're right."

"Girls, we'll only need a half-hour or so to practice your duet later," Aunt Sue says, interrupting us.

After our last class, Janie and I meet back in the choir room and we both sit in the front while Aunt Sue gets ready at the piano. "Okay, let's take it from the beginning."

She begins to play and the notes seep out of me as my voice takes over. Janie and I sing together and it sounds amazing. Music is an escape I don't make use of as often as I should. I forgot how much I loved to sing with someone else, to feel the emotion of another person through the notes. Janie's become too close to me. Jackson, Colter—all of them. I've done a horrible job of pushing any of them away.

We finish practice and Janie turns to me before leaving. "So, I found another random awesome eighties movie, *Can't Buy Me Love*. Have you seen it? Please tell me you haven't, 'cause I really want to watch it with you."

I laugh. "I've never heard of it. Who's in it?"

"Mc-fucking-Dreamy."

"From *Grey's Anatomy*?"

"Yep. He's a geek in it, which I can't imagine. So, your house, tonight?" she says.

"Sure, why not."

"Oh, and don't forget about costume shopping on Friday."

"Got it." I smile.

She runs over and gives me a hug. I'm so surprised, I don't hug her back. "Jackson's waiting for me, but thank you. I'll see you tonight. I hope it's okay I just invited myself over like that."

"It's fine. Can't wait to see it."

She grabs her backpack and heads out the door.

I sit in one of the chairs and bury my face in my hands. "I'm such a bitch."

"Hey, you can't talk to my girl like that." It's Colter's voice, but I don't lift my head to see him.

The chair beside me squeaks as Colter sits down. He drapes an arm around my shoulder and pulls me toward him. "What's wrong?"

I lean against him and feel his heartbeat against me. "Janie. She's become a good friend and I feel like . . . ."

"Like you're a bitch for thinking about leaving her?"

"Yeah. And other people, too."

"It comes with the territory."

"I know." I lift my head and look him in the eyes. "I'm sorry, you probably don't want to talk about this with me."

"You're wrong. I didn't get a chance with Ryan. I just had to accept it. But you. You're letting me in."

I shake my head. "No, it's not like that."

"It's not? It looks like that to me."

Is he right?

He takes a deep breath and that cute expression, his smile, they fade and I watch his face go through all the emotions he must be feeling. The desperation of wanting to say the right thing to change my mind, the frustration that nothing he says will work, the feeling of being abandoned. But it doesn't matter, because Tate is gone. And no matter what I feel for him, I can't get rid of that. It haunts me constantly. His kisses are the best, his sweet smiles are perfect, but I'm going to leave them on Halloween.

"Ellery," he says with a serious tone. "So, it's not gonna be easy. It's going to be really hard; we're gonna have to work at this every day, but I want to do that because I want you. I want all of you, forever, every day. You and me . . . every day."

My heart stops beating momentarily, then I process what he actually said. It's really familiar like I heard it in the . . . . "Oh my God, *The Notebook*? Really?"

He laughs. "It was getting too serious."

I eye him playfully, arching an eyebrow. "So you didn't mean what you said?"

He lifts his ball cap and runs a hand through his hair. "I . . . well, yeah. I did." He leans over and before I can utter a sarcastic remark about him even reading Nicholas Sparks his lips are on mine and the kiss is so powerful and full of life I have to remember to breathe.

38

Colter and I are walking out to my car when I realize Dean wasn't in school today. I forgot to drive by his house this morning on the way to school. I pause in front of the parking lot and my body almost drops to the ground. He wasn't in class today. How could I forget to check? I search my mind for what he was like yesterday. Was he more sad than normal? Did he have a look in his eye? Why didn't I pay attention? I've been too busy making out with Colter to be there for Dean.

Maybe he's just sick. He could be sick.

"What's wrong?" Colter asks, getting into his front seat and buckling his seat belt.

I stand by his window and try not to show my worry. "I'm fine. Just a big test tomorrow." I lean over and give him a quick kiss, but he grabs the back of my head when I try to separate and he deepens the kiss. Kissing him is an escape into the perfect world where *Happy Ellery* lives in peace, but I can't think about that right now. "I love kissing you, but—" I mumble into his lips.

He smiles against my mouth. "Then don't stop."

We kiss for a few seconds more then I pull away and he groans. "I'm sorry. I have to study." I glance around the parking lot when I say it so I'm not lying right to his face.

"Okay. Yeah, I have to get to work anyway. Call me tonight?"

"Sure. Have fun," I say, trying to fake a smile.

He smiles and I'm lost in him again. "Always."

I rush to Tasty's and cup my eyes on the glass to see inside. The lights are off, but it's four in the afternoon. It should be open right now. Maybe they have a meeting. He has to be here. He has to. My pulse jerks around like it's on a string being pulled from behind me. I knock on the door. Two times, three. I lean into the glass again and squint to see if anyone is in the room. Okay, no one's here. Maybe they just closed for inventory or something. A small ripple of dread slithers up my body. I run to my car and get in, slamming the door and pressing the gas. I head down to Baker Street where Dean lives.

He didn't. He couldn't have already.

It's probably nothing.

You know it's not nothing.

Before I get to his house I see the blue and red lights flash in the distance. I can't tell whose house they're in front of. That same feeling jams itself into my throat, the dread, the wanting to be wrong about it all. I drive slowly toward Dean's house. I pass the white house with the blue shutters we used to ring the doorbell of and run away. I glance over at the tree where Jackson first taught us to climb. My breath comes out intermittently, like puffs out of an air gun. My foot slips off the gas as I near his house.

The lights are coming from his driveway.

Red and blue cover my vision and make me momentarily blind. I park my car and run up the road toward his house on rubber legs. The echo of my feet on the pavement sounds like an earthquake. My breathing is strained. I have to stop and bend over to catch my breath. I reach the driveway and I see Dean's dad, tears flooding his face. I look for his mom.

Maybe something happened to his mom. He wouldn't today.

Are you an idiot?

Yes, he would.

Why am I so angry? This is what he wanted. *But this isn't what you wanted.*

His mom emerges from the front door being held up by another woman who's lightly stroking her hair. I frantically look for Dean.

He's not here.

He did it.

He killed himself.

Oh, God.

I get the sensation of spinning in a circle. When I was little I would spin in circles until I fell down, and I loved it. Now I don't want to feel that. I don't want that out-of-control feeling in me. I turn toward Dean's dad and his tear-filled eyes lock with mine and there's so much in them—fear, devastation, loss. He shakes his head slowly and walks toward me. I frantically look beside me for a place to run to, but he gets here too soon. The panic in my body has reached a threshold. I want to melt into the ground. I don't want to hear what he's going to say.

You know what he's going to say.

But I don't want to hear the words.

"Ellery. Oh, God. Maybe you should go."

I close my hands into fists to keep from moving them. "What's going on? Where's Dean?"

He purses his lips together and wipes away the stray tears. His eyes grow wide and he looks in the distance above me like he can see Dean's soul. "I don't know how it . . . he just . . . God. I had no idea."

"About what?" I ask, knowing the answer, knowing how cruel it is to ask him at a time like this, but I have to know.

His gaze settles on me. "How sick he was."

What can I say to that?

"You should go. I'm sorry, but you have to go," he says, fighting tears again.

I know I should leave. But I need to know the details. No matter how sick and wrong it is. "What happened to him? How'd he . . . ." I feel the tears form before they fall.

He closes his eyes as if trying to get away from my question. He wants to burrow away. I can see it. His shoulders slump like he's given up. "He shot himself. I'm sorry. I need to go be with my wife right now."

He squeezes my shoulder and takes off toward Dean's mom and the lady holding her up.

The sky is falling. The clouds are trying to suffocate me. Guilt spirals in my mind. Over and over like the deranged Tilt-A-Whirl I used to ride at the carnival with Tate. I close my eyes and the world spins around me.

I need to get out of here.

I run to my car and slam myself down onto the front seat and just sit there, staring through the glass. I grab the steering wheel and twist my fingers around the leather. A little boy rides by on a bike, screaming at another boy. His voice is muffled, like he's inside a bubble. A guy walks his dog, staring back at the sirens with a strange, curious expression. The dog barks in slow motion.

My tears have dried up and I keep reliving all the moments I'd had with Dean. All the memories. The sadness in his eyes that matched my own.

He was like me.

He's really gone.

Oh, God. I can't do this. I can't feel. I don't want to feel any of this.

39

I speed down the street, fighting the urge to either throw up, hit something, or just drive off the bridge and end it all so I don't feel anymore. It doesn't have to be on Halloween. I can just do it now.

The Dover Bridge appears through my windshield. It's really not spectacular as far as bridges go. It's made of cement and has pockets of graffiti gracing its walls. It's just conveniently placed on top of a huge river. I get out and sit on the edge of the bridge's railing, fighting the wind that threatens to blow me off. The air's always stronger up here, like the river fuels it, like it wants to control it.

I close my eyes and try to board up the pain, but it doesn't work. This is too big to fit in a box—too real. I close my eyes and try all the tricks I've done before to empty my heart. "Alabama, Alaska, Arizona . . . ." I rub my head. "Arkansas . . . ." I lower my head into my hands. "Baltimore . . . no. Connecticut?" I uncover my face and stare down at the river. "Fucking California!" I smack the railing, then hit it again. And again until my fingers are red and raw.

I feel like I'm nine again and Dean's telling me that horrible ketchup joke. I let out a pathetic laugh then grip the railing again. "Three tomatoes are walking down the street, a papa tomato, a mama tomato, and a little baby tomato. Baby tomato starts lagging behind. Papa tomato gets *angry*—" I growl the word like Dean had when he'd told me the joke. "—goes back and smooshes him and says, 'Catch up.'" I laugh until I'm clutching onto my stomach. "That joke was so stupid, Dean!" I stand on the edge of the bridge, the wind pushing and pulling me apart as I laugh through tears.

When I do it, then he'll know. Maybe he'll finally listen to me for once. Too bad I won't be around to say "I told you so."

"Is that what you wanted? For someone to listen to you?" I say, the misty air wetting my lips. Why didn't I just listen to him? Would it have mattered?

My heart feels like it's going to beat out of my body.

His blood is on your hands.

I crumble off the ledge and slide down so my back's facing the bridge. Would he have ever told anyone what *I* wanted to do? I feel like I'll never be able to stand again. How can I stand upright while Dean is lying horizontal? Did he have a plan, too? What could I have done to stop him? He'd made up his mind. Like me. Did he know the date? Was it random? What if having a plan was a mistake? Four days. Halloween's only four days away.

Halloween used to be so much fun. I remember the year Tate and I dressed up as the moon and the sun. She was all yellow from her feet to the stocking on her head that kept getting caught on her ears. We'd made her sun rays together the night before, cutting cardboard triangles and painting the tips orange. Being the moon was easier. We just cut out a gray circle with a hole for my head and had Mom shade in the craters. She was always better at the artsy stuff than us. We ate so much candy that we stayed up until three in the morning, watching horror movies. Halloween has a different meaning now. It's ugly and there are no yellow suns or gray moons anymore. Just black shadows and ghosts of the past.

I want to love Halloween like that again. But how can I without Tate? It's only me now. No more goofy yellow sun costumes, no songs at night, no ice cream mustaches or lemonade to share. My entire face itches from tears and I want to scratch it, rip the skin from me and expose who I really am without her. Am I still me?

Like clockwork, familiar pangs of guilt sneak into my mind like a predator, stalking my thoughts, waiting to twist and destroy them. I could have saved her if I just had been more careful, just paid more attention. Dean would still be alive if I had just said something to someone. I let them both die.

Would Colter forgive me if he knew? Mom? Jackson and Janie? How could I expect that of them if I haven't even asked that of myself?

I clutch my stomach, staring over the ledge to the river below, the breath in my lungs straining to flow. How am I supposed to know what's right anymore? Everything is clouded and the puzzle pieces are jumbled in the box, and they're going everywhere and they don't fit right now.

I need them to fit.

40

A strand of hair blows into my face and gets stuck to my tears. I'm a well that's run dry, a sea vacant of fish, a sky without stars. I keep clutching at my chest as if that will help my breath to finally release. I'm not numb yet. You can still breathe if you're numb. I've only felt this short of breath one other time—after Tate died.

❦

I wobble into the living room on my broken leg, clutching the crutch with my good arm, secretly wanting to let go and fall through the floor to what's below. The room smells different, mustier. Everything's in the same place but it's empty, like the familiar's been sucked away. I know nothing's changed, but it feels like I've gone back in time and returned to an alternate universe. Somewhere along the space-time continuum, I turned the wrong way and my sister is dead in this life.

My parents walk past me, avoiding my eyes.

"Can you make sure she gets up the stairs to take a shower?" Mom asks Dad, as if I'm not in the room.

"Of course," he says after a sigh.

My dad grabs my arm and helps me up the stairs without talking. My leg cast clunks on each stair. We finally maneuver to the top of the stairs and Mom is there with a small plastic bag and a garbage bag. She hands them to him.

"She needs to wrap her casts. Can you make sure she gets them on?"

He nods.

We stumble clumsily into the bathroom and I look up at my dad for the first time. He's staring past me with a blank expression.

I grab the bags from his hands. "I can do it."

He doesn't argue, or tell me to yell if I need help. He just leaves and closes the door behind him. I lock the door, undress, and stare at the mirror, at the shell of a girl I am now. The dark circles under my eyes, my stringy hair, my chapped lips.

I want my mom.

The plastic bags provide a little protection, but I probably need to secure them better. I don't really care if water gets on my casts, though. Nothing matters anymore. Not without Tate. I've been thinking about it—killing myself. My parents won't look at me, and they've decided talking around me is easier than talking to me. Jackson's in Michigan visiting his grandparents, so by the time anyone finds out, I'll be gone. It's the only way I can escape the pain and make everything right.

Her voice won't stop replaying in my mind. I tell it to stop, but the more I try to make it go away the more it invades, amplifies, echoes.

"Sissy? What's wrong?"

I open the medicine cabinet, grab my dad's razor and extract the blade.

"Why are there stars, Sissy?"

The cut is deep as I glide it across my skin. My fingers fumble with the blade as I try again, the bag on my cast making it hard to push as hard as I want. I cut three more lines to make up for the other wrist. Maybe if I get enough cuts on this side, the cast-covered side won't be an issue.

"One more song, Sissy."

Blood bubbles on my skin and flows toward my fingers.

I turn the water on and hold my good hand under the rush of water and watch streaks of red stream down the drain. The water's hot, but it needs to be to rinse away everything that happened. It needs to be scalding. I move the shower door to the side and maneuver myself inside, balancing on one leg, holding my bagged arm to my stomach.

At first I don't feel anything but my emptying head. Before I have time to comprehend any sane thoughts, the water starts to feel like little knives slicing my skin. It burns. The droplets echo in my ears and they sound like a thunderstorm. I push against the walls and they start closing in on me, pushing, smashing.

I can't breathe. It's not coming. Breath isn't coming.

This is what you wanted.

My heartbeats fire in succession like a machine gun. I wait for them to stop, to slow down. They don't. I put my hand over my chest and blood runs down my body. I can almost see my chest palpitating with my heartbeats. I push on the glass door. It won't budge and I can't breathe and I need to breathe. I want this over, but not like this, quicker. My rapid heartbeat continues. I try to turn off the water, but my fingers slip on the knob. I forget which way to turn and the stream turns ice cold. It's freezing and the knives have turned into daggers, piercing my skin. I look down and there's so much blood, but I don't feel cleansed. I don't feel the salvation I'm supposed to.

I gather some strength and try again to pull the door to the side with my good arm, but it gets stuck. I start to push on it and it won't relent. I slam my fist on it over and over, pounding onto the fake glass. It's vibrating and I can feel it in my body, hear it echo in my head.

There's too much blood.

I shove it again with all the strength I can manage and the door releases from the hinges and shatters, sending me down with my broken leg straddling the bathtub, with my bagged arm under me.

I'm naked and broken on the floor and no one is coming.

You deserve this.

I grasp onto the sink, gulping air. I look down and my blood-red fingerprint has stained the white sink. My hand slips; my body can't hold me up anymore. I can't get enough air. The room tilts.

There's a knock on the door once, then I hear a strong kick and the wood splinters before the door flies open and slams into the wall. My dad comes in, his eyes wide and panicked.

I'm numb, unable to move. My breath has abandoned me. He grabs me and sets me on the toilet, searching my face for an explanation, but I can't respond. I want to talk, to tell him to leave me here, but my lips are sewn shut, like my vocal cords have atrophied.

"What did you do?" he gasps, his face in anguish, as if he finally notices I'm covered in blood.

My breathing has calmed but my body is a statue. It's as if I'm watching my life from above it. And I can't do anything about it.

He wraps me in a towel and starts pacing. "Your mom's going to be home soon. Just . . . we'll talk to her when she gets home."

I say nothing.

He grabs more towels, I don't know how many, and holds them on my arm, pushing my good hand against the towels. "Keep the pressure on the cuts." He retrieves his cell phone and stares at it. "Jesus Christ, Ellery."

I want to let go and let the blood just flow. It wants to, I can tell.

He leaves for a moment and returns with a flowy dress I didn't know I had. He slips it over my head as if I were a doll—carefully and quietly, watching out for my bagged arm until the dress is on.

"I have a big case coming up. I can't afford to have another daughter . . . I should take you to the hospital," he says, as if he's talking himself into it.

Before Tate died I would have cared that he was so shallow, that he only cared about winning cases and fucking around on Mom, but now? His words don't hurt anymore. I don't let them.

He lifts the towels and his shoulders relax. "The pressure's working, I think. We may not have to go to the hospital." He places them back on my arm and leaves me in the bathroom, the floor scattered in glass, my blood dripping onto plastic bags.

I'm not gasping when I open my eyes from the memory. My breath has returned, but I haven't learned a damn thing. A whole year and I'm back to where I started. I may not be able to change my past, but I can change who I hurt in the present.

I have to let Colter go.

41

I have to let Colter go *because* I love him. It's the right thing to do. I got lost in his sweet words and smiles and his bravery. He never ran away. He only wanted to help me. The least I can do is let him go so he doesn't have to go through what I just did with Dean.

No one deserves this.

I get into my car and turn the heat on full blast. My cell's screen displays his name and I try to think of any way I can end it over the phone and not look like an asshole in this scenario. I suppose I'm the asshole no matter what, so I call him.

He answers on the first ring.

"Hey, beautiful. How are you?" he says in a gravelly voice laced with concern.

My heart plummets into an empty abyss.

"I'm fine."

"You don't sound fine. What happened? Are you hurt?" he says with panic in his voice.

"Dean Prescott's dead. He shot himself this afternoon."

Silence.

"Oh my God."

"Can you meet me at The Beanery?" I ask.

"Yeah, of course. I'll be there in ten minutes."

Fifteen minutes later we're sitting across from each other, the only people in the small place. It's late and most people are on to decaf by this time. Last time we were here wasn't much better. It seems to be where all horrible conversations start and end.

"I didn't know the guy, but that's really . . . shit." He grabs a sugar packet and shakes it back and forth.

"He was my friend. We knew each other when we were little. Jackson was friends with him, too, back then."

This is when I should tell him I knew. Maybe he'd understand.

You should let him go.

You're right.

He reaches across the table and holds my hand. "I'm here for you, you know that, right?"

I nod, but avoid his eyes. I can't see the pain when I tell him goodbye. I flip the edge of the plastic drink menu, then push it back. Nerves build, and I want to release them and scream until I don't have a voice anymore.

He quirks an eyebrow. "What is it? Are you okay?" He lays the sugar packet down on the table and gives me a thoughtful look.

"Nothing. I'm fine." It's my stock answer. I say it so much I should have it tattooed on my wrist.

He regards me carefully. "No, you're not. What's going on? It's something other than what happened with Dean. I can tell."

I let his hand go and flick my menu again, slapping it on the table. "You can tell? We've known each other for a month," I snap.

He winces in surprise at my words.

"I'm sorry. I mean . . . ." This is harder than I thought. I don't know if I can say the words to him. I don't want to say them.

You love him. Do it.

"I think we should take some time apart," I blurt out before I can change my mind.

His eyes widen a little but he doesn't look surprised. "No."

"Um, it's . . . not really a request."

"I'm not letting you push me away." He reaches for my hand again, but I slide it off the table before he can touch it. He tries to mask his hurt, but I know him now. I know his smiles and I've named his pain. I feel his heartbeat burning in my skin and sense his laugh before it happens. "You don't have a say in this."

"I'm part of this, too. You can't shut me out. I know what this is about. Dean didn't—"

"Didn't what? Mean to do what he did? He wasn't as sick as I am? Come on, Colter."

"I know you're scared but I can help. I can—"

"Save me?" I laugh, but it's not funny. "You want me to get better? You have to let me do this," I lie. It's so hard to do this, watching the depths in his eyes. "I'm wrong for you. We both know it," I whisper.

"I'm in love with you. Not the high school kind, the real kind. The kind even Nicholas Sparks couldn't put into words."

I close my eyes and fight the barrage of tears that want to flood out. "You knew this was going to end one way or the other. I'm doing this for you."

"No. You're doing this for *you*." He's grasping the table so hard his knuckles have turned white. "Don't do this." He looks down at his fingers and loosens his grip, tilting his head to the side with a sincere, frantic expression. "We can slow things down. I can . . . I don't know, call you less, if you want, just don't shut me out of your life." He sounds desperate and his breath is accelerating with each word.

I swallow the bile that slides up my throat. "I have to. I'm sorry." I shove my menu to the edge of the table and get up.

He grabs my arm. "You love me, too. I know you do. You can't lie to me. I can see you, the real you."

I want to say it. I do. But I have to say something that will get him to leave me alone. Forever. Something I should have said a long time ago. I paste on a serious face, fighting the tears that want to burst. "I can't be the one to redeem you from what happened to Ryan. That's not love." I squirm from his grasp and run out of the restaurant and into the moonlight. I don't look back.

The moon's rays coat my skin as I drive home. I roll down the windows and let my hair fly around my face. I swipe away the millionth tear I've shed in the last half hour. Leaving him is the hardest thing I've ever done and I don't know how I'm going to make it. I have to last four more days. It was so stupid to fall for him. It was always going to end. He had to have known that. Did he really think he'd change my mind by getting me involved in Atticus's dance, by telling me he loves me?

It's as if there's this invisible connection pulling me toward him, making me want to change everything I want to do. I have to sever it or I'll never go through with my plan. I've been careless with his heart. Mine can take it, but he's lost his brother already. I glance behind me, and debate going back and telling him I love him. That if things were different I would be everything he wanted me to be, everything I want to be. He'll see this is best. Everyone will.

My mom isn't home when I arrive, and the stairs sink slightly at my hard steps. My room is the same. Empty and bare and cold, like I've become while keeping these secrets. I grab the Duran Duran poster and roll it up for Jackson. My calculus book is in my bag. I can give that to Janie later. I have nothing to give to Colter.

You've already given him something—your heart.

42

2 Days

Dean's adorable green eyes stare out from a welcome-mat sized photo beside a fancy bronze coffin at the front of the funeral parlor. Jackson, Colter, and I are standing at the back of the room, adding to the sea of black. Colter and I haven't said a word to each other since the night at The Beanery. Jackson keeps glancing between us, like we're broken robots in need of repair.

"What's going on?" Jackson says with one eyebrow arched at me.

"Don't," I say.

Colter raises his eyes to me at my words and the expression in them is anger mixed with despair. I have to look away.

Jackson holds up his palms. "Ooookay."

Dean's parents are in the front, fielding relatives and friends of the family. Some other kids from school are here, but not many. I hadn't planned on Colter meeting my mom for the first time at a funeral, but it was bound to happen sometime. I just wish we were still together. I can't tell her we're not. She'll ask questions, and I just can't have any more questions in my mind right now. I spot her coming through the door as she's taking off her fuzzy hat. I watch her so I can memorize her. I watch her when she doesn't know I am. No matter what's happened in her life, sincerity flows from her movements. In the way she adjusts her shoes, tucks in her shirt, moves a brown curl out of her face. It runs in her blood. She finishes taking off her coat and carefully hangs it on the small coat rack by the door. She takes a deep breath and rubs her hands on her pants—a nervous habit I recognize in myself. She looks up and I wave her over.

My heart starts this weird stammer, like it just woke up from a yearlong hibernation. Colter's talking to Jackson and has no idea my mom's coming. I should warn him.

Mom grabs me in a huge hug and holds me. I want to let go. It feels too real. I don't want to be in this moment, hugging her at Dean's funeral.

She lets me go and has that sincere smile on her face. "I'm so sorry. He was so young. I just . . . it doesn't make any sense."

Colter and Jackson turn around and see Mom. Jackson bear-hugs her and they exchange *how are yous* and *I'm so sorrys*. Jackson tells her why Janie isn't here—a family trip to her sick grandpa's.

Colter and I stand awkwardly near each other, still not saying a word. He bites his lip and shoves his hands in his pockets.

"Mom, this is Colter," I say as Mom turns his way and holds out her arms for a hug.

Colter graciously hugs her back and surprisingly, it doesn't look awkward at all. She lets him go after a few seconds, but Colter is smiling. "It's nice to meet you, Mrs. Stevens."

"Please call me Dahlia."

"I'm sorry we have to meet like this," he says, running a hand through his hair.

"Me too." She sighs and I can tell she's trying to think of something else to say. "You'll have to come for dinner soon. I make a mean pasta primavera."

"Um, sure," he says awkwardly, rocking back on his heels.

"You haven't made that in months, years even—" I start to say.

"Shhh, he doesn't know that."

We smile politely, then like a vacuum, all the smiles and laughs are sucked out of the room as everyone starts taking their seats.

I look around for Jackson and find him sitting and staring at Dean's casket with glossed-over eyes, his hands neatly in his lap. I take a seat beside him, my mom sits on my other side. Colter sits next to Jackson.

The pastor of Dean's church stands up at a podium and fidgets with his Bible. "It's hard to make sense of what happens in this earthly world to make someone want to leave it. Dean was a child of God, and although his exit was premature, he is with his heavenly father now." The pastor steps down after saying a few more religious things about heaven and God's path.

To be honest, I'm surprised that he said Dean's with his heavenly father. I'd been under the impression that most religions thought suicides went to hell. I guess that's just too awkward a thing to say at someone's funeral.

Dean's mom steps up to the podium, tissues in hand, dabbing her red nose. She balls up the tissue and sets her fist on the podium, leaning toward the microphone. "My little boy loved adventures. He used to climb every tree and hike every path. One time, he . . ." she says, pausing to cry a little with the rest of us. "He . . . was, I think, seven when we visited Mount Saint Helens. He wanted to climb up every trail. Garret and I—" She pauses and wipes her nose with the balled-up tissue. "We weren't that old and we didn't exercise much. But Dean, he wanted to go to the top. We didn't quite make it to the top, but we came close. Dean was okay with that, but he told me just this year that he wished he had gone to the top so he could have seen . . . ." She cries harder now and gives up on the tissue. "He wanted to see what life would be like from the top of a mountain. He wondered if everything got small or if it stayed the same, but we just got bigger." She steps away from the mic for a moment and gathers herself before stepping back up to the mic. "You can see the top of any mountain now, my son. Any mountain you want."

What is it about funerals that make people want to be poetic? Just say what you really feel. He left the world on his own. Get mad. Get angry at him for doing it. You want someone to pay, but there's no one left to blame. None of it matters if he's not here. They're all empty words and sentences. Be mad at God for making us have a choice. Be angry at nature for giving us hearts to break. But be honest.

When Dean's mom steps away from the podium, she accidentally hits the mic and it makes an awful screech. We all cringe and some people instinctively cover their ears. For once I don't. Suddenly it makes sense. That awful sound at the end of her haunting words. Life is beautiful until the mic screeches. Until the sun comes up again. Until you kill and can't take it back.

Without will, I want to see Colter, see how he's reacting. My gaze finds his and I expect a sad expression but it's the opposite. He's gritting his teeth with his jaw locked tight, his hands in fists at his sides. Jackson's eyes are wide and glassy, like he's been staring at the sun too long. Mom's cheeks are streaked with black mascara.

This is what the people I love will look like when I die. What their tortured, withered faces will form into.

43

1 Day

I can't stop crying. I cried so hard last night I almost got sick. This is so fucking hard. I've never felt something like this before. I wish it could trump all the other feelings I wake up with every day. I want so badly not to have to hurt anyone else. Memories of Dean's funeral cycle through my brain like a flip book. I keep trying to stop them, but I'm forced to watch everyone's faces change expressions in succession. I think of Dean's mom and her balled-up tissue, and the story she told about the mountain, and how I didn't even know Dean that well, and how I'm mad at him for not telling me that story. Maybe I could have asked him to go to the top of that mountain.

He won't ever get to the top and it's your fault.

Closing my locker, I sense someone behind me. The voices in the hallway lower to a hum. I don't want to see him. I'm afraid to turn. Before I can, Jackson's beside me, leaning on the locker next to mine.

"How's it going?" I gaze up at him and he grimaces. "Yikes, that bad, huh?"

I know what I look like. My hair *is* brushed, but just barely. My clothes are wrinkled, and my face looks like I won first prize at a death-warmed-over contest.

"Well, Colter looks like shit, too, if you're wondering."

I slam my locker door. "I wasn't."

Jackson catches my eye. "He's miserable. Anyone can see it. Why are you doing this to him?"

"Don't worry about it."

He gives me the Jackson look. The one that says he doesn't believe me, that I'm lying, trying to push him away. "You're an idiot."

"I know this." I motion toward the door across the hall. English. I should just skip. It doesn't matter anyway. It's not like I'm going to graduate. But school, classes make the day go by. If not, I'll just sleep for hours and hours and I'll never wake up, not even to eat. When I do that, Mom gets worried and she gets all hover-mom. I can't have that. I have to play the game. I'm so close now. As long as Colter doesn't say anything. He wouldn't break his promise to me, would he? I haven't broken his yet.

Jackson cocks his head toward the door to English as Colter crosses through it. My heart drops into my feet. I lean against my locker and catch my breath.

"At least think about changing your mind," Jackson says. "And brush your hair, for God's sake. You're starting to look like the girl from *The Ring*." He gives me a somber smile, then he's gone.

I shuffle into English, arranging my hair in front of my face like a curtain. Jackson's right. I probably do look like the girl from *The Ring*. I hurry to my seat, avoiding Colter. I can't see him, see his eyes, his lips. If I do, it will be over. I open my English book and stare at the pages; the words blur, and my heart starts pounding and echoing in my ears. I cover them and hunker into my desk. I must look crazy.

Class goes by fast and I succeed in not looking at Colter. I get up and hurry out the door, except someone's there at the same time and we do this awkward dance of who's going to go first. Then I realize it's Colter, and our gazes lock together through the curtain of my stringy hair and the same sequence of emotions repeat, as if ticking them off like days in a calendar—love, safety, heartbreak, guilt, shame, love, regret, love. The huge bags under his eyes have purpled on his colorless face and his whole expression is just . . . wrecked. And I know, without a doubt, this is how he'll look when I'm gone.

Why did I have to have this stupid plan? Why couldn't the gun have just gone off like it was supposed to? Why did he have to get so close to me? I try to think of something to say to make it better for him, but nothing comes. Our eyes meet for a brief second and I'm out the door, running to the exit. I can't do this. I only have a day until Halloween. I make it to my car and lean against the window. I slam my fist on the glass and I let out a scream that sounds more like a growl.

"Sounds like you're taking this as well as me."

I jump at Colter's voice and close my eyes. Why can't he just leave me alone? I flatten my palms on the window. "Go away."

"No."

I cry out—the growl and scream. "Please."

"It's been three of the worst days of my fucking life."

I turn around, whimpering softly, my chest convulsing from the crying fit. He looks so weak, so different from that confident, optimistic boy I met. I did this to him. "Me too."

He moves closer and I push my back flush against my car window. "Why are you doing this to us?"

He has every right to ask, but he already knows the answer. "You know why."

His eyes go wide; then they relax. He takes a long breath in. "You haven't changed your mind. I failed you." He shrugs, defeated.

I'm sure he can see the confusion and pain on my face. He's known and hasn't said anything. "You didn't fail me. I just don't understand why you keep trying."

He looks up at the sky as a small tear slips down his cheek, leaving a shiny path. He lets his gaze fall and centers it on me. "Because I love you, Ellery. And when you love someone you want to take away their pain." He wipes the tear away and straightens his posture like he's trying to prove he's not going to be affected by it. "I'm not sure how long you'll keep me around. But I want to be with you more than I've ever wanted anything. I've seen how stubborn you are. I'm not stupid. I can see it in your eyes. I've seen it before."

"In Ryan's."

He nods. "I knew he was depressed. I tried to help him. I even called the hospital, but I hung up before I could tell anyone. I couldn't do it. I couldn't betray him." He looks at something in the distance. The hair sticking out of his cap blows onto his forehead and he has to shove it away. "I kept pushing him after that. Over and over, and he kept telling me it didn't matter." His gaze travels back to me. "I'm not going to push you. If you want to die, I can't stop you. I know that," he says quietly.

I want to tell him I'm fine and have it be the truth. I'd do anything to get that expression off his face and have his other one return, the one before he met me. "Are you going to tell?"

He lets out an exasperated groan. "I have to. I know I should." He lifts up his hat and runs his hand through his hair. "Please don't make me do this." His eyes are desperate, confused, scared. "I told you I'd give you till Halloween, but I can't ignore . . . ." He starts to pace back and forth, pounding his fist into his leg.

I need to stop this. I grab him and pull him closer. "Colter."

He grabs my shoulders like he did at the cemetery. "Tell me you won't do this. Tell me you'll change your mind and be with me."

"I . . . ."

His fingers are cutting into my shoulder, but I don't think he realizes it. "Please," he pleads, his eyes alight with desperate hope and his breath visibly shallow with worry.

Tears start sliding down my cheeks. Can I lie to him again? Would it even work? He's so desperate I think he'll believe anything, and that makes me a horrible human for what I'm about to do, but I have to do this. I travel down the rabbit hole and box up my feelings for Colter enough to lie to him once more. "Okay," I assure him. "Okay."

He releases his death grip on my shoulders and strokes softly where his hands were like he's apologizing. His eyes light up in relief as more tears fall from them. He gives me a sly smile that melts me into the car. He inches closer and wraps a tendril of my hair around his finger, letting the strand slip through his hand.

I've never had anyone love me before. Not a boy. Not someone who kisses me. It feels like a foreign language. I can't speak love. I wouldn't know how to form the words.

I slide my arms around his waist and pull him to me. He cradles my cheeks and pulls my mouth to his. I can taste his salty tears on my mouth; they're mixed with mine and our noses are snotty and I don't care. His stiff body softens and melts into mine and it feels so fucking right. I kiss him like the answer to life is on his lips. He kisses back like it's the last one we'll ever have. I cry more and the tears fall into our joined mouths. I don't stop. I start to whimper, but the kiss continues. I can feel him shaking, and I'm shivering in the cold air. I run my hands through the back of his hair, letting his cap fall to the ground. He adjusts his mouth to mine as if our lips were born attached each other. If I let go, this will all be over, and I don't want this to ever end.

He halts the kiss and moves his forehead to mine. "I'm not going to leave you, okay? So stop pushing me away."

I nod and wipe tears from my mouth. I'm not sure if they're his or mine.

44

Halloween

It's Halloween and I've put on my *Happy Ellery* mask so I can make it through the dance. I'm doing this for Colter, for Atticus and his friends I've promised to be here for. Everything around me is blurred, like I'm watching my life through a foggy window. I bar up all the bad thoughts and concentrate on the dance.

One moment at a time.

Colter and I pass a punk rocker dressed similarly to me, a girl from *Grease*, four Michael Jacksons and even some girls dressed as Molly Ringwald in *Pretty in Pink*.

"*Grease* wasn't the eighties."

"You're the only one who knows that," Colter says, wrapping his arm around me.

My leather pants are making my legs chap already, and I'm seriously regretting the pink wig. My head itches so bad I'm sure it's cock-eyed by now. Colter's hair is spiked, and he has holes in his jeans and a red leather jacket like Michael Jackson. I really want to scream that the eighties were more than just Michael Jackson. Where's Duran Duran? Madonna?

Oh, spoke too soon. A girl with blonde curls and cone-boobs passes me on the right.

"I've never seen so much neon before," Colter says, scanning the parking lot.

"I know. And neon was really more of an early nineties thing, but whatever. There's a lot of people here," I say. "Where's Atticus?"

241

He shrugs. "He left before me. Guess he's too good for his big brother." He looks a little disappointed.

"Maybe he'll get lucky tonight," I tease.

Colter's eyes go wide and he smacks me on the ass. "Take that back."

I laugh. "Did you have *the talk*?"

He grabs me and pulls me up for a quick kiss. "There's no way my brother's getting laid before me tonight." He grabs my leather ass and pulls me up to his lips again, hiking me up his body. We kiss for a few seconds before realizing we're at a kid's dance.

I slither down his body onto my feet. "If you're a good boy, maybe I'll let you see what I have under the leather." I can't believe that just came out of my mouth. It's as if I am a different person around him.

He groans, then pulls something out of his pocket. Pink plastic earrings. Totally eighties-worthy. "My mom wanted you to have these," he says with an excited expression on his face.

"Um, what?"

"She said it's a peace offering." He grins.

"What did you tell her?"

"I just made her understand that if she didn't accept you, I was leaving. She came around pretty fast after that." He hands me the earrings.

"They're not going to emit poison into my ears or anything, right?" I say, shoving them into my ear piercings.

"I doubt she used the strong poison; that's reserved for her really bad clients. You're safe." He shows his toothy, goofy grin.

I laugh. "Thanks? I think."

He wraps his arms around me and kisses me on the head. "Let me worry about her."

We enter the dance and the music is blaring from twenty speakers. The ballroom looks completely different. Skeletons, various spider webs, and ghosts hang from the ceiling, and orange and black accents drape the walls. The cobwebbed photo booth has a line at least twenty-five people long. Kids are laughing and dancing. It's a scene right out of a corny scary teen movie. I'm just waiting for a big pail of pig's blood to land on my head.

Colter spots Phillip on the other side of the dance floor and waves him over. I slink behind Colter, afraid to look Phillip in the eye. I've been avoiding him since the night we kissed. Phillip walks over and grabs Kirstyn on the way, and I huddle even farther behind Colter, wanting to be anywhere but here. Colter looks back at me like I've lost my mind and pulls me up next to him. I start to pace in place as Phillip and Kirstyn join us. Phillip's dressed as Prince, complete with the pointed boots and shiny purple jumpsuit. If I weren't so nervous, I'd be laughing my ass off at how he looks. Kirstyn's dressed as Madonna. I'm not sure why I was worried there'd be no Madonnas. Everywhere I turn there's blonde hair and cone-boobs. Kirstyn is sans cone-boobs, but she has tassels hanging from a makeshift bathing suit lined in gold. I spot Jackson and Janie on the other side of the room. They wave and gesture for me to come over to them. From far away they look like two of the Village People.

Phillip and Colter knock fists. "This is fuckin' lame, dude," Phillip says. "I didn't know I'd have to come to this shit."

"You're dressed as Prince." Colter laughs so loud I could hear it over the music. "You know you wanted to come just to wear that outfit."

Phillip purses his lips and glares at Kirstyn.

"It's all they had left," she says, grabbing his arm and wrapping hers around it.

I cringe.

"Nice outfit, Ellery," she says.

"Thanks," I squeak out, even though I'm sure she doesn't mean it.

Phillip looks at me once then turns his focus on Colter. "So, you guys a thing?" he asks.

My heart burrows into my stomach. I adjust my pink wig.

"You could say that," Colter says, grabbing my hand.

My hand starts on fire at his touch and I want to be anywhere but here. "I'm going to meet up with Jackson and Janie," I say, inching away from Colter. He looks down at me with a sympathetic expression. He knows I need to leave, so he slowly lets go of my hand and I sneak away, steadying my breath.

Jackson's wearing chaps and a cowboy hat, and Janie is dressed as a sailor. Jackson wraps his arm around my shoulder. "Is that Phillip dressed as Prince?" he says through a laugh.

"Really? You're dressed as a Village Person, and you're making fun of him?"

"A Village *Person*?" He laughs and lets me go to sidle up next to Janie. "I'm a cowboy," he says emphatically.

"And I'm a naval officer," Janie says with a straight face, then cracks up quickly after. "Nice leather pants. Good luck getting those off."

I scratch under the leather at my waist. They've been stuck to my skin like suction cups. "Let me remind you, these were your idea."

She laughs and sips some punch. "The decorations turned out nice."

"Better than I thought they would." I search the room for Atticus and find him in the corner with Grace. He's dressed as some punk guy with spiky hair and a chain wallet. Grace is Cyndi Lauper, complete with electric orange hair glowing in the lights. They're huddled together, whispering and laughing.

"Uh oh, that doesn't look good," Jackson says, nudging his head to where Colter and Phillip are.

I turn to look and Colter and Phillip are glaring at each other.

Oh, God. I shouldn't have left them all together. I say goodbye to Jackson and Janie and make my way toward Colter.

"She's fucking nuts, Colt," I hear Phillip say, his back turned to me.

Colter wipes his hands on his jeans with a confused, angry expression. "She's not crazy."

Mortified, I hide behind a pillar nearby. I can't get in the middle of this.

"Did she tell you Jackson had to rescue her from the cemetery?" Kirstyn says. "I saw it. He had to carry her. She was freaking out."

"Her sister died. She's having a hard time, that's all."

"She said she wanted to kiss me. We kissed and she tossed me off her like I tried to fucking rape her," Phillip says. "I'm telling you. Drop that bitch now before she fucks up your life."

Colter's hands form into fists. His face reddens and his eyes narrow.

You should show yourself. You can stop this.

"I mean . . ." Phillip says, obviously ignoring Colter's closed fists, ". . . she might be a good lay. But—"

Colter cuts Phillip off with a punch to his face. Phillip flies back toward the pillar I'm behind. I jerk away and stand there, stunned and unable to move.

Phillip adjusts quickly, flies back to Colter and punches him in the stomach. Colter bends in half, then they're on the ground.

Kirstyn sees me in the corner and starts yelling. "Happy? You did this!" she screams.

I hurry toward them and try unsuccessfully to grab Colter's arm and pull him off Phillip. "Colter, stop it. He's right. Stop!" I yell.

Colter looks up as Phillip connects one last time with his face, and they both stand up.

"We're at a kids' dance, for Christ's sake," I say.

I hold Colter away from Phillip. Both have bloody faces and are wiping them.

One of the older chaperones is walking our way with a stern look on her bony face.

Colter's still fuming, trying to get me to move. I push my hands on his chest, pull down his chin and look him in the eyes. "He's right. I'm totally fucked up. So stop defending me."

I turn to Phillip; he's wiping his bloody nose, glaring at Colter. "You may be an asshole, but you're right about me. Do you want a fucking medal?"

Phillip gives me one last glare, then stomps off with Kirstyn at his side. The chaperone stops them. I can't hear what she's saying, but she's staring at his face. She shakes her head and glances over at us.

Colter bends over, holding his stomach, so I lean down to his line of sight. "We need to get out of here."

He wipes his bloody nose, but doesn't say anything.

I grab his hand and pull him to his car. He's sluggish and resists me the whole way. I take his keys from his pocket and get in the front seat after opening the passenger door for him.

"We have to sing. We have to go back," he says.

"Are you kidding me? Look at you. Besides, the frigid bitch in there doesn't look happy."

"You have the duet with Janie."

"It just became a solo, now shut up."

He's silent the rest of the drive to my house. My mom's at work and the house is eerily dark. He shoves the car door open and storms out. He stops in front of the door as if realizing for the first time we're at my house.

He turns and looks at me. "Why are we here?"

"You're hurt. I need to clean you up."

He glares at me. "Why'd you say that?"

I search my brain but can't find anything. "Say what?"

"That you're fucked up. That Phillip was right. Why'd you say that?"

"Because I am."

45

Colter grits his teeth but says nothing. I drag him indoors and we make our way to the bathroom. I point to the toilet. He reluctantly sits and his expression is one I've never seen. He's angry. Really angry. At me. I grab some ointment from the cabinet and grab a washcloth from the drawer next to the door. I raise his chin and look at his face. It's bruised and bloody, and he has a huge cut on his cheek from something.

"Does Phillip ever trim his nails? Shit, that's deep."

Colter just glares at me, his eyes full of sadness and worry and more anger. I try not to look at him. I dampen the washcloth and start wiping at the cut to clean it off.

He hisses in pain.

"Sorry. I'm almost done." I lean over and apply some of the ointment, spreading it against the cut, and finish wiping away the rest of the blood. His nose and eye are bruised and the cut is deep, but he's okay. "My hero," I say, leaning over to kiss him on the cheek. "I've never had anyone do anything like that for me," I say, kissing him on the nose. "Thank you." I kiss him on the lips, but he doesn't return the kiss.

I open my eyes and he's glaring at me again. "He called you a bitch and you don't even care. I'm the only one who cares. And I care too much."

He jerks up out of the seat and starts pacing like he did yesterday at school. "I still see it in your eyes."

I look away from him.

He turns abruptly toward me. "You said you were going to try." He laughs angrily. "I'm such an idiot. I believed you."

I don't know what to say to that, so I say nothing. I can't lie to him anymore.

He closes his eyes so tight even tears can't escape. Anguish is painted all over his body, in his posture, his face. "I can't lose you like I lost him. I can't." He opens his eyes and runs a hand through his hair, making the gelled pieces stick up. "I have to believe you came to me for a reason. That somehow, because of what happened to Ryan, you were sent to me. And I'm failing, and I don't know what to do. What can I do?"

I grab his face, center my focus on him, and say the one thing I know that will make him feel better, that will end his rant. "I love you." As I say the words, I believe them. I feel them. It's me saying them, not *Happy Ellery*.

He gets a surprised look on his face, and then I'm buried again in the depths of him. I kiss him first, then he kisses me back, hard, desperate. He moves me out of the bathroom and into my room. He backs me up against the bed, and I'm lost; I'm not thinking of anything but him and his body touching mine. He's tentative with me. But I coax him onto the bed. He lies on top of me and his body feels warm and safe, and for the first time in a long time, I'm not scared. I know what I want.

It's him.

He moves from my lips to my neck, trailing kisses down my skin, leaving me shuddering in the wake they create. He stops and looks at me.

"Are you sure you want to do this?"

I don't hesitate. "Yes."

He continues kissing me while trying to shrug out of the red leather Michael Jackson jacket. He's struggling, and I'm trying not to laugh because I know it'll ruin the moment, but I do. He finally gets one arm loose and shakes his other arm, trying to get the jacket to slide down. He looks at me and rolls his eyes. I grab the sleeve and pull it off. I yank off the pink wig and curse myself for wearing leather pants—they're like a chastity belt. He tries to pull them off seductively, but fails when the leather won't budge. I laugh again and find a way out of my pants without using oil. He's kissing me between pulling off his shirt and his sparkly silver socks. Each piece of Michael Jackson's wardrobe flies from my bed onto the floor.

"Show me your tattoo," I say, remembering him mentioning it.

He turns over and there are words printed on his side. "*It is what it is?*" I say, running my finger over the dark blue ink.

"Yep."

"That's . . . interesting."

He smiles, curling me into him, our skin molding together like hot candle wax. In moments we're fully naked, staring at each other. I cower a little and try to cover myself up, ashamed—not of my body, but of letting someone see it, letting someone into this part of me, the secluded part I keep hidden. His mouth turns up in a half-grin as he pulls a condom out of his wallet. He turns quickly, then lowers himself onto me and continues kissing me until I can't breathe. It hurts at first. My body's small and I'm afraid to let him in. But as his hands search everywhere his kisses have, I start to feel that familiar warmth. Our bodies fuse perfectly together, like the fucked-up puzzle finally fits, and its corners are messy and wonderful.

Afterward, we lie in each other's arms. His sweaty body is curled up next to mine as if he needs me to live. He's breathing softly into my neck, causing the tiny hairs to twitch.

It's too much.

46

The walls start closing in on me again and I wonder for the millionth time why I can't just be happy without a trade involved. I try to move from his grasp, but he pulls me back in, mumbling something sweet I can't hear because my heartbeats are echoing, so loud in my ears.

The heat starts, the searing blaze in my stomach. It crawls, grasping my blood as it travels up my throat. I don't want to run. I don't. I want to stay in his arms and be normal. I struggle away from his grip, and he sits up and curls the sheet over himself. He looks so vulnerable, like I could tip him over with a feather. It's like he knew I'd do this, but he hoped I wouldn't. It breaks me. He's too close. He's gotten too close.

I toss on jeans and a T-shirt. "I have to . . . I need to go somewhere. I'm sorry," I say, darting out the door.

"Ellery, wait!" he yells. I can hear his feet stomp on the carpet, like he's jumped from the bed.

I get in my car and take off, cursing myself for leaving him behind, for running away again. I drive to the one place I know I need to be right now.

The cool air blows hard as the sky opens up for me. The moon's rays guide me toward the edge of the bridge's railing. I heave one leg over the cement, followed by the other. A car passes and I duck down. My eyes find the river below. In the dark it's hard to see the movement of the water, but the rushing makes a constant *shhh* sound as it flows violently under the bridge.

Another car passes by and I raise my head again, grasping onto the ledge of the railing. All I have to do is let go. There's no way I'd survive. The water is cold and unpredictable. The icy air blows my hair into my face, coats my throat, and numbs everything inside me. My arms break out in goosebumps. I close my eyes. There's no miracle to save me this time.

The engine of a car rumbles behind me. I duck again, but the tires scrape on the gravel. Someone's here. I turn and see Colter's Escalade.

"Fuck me," I say into the night.

I hear a door slam and I look at his face. It's full of pain and anger and something else. He looks tired. Tired of fighting for me. Tired of worrying if I'm going to run every time he says something or does something.

I'm tired, too.

He's in a grubby white T-shirt, but he left the Michael Jackson coat behind. "What are you doing? Do you even know anymore?"

"No." I hear my voice. It's coming out weak and soft. "I thought I could do it. Try to be the real Ellery, not the fake one. I was the real one with you. She was happy. You made her that way." I'm shivering from the cold and the encounter and him. The clouds have moved in front of the moon, making my shadow disappear—but only for a moment. I know it will come back as soon as the moon does.

"Then what's the problem?" he asks with desperation in his voice. "What do I have to do? Tell me. I'll do it."

I clench my fists and try not to yell at him. It's not his fault he doesn't get how it feels. "See, that's what people don't get. There's nothing you can do. Nothing anyone can."

He gives me that pitiful look. I don't want that look. "Don't do it. Please."

"I have to. There's no other way to get rid of everything inside me."

He inches closer to me. "Your life could be better. I'd make sure it was better."

That guilt feeling churns inside me, making a mess of my emotions. "You can't fix me. I'm broken," I say, softly.

He pounds his fist on the side of the bridge, making a noise that's not a yell or a groan, but a combination of both. "Talk to me. I'll help you. It doesn't have to be like this."

"It does."

He turns and grabs my shoulders. "I can help you, you just have to let me. I'll do all the work." He lowers his head. "God, I feel so fucking helpless."

"I never asked you to help me." I slump in his grip.

He lets me go and backs up, shuffling his feet on the cold asphalt. "I love you, so stay. Stay for me. Fuck everything else right now," he says between uneven breaths.

"I wish I could. I'm sorry." I have to turn away from him and look at the river. "But loving me isn't going to make me better."

He grabs my arm and twists me back around. "Why?"

"Because," I say, trying to form the words I'm thinking. "Because, I wasn't waiting around for some guy to love me."

He glares at me, clenching and unclenching his fists like he wants to hit me. I know he won't. "So, I'm just *some guy* to you. You're so fucking selfish. You say you love me but you're still going to leave me—your life, before you've even done anything with it."

"I lived this life and it spit me out!"

He eyes me suspiciously. "What aren't you telling me?"

"It's my fucking fault she's dead."

He sighs. "We've been over this."

"You don't know the whole story. No one does."

He folds his arms across his chest with an impatient tilt of his head.

"My dad was cheating on my mom. I knew he was for a while. On Halloween, it all kind of blew up and we fought. I think Tate heard us and got scared. God, it's all my fault. I should have just told my mom when I found out, but I waited."

I take a deep breath and fight not to break down. The memory of that night seeps into my brain like liquid.

❀

"You're a liar!" I yell, running up the stairs.

"Don't walk away from me," Dad says in a dark tone.

"Go see your girlfriend and leave me alone," I say under my breath. Or at least I thought it was.

"What did you say?" he says, storming up the stairs.

I run into my room and slam the door, shaking from fear and adrenaline. He bangs on the wood, causing me to wince at each thump. I back away from the door, my breath sputtering out of my lungs.

"This is unacceptable, Ellery."

"You promised me you'd stop seeing her," I say to my closed door.

"I did. Where did you hear otherwise?"

"I heard you. I know you went to meet her."

"That's ridiculous," he snaps. "Where did you hear such a fabrication?"

I hate when he uses his ten-dollar words to make me feel stupid or make himself seem more important. "I'm going to tell her."

"No, you won't," he says, in an eerie, threatening tone.

"You can't stop me."

"Just keep your mouth shut," he rumbles. I hear him walk away and my anger grows from a small flame into a huge fire.

"Fine, *Daddy*," I whisper.

I scan the walls of my room. All the posters and colors and happiness stare condescendingly at me. I tear down the first poster. The crunching of the paper fills the room. It feels good. I freed it, gave it a reason to exist. I rip another down and go on a spree, obliterating everything off the walls. The flimsy paper buckles under my fingers and it makes me feel powerful, like I can conquer the world. It only lasts a moment. I fall onto my bed and the tears come again, violently. I ache for something and I can't figure out what. It's something out of my grasp.

I can't do this anymore. I scratch at my eyes wanting to hack out the tears. I don't want them anymore. I gouge my nails down my face until it's raw and my nails are stained with blood. It doesn't make me feel better. Pain is only a temporary relief.

I grab my keys and run out the door, my face bloody, my fingers stained red. My dad is gone.

You have to tell her.

Rain pounds hard on my face, causing my eyesight to blur. I let the droplets coat my skin. There's no going back. He'll hate me. She'll hate me. Tate. Oh, God. What will she think?

No. I have no choice.

With wet hair and soaked jeans, I climb into my Escape and take off, my tires sliding down the driveway. I push hard on the gas.

You're doing the right thing.

The icy rain pelts on the windshield, pounding like large wooden sticks banging on metal. My tears and blood have dried and the residual burn has left my skin stiff. The gentle swipe of the windshield wipers is the only sound. They swish back and forth. Back and forth. I glance in the rearview mirror and wince at my appearance.

You really are crazy.

Bile gathers in my throat. I swallow it down and cross over the bridge.

It all happens in a slow bubble—a blip in time.

Slipping on the puddle in the road. My car smashing into the railing, careening off the Dover Bridge toward the rushing water.

The descent lasts for hours and seconds at the same time.

"Sissy?" A small voice travels from the back seat.

The despair is instant. Everything in what was left of my life just changed. My thoughts, my actions. My heart separates into tiny pieces.

"What's wrong?" Tate says, emphasizing the G at the end of *wrong*, like she always does.

I yank my foot off the gas and look back into her pure brown eyes, so innocent and confused. Time is frozen.

How could she be here?

"Buckle up! Hold on!" I scream, holding my arm behind me in a weak attempt to shield her from the impact. She tumbles forward, legs and arms flailing, her face twisting in pain and confusion.

I try to grab her, but my hands find empty air.

That was the last image I saw. I don't even remember hitting the water or how the hell I survived. The doctors told me it was a combination of how the car was made and sheer dumb luck. It should have been me at the bottom of the river.

"I was on my way to the hospital to tell my mom about my dad when my car slipped and smashed through the bridge. I don't know how fast I was going. But it was fast enough that I couldn't control anything. The car started falling toward the water when I heard her voice, and I knew she'd snuck back there to hide from us, from our fighting. She had nowhere else to go to get away."

I sit down on the railing and face the river. He walks up behind me and pulls me into his chest, placing his chin on my head.

Safe.

"I watched her die. I saw her little face go through the confusion and then the reality that this was it for her." I wipe acidic tears from my eyes. "I couldn't comfort her. I was trying to figure out how to save her. I thought I was going to die, too, but I didn't care. I needed to save her. Have you ever watched someone the moment they realize they're going to die? I don't mean when they saw it coming. I mean when they have no idea and then—boom. They have seconds. *Seconds* to come to grips with it."

"Jesus," he says softly into my hair.

"I tried to put . . . I put my arm out, but it was hopeless."

"I'm sure you did everything you could." His warm breath rustles my hair.

"I should be down there. I deserve to be down there in that water, so I can feel what she felt. So I can somehow make it right."

"It won't make the world suddenly balanced. Do you really think your sister would want you at the bottom of the river?" he says, glancing down at the water below us.

"She looked up to me and I let her down in the worst way you could. I did *nothing* to save her."

"She loved you. You were her big sister. She'd want you to let this go."

I turn around and push his arms off me. "You don't know that. You didn't even know her."

"My brother wouldn't want me to kill myself for not helping him. I could have saved him. If I would've told someone, he'd still be alive. You don't think I suffer every day with that?"

"Do you think that would have really stopped him? If you told?"

"I'm never gonna know." He locks his jaw like he does when he's seriously pissed. "You're taking the easy way out. Just like he did."

"You think this is easy?" I flip my legs back over the side of the bridge and move closer to the edge. I hear his intake of breath.

"No, I can't even imagine what you've been through."

"My dad blames me for her death. He won't even speak to me."

He places his hands gently on my shoulders. "He's an asshole, but he's not worth dying for."

"You make it sound so simple."

"It's not, but it can be."

I take a deep breath and stare down at the water below.

Soon.

47

The air on the bridge has thickened with the truth. It's charged with it. Everything I've ever kept secret is pouring out of me like it's made of liquid. I twist on the ledge toward him so he can hear my next words. "I knew about Dean and I didn't do anything," I whisper, hanging my head. Might as well confess all my sins.

His eyes widen in surprise. "You knew what he wanted to do?"

I nod. "We talked about it—killing ourselves. He didn't want me to, and I didn't want him to." I let out a hopeless laugh. "It's ironic. That I wanted him to live, but I did nothing to help him. I told no one, and he told no one about me. It was like this secret deal."

Colter lets go of my shoulders and backs away slowly.

"I drove by his work and house as much as I could. I watched him from afar, but you know what the really fucked up thing is? By the end, I wasn't sure I was watching him because I was afraid he'd kill himself, or that I was fascinated by the fact that someone else wanted to do it too." I take another deep breath in. "Do you see what you've fallen in love with?"

Before he can stop me, I swing my legs over the bridge's edge and look down at the rushing water.

"*Ellery.*" There's panic and fear in his tone, but I fight to ignore it.

Killing myself is the logical move. I've hurt so many people. It's my fault that no one will ever find out that Dean had a sense of humor, or that he knew a lame joke about ketchup. Or that underneath all that gruffness there was a sweet soul. It's my fault that I'll never hear Tate laugh again, that she'll never meet Colter. She won't ever get married, or kiss a boy, or graduate, or be Auntie

Tate to my kids. She'll disappear from my memory, slowly at first, like test questions I studied so hard for and knew all the answers, just to forget them the next week. Her hair will fade to gray, then her brown eyes will turn colorless, her smile will blur. She'll be gone for good.

"No, Colter. This is me. I'm a horrible person." The cold air circles around us, and the moon is hiding as if it's ashamed of what I've done, too. I rake a hand through my hair to put it back in place. I turn my head and look behind me at him, wavering. "Don't you get it? I deserve this."

In one swift movement, Colter swings one leg over the railing and straddles the cement. "Okay, so you want to jump. Then let's jump."

My heart stalls and my breath along with it. "Colter, don't."

He moves his other leg over and dangles both legs off the edge. "What? I don't deserve to die? My brother's death is on *my* hands. Wouldn't this make the world right again?" He leans forward and I throw my arm out in front of him.

"Stop it. I know what you're doing."

He shakes his head. "How would you feel if I jumped? Right now."

"I . . . you're not going to jump." My breath is back and it's fast and unpredictable. My whole body fills with a different feeling—fear of losing him, and it's like I'm watching Tate smash into the windshield in front of me again. A knife is slowly being dragged across the entire surface of my skin. Nothing matters but getting him off this bridge.

"How do you know I won't?"

"Stop it," I snap.

"Why, Ellery?" he says in his security officer voice. "Why do I need to stop?" He looks over at me expectantly, holding the railing with both hands lightly, leaning forward.

"Because . . ." I love you and need you and can't imagine the world without you in it. Because your little brother wouldn't have you to look up to, and your nieces wouldn't have you around to teach them how to steal candy. Because being left behind without you would be devastating.

"Because why." He leans forward more and I panic and scramble off the railing.

"Stop it!" I yell, covering my ears and closing my eyes. I crouch down onto the ground and start naming my states. "Alabama, Alaska."

Colter's arms wrap around me and every cell in my body longs for him. He's broken me in every way, but I love him. "Ellery, I'm sorry. Please. Oh, God."

I look up into his eyes and fight to control my breathing. "I can't lose you," I say.

"Never," he says, wrapping me in his arms. I fold myself into them as he rocks me gently in the wind.

❀

He pulls up to my house a half hour later and turns off his car. "I think I should stay with you tonight. I can sleep on the floor."

My body aches to be by his. I let him take me from the bridge, and my mind keeps coming up with reasons to run, but I can't leave him.

"My mom won't be home until seven tomorrow. You can sleep with me."

He leans over and kisses me lightly on the lips. "I talk in my sleep."

"I kick in mine."

We get out of the car together and go inside. The air is still charged from our fight, from all the words we said. We left everything on that bridge, and all I want to do is sleep.

48

1 Day After

Morning comes quick. I wake up without Colter's arms around me and I feel naked and vulnerable, something I haven't felt in a long time. It's the day after Halloween, and my plans once again have been foiled. The sun's rays paint my walls a dull yellow, illuminating the starkness that has become my room. An uneasy feeling makes its way through my body.

I have no plan.

I need a plan.

The covers feel like sandpaper. The walls creep forward as if they're on wheels. The walls start to morph into shapes and devilish smiles. I scramble out of my room to the stairs, breathing heavy.

Where's Colter? What time is it?

I didn't look when I woke up. I always check the time in the morning; it's part of what I do every day. I hadn't stopped in the bathroom to get ready before coming down the stairs, either.

What's wrong with me? I swallow hard and brace myself on the banister. They're just stairs.

The air thickens and it's hard to breathe, like I'm sucking in molasses and it's oozing into my lungs. The stairs start pulling me into the floor, farther and deeper, until I'm sinking into the wood. It's sticky and my feet drag as I try to get off the steps. Shadows emerge from the wall, clawing and trying to get inside me. I try to hold on to whatever I can find, but my hands come up empty.

I'm suffocating again. Life's crushing me, folding me, twisting my body. "Air," I say weakly. "I need air."

"Ellery?" Mom says, softly. "Are you okay, honey?"

Fighting to take a breath, I follow my heavy feet off the stairs toward her voice, yanking my legs from the liquid wood and closing my eyes to make the shadows disappear.

It's not real. *Alabama, Alaska, Arizona . . . Arkansas.* Breath starts to flow into my lungs, lifting the thickness away as fast as it came.

The living room is bathed in the same dull hue as my walls, but the rays are tinted green, like the curtains. My heavy feet start to sink again when I see who is sitting on the couch across from my mom. He hasn't changed since we saw each other last. His beard is trimmed more and his glasses are different—thicker and hipster-ish. He still wears those stupid brown loafers.

I shut my eyes and take a gulp of clear air. "Dr. Lamboni."

49

Colter told. He really did it. My body doesn't heat like I expected. It's too tired from trying not to sink into the stairs.

Dr. Lamboni gives me a grim smile that says more than his gaze. His eyes are glazed over, like he's had more coffee than food in the last twenty-four hours. "Hi, Ellery," he says in that annoying, soft tone I remember too well.

"Honey, Dr. Lamboni just wants to talk to you," my mom says, looking to the side of me, avoiding my eyes. She has a towel between her fingers she's trying not to destroy.

She's lying.

He nods in agreement with Mom. "I'm not here to make things worse for you. Please understand that. We only want to help."

He told. Colter really told on me. Part of me never believed he was capable. No, maybe Mom found out some other way. He would never tell on me. He loves me. He knows what this would do to me. "What is this about?" I ask, somehow willing my voice to speak through the haze of dull color coating the room.

Mom pulls the towel once through her fingers—it's the one with the big turkey from Thanksgiving. "Honey, he's here to help you." Her voice wavers and it's then I notice the black tear streaks down her face. "Please sit."

The room starts to spin, my weighted feet sink more, my heartbeats don't know what to do. "Who told you?" I ask, hoping the answer isn't Colter. Hoping the one person I trust more than anyone didn't betray me. Didn't break my heart more than it already is.

"That's not important."

"It's Colter, though. He's the only one it could be."

Dr. Lamboni takes a breath, but doesn't say anything. The words are written all over his tanned face.

Numb from my toes to my hair, I grab the side of the couch and take a seat next to my mom. I stare at the stripes painted on the wall while they talk about how long my hospital visit will be, how long I'll be required to have someone around me, the rules.

Mom cries. Dr. Lamboni soothes her in that soft voice, the patronizing one he used on me. She covers her face with her hands, the only time she drops the towel.

"We have to tell her father. He should be here," Mom says to him.

"No," I say, with the only conviction I have left. "I don't want to see him. If you call him, I'll find a way to do it. Don't you dare," I scream. I pick up the lamp and throw it hard across the room. It shatters against the sunshine walls and it feels familiar, like the time I tore my posters off the wall and shredded them. "He's not ever coming near me again!" I yell and pick up the matching lamp on the other end table, arching my arm so I can bash it against the wall when a sharp jerk pops me out of my rage. I'm breathing hard, and the hand with the lamp in it is trembling, threatening to drop the contents to the floor. Before I can blink, the lamp is swiftly removed from my grip and I'm grabbed by the other arm. Dr. Lamboni keeps a tight grip on me and gently guides me toward the chair in the corner.

Mom widens her eyes, and the shock and surprise on her face knocks me out of my numbness.

What did I just do? "Mom?"

It doesn't matter. It's over.

"Oh, Ellery," she says, wringing that towel within an inch of its life. They both stare at me carefully trying to assess my stability, I suppose.

"You need to pack some things. We should get you to the hospital."

"Aren't you going to ask me if I'm a danger to myself?" I snap. "You're going to believe Colter's word over mine?"

Dr. Lamboni pinches his nose with his fingers, then turns his hard gaze on me. "Yes, I believe him."

I jerk up from the chair and Dr. Lamboni and Mom rise quickly, as if they need to catch me if I run. This is how my life is going to be from now on. Someone always watching.

"I'll help you pack," Mom says in a somber tone.

I turn to her and crease my eyes like I do when I need her to believe me. "Mom, Colter's lying. Can't you see he's turning you all against me?"

She closes her eyes and a small tear slips down her cheek. "Do you want me to pack for you?" she says in a strained voice.

My shoulders drop and I admit defeat for the moment. "No, I can do it."

The stairs don't sink when I step on them. Real life has snapped back, and it's worse than the horror of the ground sinking. Mom follows me up the stairs and watches while I pack my life into a small pink and white suitcase—I never got a new one after I went to Disney World in fourth grade.

How could Colter betray me? *I'll give you till Halloween,* he'd said. Perhaps he always was going to tell. Maybe he doesn't even love me. This was all a big ruse to get me help, get him *his* salvation and deny mine. I wish it wasn't too late to take my heart back from him.

Carrying my pink suitcase, I walk out with Dr. Lamboni and Mom, and head to the unknown.

50

The hospital is the scariest place on earth, I'm convinced. It's where people go to die. How can that be anything but horrid? Because I didn't actually slit my wrists, we've been waiting for an hour and a half to get a room. I'm told once I'm in there a psychiatrist will evaluate the level of suicide-ness I have. As if there are categories. Today I feel a quarter suicidal, part suicidal, half normal. It's insulting. All of it.

I'm on my second Dr Pepper when the nurse finds us and directs us to a room on the same floor. We walk in and it reminds me of my room at home—stark and naked, but it smells like bleach and whatever detergent they use for the sheets . . . and my mom. She smells the same when I hug her.

The nurse is young, maybe twenty-three, and she's in light blue scrubs with rubber duckies on them. My mom has the same kind. "You can take a seat in the chair if you want. Dr. Chambers is just going to ask you a few questions."

Dr. Lamboni whispers something to the nurse and she leaves. He nears the doorway. "I'm going to leave, but I'll just be down the hall. I have another patient who needs to see me." He smiles at me; it's sincere and it makes me squirm in my chair. He knows a lot about me that no one else does. When someone holds your deepest secrets like that, it makes you uneasy when you're around them, like they will tell at any moment. "Dr. Chambers is great. You're in good hands," he says, then leaves.

Mom finally takes a seat in the other chair in the room, leaving the hospital bed vacant. "Do you want me to get you something to eat?"

"No, I'm fine."

She grabs onto the sides of the recliner. "You're not fine. How long has this been going on?" she asks softly, kneading the fabric of the chair between her fingers.

"Nothing's going on."

"Ellery, dammit!" she yells, rising up from the chair, her breath heavy. I flinch at her tone. "Don't lie to me."

Resist her. If you tell the truth they'll keep you here forever.

"I don't know."

"Ellery," she growls.

"A while."

"I don't know what to say. I should have seen it. I'm sorry."

"Mom, it's not your fault," I snap, not wanting to, but I can't help it. I'm so angry I don't know how not to snap at people right now. It's as if the anger has captured and possessed me.

The doctor comes in soon after and takes a seat across from me while Mom heads out to get her fourth cup of coffee. He's a small man, thinning hair, bow tie with red stripes on it. He grabs a legal pad and writes something down.

"Are you going to harm yourself?" he asks, his pen poised.

"No."

I mean, what else can I say? Um, yes. I'd like to do it with that tongue depressor. Do you think it pierces skin?

"Are you going to hurt others?"

"No," I snap.

"Have you made any plans to harm yourself in the future?"

"No."

He pauses to write something down. "What do you think your suicide would achieve?"

I'm ready to say no again when I realize what he's asked. No answer comes to me. Which I don't get, because it's all I've thought of since the gun failed to do its job. "I . . . ." I didn't know about this one. "I guess . . . the pain would be gone."

"Whose pain?"

"Mine. Everyone's."

"Do you have any hope, Ellery?"

Shit. These are harder than I thought they'd be. I glance around the room. The window's curtains are a deep shade of green, Dr. Chambers's jacket is denim blue, the door is gray like the moon.

"Ellery?" he repeats.

"Hope for what?" I ask, hoping maybe he has the answer.

"You tell me," he replies.

"I don't know."

He takes a deep breath, closes the legal pad, and adjusts his bow tie before scooting out of the chair. He makes his way toward the door, and gestures for someone to come inside.

The nurse comes back in and gives me a small smile. What do they know about me that I don't? Where's my mom? Are they going to strap me down? Panic fills my body at the thought, and I glance down at my shaking hands. "What's going to happen to me?" I ask Dr. Chambers before he can leave.

He turns with a concerned expression. I try to stop my hands from shaking by sitting on them, but they won't still. "You'll have to stay for a few days, but after that you can go home. We just have to make sure you're safe. Okay?" he says, with sincerity in his voice.

Tears start to flow down my cheeks. "I want to go now."

He sets the legal pad on the chair and the nurse checks something in the hallway. He sits down again and regards me carefully. "I can't let you go. We both know you've been lying for a long time. And there's nothing about that interview that was the truth, except maybe the last couple of questions." He leans back in his chair. "I'll be back tomorrow and we can talk more." He stands again and picks up his legal pad. "Do you need something to help you sleep?"

I shake my head. "Is my mom coming back?"

"Yes, she'll be back. You don't have to go through this alone." He slides out of the room and stops in the doorway. "I'll see you tomorrow."

I nod as the nurse comes back in. She hands me a gown, but doesn't leave the room. She apologizes for it.

She doesn't know. I've never felt more alone in my life.

51

2 Days After

The morning sun casts yellow into my hospital room. The color is brighter but more fake than it is at home. I miss the dull yellow of my room.

Mom hasn't left my side all night. We played cards like we used to until midnight, when the day finally caught up to me. She told me Colter wants to visit. Jackson and Janie, too. I told her I'd only be willing to see Jackson right now. He's supposed to come early before school today. I put on some jeans and a shirt before he visits and wait, staring out the window at the cars going down the road.

Dean's not out there anymore, riding past my house on his bike, climbing that stupid tree in his neighbor's yard. My chest aches every time I think about him, like it's a wound that won't ever heal. My partner in death, but I'm not dead. Was it always going to be this way? Would I have done it if Colter never came to get me?

"Hey, Ellery Bellery," Jackson says from behind me.

I turn around and his face is full of . . . normal. He's not sad or ashamed or guilt-ridden. He's him. I run and wrap my arms around him, hugging him close. "I'm so glad to see you," I say, his shirt muffling my voice.

"Me too. I'm going to try to restrain myself from hitting you upside the head. But it will be hard."

I let him go and lower my head, taking a seat on the end of the bed.

He takes a seat on the chair that Dr. Chambers sat in last night, crossing his legs, then uncrossing them. "Nice digs."

"Jackson Gray."

"What? My grandma had to share a room with a guy who smelled like cabbage farts. Trust me, this is better."

I laugh, and it feels strange to laugh right now. "It's like prison. They stand outside the bathroom while I go."

"Do you blame them?" he says, putting on a serious face.

"No." I shrug.

"Do they have you on happy pills?"

"Not yet, but I suspect they will start soon."

He nods and searches around the room, crossing his legs again. "You have a flat-screen in here."

"Yep."

He takes in a deep breath. "Colter's worried about you. He thinks you hate him."

"I don't want to talk about him."

He gives me a stern look, the same one he gave me when he picked me up at Kmart the night I tried to return the gun—the night that changed my life. It seems so long ago. "I would have told, too, you know. Sooner than he did, actually."

"I said, I don't want to—"

"I know what you said," he says, cutting me off. "What's going on? Do you really want to kill yourself?"

"Most of the time." It's the truth. Now, that I'm here, I might as well face it. I didn't magically not want to kill myself the moment I stepped into the hospital. Although it seems like trying three times and failing maybe means something, that maybe it was never supposed to happen. If I try a fourth time and fail, what does that say about me? That I'm determined, or just stupid? Did Dean try before and fail? Would he have visited me here, too?

"Okay, now that we have that straight."

"I don't want to lie to you anymore," I say. "I'm tired of lying to everyone."

"Then don't," he says softly. "Talk to me. I'm here. I've always been. I always will. Just let me in."

"You don't want to be let in."

"Don't tell me what I want. I'm your best friend." He lifts his chin and gestures to himself. "Unload. I can take it."

Truth bubbles up like acid in my throat. I want to tell him everything, but I could lose him. "I knew about Dean wanting to kill himself." He doesn't react to those words like I thought; he's still leaning in, listening intently. "I knew and I didn't do anything. I didn't want him to die, but I felt like if I said something I'd be a hypocrite, because he knew about me, too." I take a deep breath. "I tried to kill myself with a gun the night you came and got me at Kmart. I blame myself for my sister's death. My dad and I had a fight and she snuck in the car and I slipped . . . ." Tears start streaming down my cheeks and I wipe them away violently. "I'm in love with Colter, and I hate him, too."

Jackson wraps me in his arms this time and strokes my head gently.

"I'm sorry," I say, hugging him tightly. "I'm so sorry."

"I know you are."

"I love you, you know."

"I know," he says gently. "Me too."

"Honey? You have another visitor." Mom says, peeking her head into the room. She sees me in Jackson's arms and pauses. "I'll have him wait until you're finished."

"It's okay, Mrs. S. I think we're good." Jackson loosens his grip on me and gives me a quick kiss on the cheek. "I brought Colter. You'll thank me later."

"But—" He's gone before I can get out any more words.

Fucking Jackson.

52

Nerves build up in my blood at the mention of his name. Colter's here and he's coming in and he betrayed me. How can I love and hate someone so much at the same time?

"She doesn't want to see me, Gray," Colter says outside my door.

I lean in to listen better.

"She does. Look, she's kind of weepy, so go easy on her."

Weepy? That little shit.

"Does she want to see me?" Colter asks in his pitiful voice. He seems so unsure and it kills me and I want to put him at ease, but I can't because I hate him too much right now.

"Just go in. She can always kick you out," Jackson says.

The door squeaks open and I adjust myself on the bed. Should I sit or lie down? I didn't check my hair. Are there tear streaks down my cheeks?

"Hey," he says softly. His expression is somber, but I can see he's trying to look hopeful and sincere through the pain around his eyes. He has a book tucked under his arm.

I want to run to him and wrap my arms around him like I did with Jackson, but I stay on the bed. I don't say anything as he sits in the chair Jackson vacated. He takes the book out from under his arm and sets it down on the armrest of the chair.

"What book is that?" I ask.

He smiles and I melt. "*The Notebook*."

Tears fight to come out of my eyes. "Why would you bring that?"

"I thought I could read it to you."

A noise comes out of my throat. "I can't believe you spent money on that."

He quirks his mouth to the side. "Actually, it's my mom's."

"Your mom has bad taste in books."

"It's really not that bad. It has its moments, ya know? Like there's hope."

Like there's hope for us? For me?

He glances around the room and cringes. "I hate hospitals. There's so much death."

"I know. It's so depressing," I tease.

He gives me his exasperated look, the one I bring out in him, the one someone who loves you can manifest out of nowhere. I've seen it several times. He lays the book down on the movable table tray beside him. "I'm sorry." He shrugs. "I know you must hate me for what I did."

"You're right. I do."

He closes his eyes and leans back in the chair, rubbing his jeans with his palms. "I had no choice. I gave you till Halloween. I kept my word, but you didn't keep yours. I tried to help you, join you. I just didn't have anything left to try but this."

"You betrayed me."

"I know." He lifts his chin and scoots forward, resting his elbows on his knees so he's closer to me. "I would do it again."

"Everyone would have been better off. The world would have finally made sense."

"You mean, the way Dean's death made the world better? What did it feel like when you learned about what he did?"

I search my mind and heart for the feeling and find it buried deep in a place I never wanted to go again. I try to put it into words. "Like nothing in my life would be warm or sweet or happy again. Like everything would wash away forever, and get replaced by only shadows of memories instead of real ones."

"Now I want you to think about me. How do you think it would have felt for me to find out that you . . . ." He clears his throat. "How would you have felt if I would have jumped off that bridge?"

My stomach starts churning and my heart starts beating off rhythm as my eyes fill with tears. My body feels depleted, like a hollow abyss with nothing to fill it. "Agonizing. Like all the worst pains I've ever felt hitting me all at once, breaking my body and mind and heart at the same time until there are only shards remaining." It comes out a little more dramatic than I intend, but it's the truth.

He gives me a pointed look. "I wouldn't have been the same without you. My whole life would have been changed and defined by that one moment where you chose pain over life. I want to say I'd be okay. I wanna say that your death wouldn't have haunted me forever, but it would have. You can't love someone that much and expect to come out the other side the same person. It doesn't work like that." He leans in closer. "When you were on that bridge, I saw flashes of what my life would be without you, and it made me want to get on that bridge, too, made me want to do anything to stop you." He bites his lip as tears film his eyes. "I know you can't live for me or for anyone else. But at least live for you. Don't live for your sister, or Dean, even. They're gone. I'm sorry, I know this isn't what you want to hear, but they are. They aren't coming back."

His words hit me like a truck. All the questions I've been asking, all the pain—is that what I've been doing? Living for her? "But it's my fault she's dead. And Dean," I say, but the words don't sound the same anymore. I'm not sure I believe them. It's as if they're coming from someone else's mouth.

He shakes his head and moves to sit on the hospital bed with me. "It's not your fault. It's not mine that my brother killed himself, either. Watching you go through this, being with you . . . I know that now. I was a shell of a person before I met you. My brother haunted me, too. I never even realized how much I blamed myself until I saw you do the same thing. Then I wanted you to let go, too. I wanted you to be free, like I was starting to feel." He reaches over and covers my hand with his. "You're free, Ellery."

"I'm not." Am I? Is that all it takes?

"You are. Let them go. That's all you need to do. They're ready. If they were here, they would tell you the same thing. Search your heart for the answers."

I squeeze his hand and weave my fingers through his. "It's not that easy."

"I know it's not." He lifts my hand to his lips and kisses it gently. "But I'll be here for you as you go through this. You're not alone."

I unhook my fingers from his and wipe my tears away. "I really fucked up, didn't I?"

"Yeah, you did," he grins. I push him in the side and he chuckles a little, breaking the tension. "How about I read some of that book."

"Really?"

"Yes, it's our book."

I let out a groan-laugh. "No, it's not. It's our anti-book."

He arches an eyebrow, grabs the book, and turns to the first page, leaning back against the wall. Before he can utter a word, he closes it and jerks his head up like he just had a spontaneous idea. "We need an anti-movie, too."

"Define the terms."

He quirks his mouth to the side. "Corny lines, unrealistic plot."

I search my mind for a movie with lines as corny as *The Notebook*. "I've got it."

"Me too," he says with a huge smile on his face. "Okay, we'll say them at the same time."

"Yeah, that's not corny at all."

"*Shush*. On the count of three. One, two, three—*You've Got Mail*," he says at the same time as I say, "*Jerry Maguire*."

"Oh, that's a really good one." He lowers his head to get it even with mine. "You complete me," he says with a goofy grin on his face. I shove him, and he grabs my arms and pulls me into his chest and wraps me in his arms. *Safe*. "Say it."

"No," I say through a laugh, pushing on his chest.

He squeezes me and whispers in my ear, "Say it."

"Come on, I would never be able to look at myself in the mirror again."

He kisses my ear and blows gently into it. "Say it," he whispers, causing me to shiver.

"No," I whisper.

He moves to my neck and kisses me, whispering each time for me to *say it*.

I never do.

53

May 15

"Where are we going?" Colter says as I drive down the street to the zoo.

Dr. Chambers thought it would be good for me to return to the zoo with people who are important to me. It's hard to believe it's been six months since I started therapy, and Colter's still around. I'm so fucking lucky.

He laughs as the zebra-painted sign comes into view. "The zoo? I haven't been here since I was like, twelve, I think?"

I pull into a parking spot and give him a peck on the cheek. "I used to take Tate here. I haven't been back in a while."

It feels good to say her name out loud without guilt pounding in my head. Therapy was a lot harder than I thought. Not that I thought it would be easy, but facing every nightmare I'd ever had wasn't something I was prepared for. Now my mind is contained in little orange bottles, but Dr. Chambers says I won't have to take pills forever, just until I can figure some stuff out.

I've found a way to forgive myself, or something as close to forgiveness as I can manage. I won't forget. I can't. But letting go of what happened made me feel like I could do anything. Be anything I want. I never thought I'd ever feel that way again.

Colter grins like he just stole something he's not supposed to have. "You know, I've never made out at a zoo before," he says, raising his eyebrows.

I smack him in the arm as we get out and walk through the zoo entrance. The sounds of the birds and the monkeys take me back to when I would take Tate. I can see her chasing the birds, trying to fly away like them. I smile, but a streak of discomfort soars through me.

I look up at the sky and breathe in and out, thinking of the positive affirmations Dr. Chambers taught me until the calm surrounds me again.

You have a good life. You can do anything.

I'm incredibly grateful that I only have to say the words in my head. Even I know how lame they would sound out loud. I do write them down, with every other thought I have, in an ugly journal with a sun on the cover.

After we've paid to get in, I drag Colter to the goat corral. Jackson and Janie are meeting us in a few minutes at the tiger enclosure. Atticus is coming too, with Grace. They just got back from Disney World.

I wanted to bring Colter to the goats alone. I had to see them again.

He gives me a look. "Really? The goats?"

"Yes, the goats. Tate used to love this place."

Colter puts a quarter in the machine, turns the knob, and pellets fall into his palm. He leans over and feeds one of the goats. His smile is that of a kid, a seven-year-old boy who visited the zoo with his family. It's crazy how certain movements, certain scenes in life bring you back to such a young age. But I see that in him, in his expression. He pets the goat on the head then laughs, wiping his hands on his jeans. He joins me and nudges my side to let me know he's there.

The pen fills with giggling kids. I watch their trepidation as they go to pet a goat for the first time, yanking back their tiny hands and giggling that way only little kids can.

"I used to think of the goats as trapped and miserable." I take a breath in and close my eyes for a brief moment, then open them and see the sun's rays, the laughing children, Colter's smile. "But now, I see how happy those kids make them. How their lives would be boring without anyone in it to scratch their ears or feed them pellets from the machine."

"I love how philosophical you've gotten post-therapy. It's sexy," he says, moving closer to me.

I chuckle and roll my eyes. "I guess it took me a bit to realize that not everything's a trap."

Grabbing my hand, he pulls me into him. "I'd like to trap you behind that barn over there."

I laugh and smack him on the chest. "Stop that. *There are children here*," I say in my teacher-y tone, mocking him.

He wraps his arms around my waist, tilting his head close to my ear. "Good. I perform best in front of an audience," he whispers, then grazes his lips under my ear, trailing sweet kisses across my jaw until he reaches my mouth and covers it with his.

I'm not sure what made me want to live again. It wasn't a bunch of grand epiphanies or gestures; it was more like each puzzle piece of my life finally created something whole. All the torn edges and tattered corners of each moment mattered a little less. *Happy Ellery* didn't exist separately anymore, because she was me. My smiles grew wider, my heart beat stronger. It all finally made sense. Life. How unpredictable and messy and beautiful it could be. I know; I can hardly believe those words are coming out of me without a hint of sarcasm (well . . . maybe a little).

Dedication

For Grandma, who taught me so much I will never forget.

Acknowledgments

I lost my dad to suicide when I was sixteen. I had no idea at that time how much it would change my life, but I'm thankful that something positive was born out of something so tragic, that I was able to live my doubts, fears, and questions through Ellery. Thank you for choosing to bring Ellery into your life too.

This book couldn't have happened without the support and encouragement of my agent-of-awesome Christa Heschke. I'm so thankful for my editor Jacquelyn Mitchard who championed Ellery and this story, and who took a chance on me. Thank-you to Bethany Carland-Adams and the team at Merit Press and Simon & Schuster who have been supportive and continue to be supportive throughout my debut journey. A big shout-out to Judith Engracia who saw the potential in this story (and me) in the very beginning.

Writing can be a lonely world without friends to share this journey with. Huge thank-you to the bloggers and readers who have shared such heartfelt messages and reviews. You brighten my day.

If you feel you are in danger of harming yourself, please reach out. Talk to someone you trust or call the number below. Remember, you are loved. Never *ever* forget that.

For more resources on suicide prevention please visit afsp.org or call the National (U.S.) Suicide Prevention Lifeline: 1-800-273-8255.